Praise for *Boop and Eve's*

"Three generations of women, one agonizing secret. Boop and Eve will steal your heart as they travel together—one seeking her future, and the other forced to face her past. Sheriff's novel will make you laugh and cry, sometimes on the very same page."

—T. Greenwood, award-winning author of
Keeping Lucy and *Rust & Stardust*

"Debut author Mary Helen Sheriff has woven a contemporary, heart-warming saga about women, for women. Peppered with surprises and humor, her story follows three generations of a dysfunctional family through their hurt, anger, and regret toward reconciliation and hope."

—Pam Webber, best-selling author of
The Wiregrass and *Moon Water*

"*Boop and Eve's Road Trip* is a delightful, funny, poignant ride filled with laughter, tears, and mystery. It is both a physical and emotional journey that Boop and Eve undertake, and the healing they both experience is something that might just heal a little part of everyone."

—Kathy Hepinstall, author of *The Book of Polly*

BOOP AND EVE'S
ROAD TRIP

BOOP AND EVE'S ROAD TRIP

A NOVEL

MARY HELEN SHERIFF

SHE WRITES PRESS

Published 2020
Printed in the United States of America
ISBN: 978-1-63152-763-0
ISBN: 978-1-63152-764-7
Library of Congress Control Number: 2020907889

For information, address:
She Writes Press
1569 Solano Ave #546
Berkeley, CA 94707

She Writes Press is a division of SparkPoint Studio, LLC.

In loving memory of Hootie

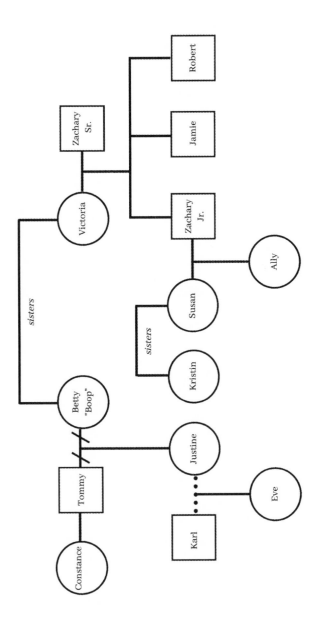

FAMILY TREE

CHAPTER 1

Boop loved her daughter to the moon and back, but Justine had a way of sucking the joy out of a room faster than a vampire bat. When she'd invited herself and Eve to Christmas at Boop's condo in Florida, Boop could hardly say no. She was grateful for any morsel of affection Justine threw her way, and she jumped on any chance to protect her granddaughter, Eve, from Justine's barbed tongue.

"So you signed up for Textiles 1 next semester?" Justine asked Eve. As Justine passed the scalloped oysters, Boop couldn't help but admire her manicure. Boop's own nails were more ripped than wrapping paper on Christmas morning.

"Yeah. It sounds awesome. The professor is supposed to be cool." Eve's slight gasp and ducked chin prior to her breezy response suggested a tension that confused Boop.

"That's nice." Justine widened her smile and batted her eyelashes, conveying, in her own way, quite the opposite. "Only, don't you think it's missing the point?"

Eve's entire body tightened, as if preparing for a pummeling. "What do you mean?"

The hairs on Boop's arms tingled.

"What kind of job could you possibly get with that? Laundress, tanner, knitter? Oh, I know—maybe you could work in a fabric store and teach sewing classes." Justine took a sip of water. No fattening eggnog for her. "You should be focusing on taking courses that will help you get into medical school."

With all the sneer in Justine's voice, Boop wondered if she'd gotten the words "fabric store" and "whorehouse" muddled up. Justine's tunnel vision around Eve's attending medical school was borderline obsessive-compulsive. Medical school was Justine's unrealized dream, and she made no bones about blaming Boop and Tommy for their failure to support her and push her toward success. Boop couldn't argue with that. They'd been lousy parents.

No one would ever accuse Justine of not pushing Eve. As for supporting her—let's just say Boop and Justine had vastly different definitions of "support."

Since the relationship between Boop and Justine was perilous on the best of days, Boop avoided conflict when she could. Occasional light meddling for Eve's sake was the exception. "I reckon studying art makes a girl well-rounded. Justine, this here corn pudding is the best corn pudding I ever ate. How do you do it?"

Justine ignored the blatant attempt to change the subject. "Well-rounded? Bah! Says the lady who got her MRS degree and hasn't worked a day in her life." She scraped the marshmallows off her sweet potatoes, leaving the butchered white goodness behind like a sacrificial lamb.

"Life was different then," Boop muttered. She scanned the row of birdhouses hanging from the railings of the stairway in search of the comfort they sometimes brought her.

"Boondoggles about scraps of cloth won't pay the bills."

Boop pulled her eyes from the birdhouses to see how Eve was faring and found her slumped in her chair like thirsty edelweiss. Her gray dress the same shade as its silvery leaves, her skin its flowers. What Boop wouldn't give to fertilize her granddaughter with a few ounces of gumption. How Eve was going to get through life in one piece, Boop did not know, but then Boop hadn't exactly managed that feat either. In her case, the strength had only come after breaking and breaking and breaking. Since Justine had wrapped Eve's childhood in Bubble Wrap, Eve was quite intact. For Justine, this was a point of pride, but it troubled Boop.

Justine had even managed to send Eve "away" to a college a hop, skip, and a jump from Boop. Not that Boop minded having Eve nearby. She loved it, but still she worried her presence was holding Eve back from the proper rite-of-passage that college life should be.

"Never you fear, I've taken care of it," Justine said.

"You what?" Eve asked.

"I spoke with Bess, and she agreed to move you into Biology 102. You'll have to call and confirm of course." Bess was Eve's dean. Justine and Bess were on a first name basis because Bess's brother was also Justine's boss Trevor. This relationship allowed Justine to micromanage Eve from afar. "What were you thinking, leaving that off your schedule?"

"I just wanted a break. That's all."

"Perhaps it has something to do with the B you got in lab?" Justine's tone was casual, but the savagery in her bite of green beans sent an altogether different message—one of predator and prey. "Bess had a talk with the TA who runs your lab—Rob something or other. He said you let your lab partner do all the work."

"Well, I—"

"He also mentioned that your lab partner was a boy." Justine sliced her roast beef with the precision of a surgeon.

Boop wondered how on earth she was going to derail this conversation with an adversary like Justine.

"Yeah, so?" Eve took a swig of eggnog and then wiped the corners of her mouth with the back of her hand.

Justine flinched at Eve's bad manners but refused to let them throw her off her game. "I'm just wondering if this boy is too distracting."

Desperate to change the subject to a more pleasant topic, any more pleasant topic, Boop clapped her hands. "Hot diggity dog! I am all ears."

"Tim's not interested in me." Eve scattered her peas around her plate.

"Any boy worth his salt would snap you up quicker than an alligator," said Boop. And really, Eve's pale skin, dark hair, and green eyes were a stunning mix. She was a looker all right, and sweet, and smart. A real catch, if you asked Boop.

"Alligator is right. Finish college first." Justine jabbed her fork in the direction of Eve's peas.

"No worries there." Eve stuffed a forkful of peas in her mouth and washed them down with another swig of eggnog.

Boop kicked herself for forgetting Eve's aversion to peas.

Justine lowered her accusing fork. "Hmm. You also got a B in swimming."

"That's ridiculous! I missed class twice, and she took me down a letter grade."

"Then you shouldn't have missed class."

"I wasn't feeling well."

Staring down at the storm on Eve's plate, complete with mashed-potato clouds darkened with gravy, raindrop peas, and green bean lightning bolts, Boop reflected that food was an underrated artistic medium. Indeed, a storm was brewing, and Boop would have to move quickly to blow it off course.

"Did you tell your instructor that?" asked Justine.

"Yeah, but she said without a doctor's note she wouldn't excuse it."

"Why didn't you get a doctor's note?" Justine used the corner of her cloth napkin to dab away some minute crumb that no else could see. Somehow her crimson lipstick still managed to look pristine.

Eve licked her eggnog-smeared lips. "Because I don't go to the doctor for my period, but I do miss swimming for it."

"Humph. I'll get this cleared up. You two keep enjoying your meal." Justine stood, picked up her plate, and strode to the kitchen sink. "A mother's work is never done." She turned on the faucet.

The sound of running water cut through their conversation. Boop let out a deep breath, grateful for the reprieve.

"Do I smell gingerbread cookies?" Eve asked Boop.

"Yep. I found my grandma's old recipe," replied Boop. "I've got such fond memories of her baking them at Christmastime every year. I sure do hope they taste as good as I remember—I'm not the baker she was, that's for sure."

"They'll be awesome."

Boop glowed under Eve's loyalty. She might've failed at motherhood, but she was doing an okay job at this grandmother gig.

"How's that roommate of yours?" Boop asked.

"Carrie's great."

"You two getting along?" Justine asked over her shoulder.

"Yep. We're actually becoming pretty good friends."

"And how's Ally?" Boop asked. Ally was Boop's great-niece, but also Eve's best friend. She'd moved out to LA a few months before, chasing after the lights of Hollywood.

"She found some top agent, and they're dating. She sounds thrilled. Seems like everything is falling into place for her," Eve said.

"I'll be a monkey's uncle!" Boop said.

Justine smirked. "She's dating her agent? Mixing business and pleasure? Not smart."

"Pot and kettle," Boop muttered under her breath.

Eve winked at her. Justine was having an unsuitable relationship with her married boss. Boop and Eve generally pretended not to notice but had upon occasion speculated on the details—out of Justine's earshot, of course.

"Ally's a grown-up. I suppose she'll learn. Now, back to you, Eve.

I have to admit, I'm concerned—two B's your first semester does not a valedictorian make."

Boop groaned, were they back to this? By golly, Justine was the walking definition of "funsponge."

Eve's face flushed. "I'll do better."

Justine turned off the faucet and spun to give Eve her full attention. "I imagine you will, but I've been giving it some thought, and I believe your little alteration business is too distracting." Eve had been taking in clothing alterations for years to earn some pocket money, impressing Boop with both her sewing skills and entrepreneurial spirit.

"No, it's not that." Eve chewed on her thumbnail. "Really."

"I'm going to have to insist that you put an end to this hobby. Get your fingers out of your mouth."

Eve stuffed her hands under her bottom. "Mo-om."

"Mom nothing. I'm dropping off your sewing machine at Goodwill before I leave."

"But I bought Heathcliff with my allowance."

"Yes, and you've abused that privilege." After wiping her hands on a mistletoe dish towel, Justine grabbed the aluminum foil to cover the leftovers. "For God's sake, who names a sewing machine? Your priorities are all mixed up. It's time you got them straight."

Eve's eyes welled with tears. Trembling, she whispered, "Please."

"Don't make this any harder."

Boop cleared her throat. "How about you let me have it?"

"What?" Justine and Eve's voices came together.

The scent of burnt gingerbread drifted from the oven. "Oh!" Boop popped out of her seat and rushed to check the cookies. "Dang it, I forgot to set the timer." She stooped to pull the pan from the oven. The gingerbread was much too dark.

Boop squeezed her eyes shut. She couldn't even make cookies without burning them. How the hell would she ever manage to make her family right?

"They'll be delicious," Eve tried to reassure her.

Justine's raised eyebrows made her opinion clear, but at least she had the grace to keep her trap shut for once.

Boop set the cookies down to cool and flashed Eve a smile of gratitude. "I want to make some new curtains and a throw pillow. I can use Eve's machine, and then when she pulls her grades back up, she can have it back. Win-win."

Justine raked her eyes over Boop. "Fine."

Boop slid three, still-warm cookies from the pan onto a plate for each of them.

"No, thanks," Justine said.

"I guess they are a little overcooked." Frowning, Boop looked down at the cookies. "You don't have to eat one, Eve."

"Of course, I will." Eve took a bite. "Yum."

"You think? Even though it's burnt?"

"I like marshmallows burnt, so why not gingerbread?"

Boop popped a cookie in her mouth. It tasted worse than the paper the recipe was written on. Eve had perfectly functional taste buds, so there was no way she thought the cookies were even edible. Boop wanted nothing more than to swallow Eve in a big old hug. Instead, she took another bite of her cookie. "Mmmm. Mm." If Eve was game to play along, there was no way Boop was giving Justine the satisfaction of admitting the cookies were a disaster.

She and Eve were a team.

"Why don't we do gifts now? Eve, do you still want to give yours first?" Justine asked.

"I guess." Eve approached the presents as if they might bite, and then handed Boop her gift with a trembling hand.

Boop found her nervousness odd. Not one to bother with precision unwrapping, she had hers open first. "A cover-up! I love it!"

Eve had clearly put real time and thought into choosing this gift. It was a nice quality too; Boop hoped she hadn't broken the bank to pay for it. She threw it on over her green pants and red blouse. "It fits just right! It even matches my favorite bathing suit. This is terrific. Thanks, Eve! Don't you just adore it, Justine?"

"It's nice." Although Justine barely gave it glance, as she finished sliding her fingers through the tape holding her box together. After opening the tissue paper, she unfolded a garment and held it up. "It's a dress. Thanks."

"Do you like it?" Eve asked.

"It's nice." Justine fingered the label. "What's this brand?"

Eve shrugged.

"Backstitch. I've never heard of it. I guess you picked it up at one of those discount stores." Justine smirked. "My daughter's so thrifty."

Why did Justine have to be so dang uppity?

"It's a nice quality, Mom. Look at the stitching and feel the fabric."

"I'm sure it is." But Justine didn't bother to do either. Instead, she refolded the dress and put it back in the box.

Eve's shoulders slumped, and she stared at the ground.

More than anything Boop wanted to light a spark under Eve, encourage her to push back against Justine, but Boop didn't play with fire lightly. Not anymore.

CHAPTER 2

Without Heathcliff, Eve worried she was nothing more than an ordinary girl trapped in a life of her mom's design. Except her mom was perfect, and her mom loved her, so it stood to reason that her design for Eve's life would be masterful. Eve knew she should embrace it. Her attempts to do otherwise always backfired.

Eve packed the dismantled dress form into her footlocker. Her mom thought her little alteration business was the distraction, but that business was a mere cover for the real distraction. The real distraction was that Eve had dreams. Big, secret dreams that did not include medical school, biology labs, aborting frog eggs, and measuring pig intestines. Eve had dreams of becoming a world-famous fashion designer.

The sketchbook that contained the drawings of her Christmas gift to her mom was stuffed in at such an awkward angle Eve had trouble closing the lid of the trunk. She shoved at it to no avail. One of the aspects that drew Eve to the world of fashion was its ability to express something of the wearer without the wearer even realizing what they were expressing. Eve herself had no desire to drape her insides on her outside, hence her typical uniform of black tank top, jeans, and flip-flops. But her mom and Boop had no such qualms, so hours had gone into attempting to capture their personalities and style. At last, she was able to push the sketchbook into alignment with the others and close the trunk.

Eve had made a deal with herself. If they had loved the gifts, then Eve would have shared her aspirations with them. She'd prayed that once her mom saw how talented Eve was, she'd be supportive, excited even. Eve should've known better. After her fledgling artist of a dad had run out on them, her mom had scoffed at anything resembling art. Ironically, Karl would never consider fashion design real art anyway.

Eve folded up her ironing board and slid it behind her dresser. The demolition of her sewing studio made their tiny dorm room feel much bigger. When she got back from class, Carrie would be thrilled. Even she didn't know about Eve's dreams. She, too, had been hoodwinked by the little alteration business illusion. Ally was the only person who knew about Backstitch. She'd even worn a bunch of Eve's designs.

With Heathcliff, Eve created magic, but magic was for children. It was time to grow up, to set aside her childish dreams. She snapped the case of her sewing machine shut with a finality that sent shudders down her spine.

Eve wandered over to Carrie's half of the room to look through her inventory of essential oils for one that might induce courage.

"Sandalwood: fights feelings of fear and dread." Now where was that diffuser?

Eve: Going to ask Tim out today

Eve: Wish me luck

Eve: Luck?

Eve: Ally?

Eve served her prison sentence in Biology 102, grateful that at least Tim had agreed to be her lab partner again. The reek of formaldehyde was so foul Eve had worn a mask to the previous dissections. This morning, though, she'd put on makeup (for once), which would have been made pointless if a mask covered half of her face, especially given the super attractive science goggles already covering the other half. Safety goggles were a ridiculous lab requirement. Were they afraid the pigs would come to life and gouge her eyes out? Yet another example of adults and their misguided overprotection.

Everyone said she'd get used to the smell after a few minutes, but Eve had yet to move past the nauseous stage.

Tim rolled his eyes toward the corner where several girls in form-fitting shirts with plunging necklines were squealing and prancing around like piglets themselves.

But when Eve examined the real pig strapped to the tray in front of her, thoughts of silly girls and dancing piglets vanished completely. The pig was small. Fetal. Its skin a paler and tanner version of pink than the one she'd used in her childhood coloring books. Funny, how we simplify everything as children, even colors. Eve would've given a great deal to be able to color her world with a box of sixteen crayons again (though perhaps not her designs).

Tim's gloved hand sliced from the throat to the umbilicus.

Eve locked her gaze safely on the lab book. Her hands shook. Partly because, well, blood and guts, and partly because today was the day. The day everything would change. The day Eve would take control of her life and ask a boy out. Ask Tim out. In spite of her mom; in spite of her own terror. She couldn't wait to report back to Ally. They hadn't talked in two weeks—practically forever. Wouldn't she be shocked? And proud?

Tim exclaimed over the pig's scrotum.

Eve followed his pointing finger and instantly regretted the tater tots, Lucky Charms, and Devil's Mess she'd had for breakfast.

Tim folded back the skin and muscle to reveal its gummy internal organs—the stomach, the intestines, the liver. . . .

Eve swallowed down the stomach acid leaking into her mouth. She needed to stop watching but couldn't seem to help herself. The combination of "peer-through-fingers-while-watching-horror-movie" syndrome and Tim—with his cute chin dimple and streak of bleached hair on his otherwise dark head—was irresistible.

Did Tim find her irresistible? When she asked if he wanted to grab a coffee with her after class, would he jump at the chance? Maybe he'd been trying to find the nerve to ask her out. Just last week he'd mentioned being interested in someone, and he'd said it with heavy significance—as if the "someone" was actually her. Then, yesterday, he'd referred to her as a "babe." Not Eve's favorite word but, coming from Tim, she'd take it. So today was the day.

Tim held up the pig to drain its bodily fluids.

Eve's stomach rumbled.

Now. She'd do it now. She crossed her gloved fingers. And opened her mouth.

He turned on the faucet to rinse out the body cavity, and that's when it happened. That's when he sprang it on her.

"So . . . I've got something I want to talk to you about."

Eve blushed. Was he going to do it? Then she'd be off the hook. A wave of relief washed over her, but Eve was surprised to note a twinge of disappointment too—now she'd never know if she could've screwed up the courage. Whatever—was she crazy? Tim was about to ask her out, and she was worried about tests of courage?

"I've been wanting to talk to you for a long time, but I couldn't find the guts." He held up the dead pig when he said "guts" and wiggled his eyebrows at his cleverness.

Eve gave him an encouraging smile. Her heart raced, preparing for one of those moments.

"I'm pleased to announce," he drummed his stained gloved fingers on the lab table's edge, "that Carrie and I are a couple."

"Wait. What?"

"I know right? Crazy. She wanted to be the one to tell you, but we flipped for it, and I won. Isn't it awesome?"

How could Carrie do this to her? They were friends. Roommates. But then Carrie didn't know about Eve's crush, did she? Damn! Why hadn't Eve confided in her?

The smile on Eve's face froze in place like a clown's. "Awesome. Right." She blinked, glad now for the goggles. Sweat broke out on her forehead. They were wrong—she wasn't getting used to the smell.

Tim offered Eve the scissors. Without giving it any thought, she took them, and snipped. The bone crunched. Eve ran to the trashcan and said hello to her breakfast for the second time that day.

"Oh, gross!" the girl nearest Eve said.

Eve could feel the eyes of the whole lab drilling into her hunched back.

Tim's voice came from behind. "You okay? Why didn't you say something?"

"Leave a message after the beep."

Beep.

"Ally! I blew it. Tim is dating Carrie now. Can you believe it? I'm so upset. Call me."

Two weeks later, outside a frat house, Eve was almost certain that the gold tooth flashing from the fratboy's mouth was part of his pimp costume. Nevertheless, if it were possible to catch an STD from a glance, then this guy would've just given Eve chlamydia. Carrie had persuaded Eve to borrow an outfit for the party—black leather skirt, fishnets, bodice trimmed in rhinestones. "Pimps and Hos" was the unfortunate party theme.

"What's up? You hos on the list?"

List?

When Carrie first mentioned going to the party, Eve had shot down the idea. However, Eve was trying hard not to let on to Carrie how much her new relationship with Tim had crushed her. After all, Carrie hadn't known anything about Eve's feelings, and that was on Eve. Eve had no one to blame for her pathetic life except herself—and maybe her mom. Perhaps the answer lay in doing the opposite of her instincts and ignoring her mom's dictates. Tonight, Eve would be reborn as a Party Girl.

As ten o'clock crept closer, reality crept in. Eve was a frat party virgin; she'd never even been to a keg party. She wouldn't know a soul there except Carrie and Tim, who'd probably spend the evening making out in front of her.

Eve tried to squirm out of the whole thing, but Carrie wouldn't let her. Trussed up like sluts, they walked the streets. Eve channeled inner catcalls: *Hey beautiful. Damn girl. You're all grown up. Look at you. Miss Independent.* Only the voice in her head was this insincere breathy voice, so the talk came off more taunt than pep.

The guy at the door had mentioned a list. What list?

"Carrie Jamison, Tim put me on it."

Eve nipped the chipped fingernail on her pinky, worried (hoping?) that Carrie's name wouldn't be on this magic list.

The pimp at the door gazed into a binder. "Right here. Got you. And your friend?"

Carrie slung her arm over Eve's shoulder. "She's with me." Only that was wrong because Carrie was with Tim, which made being with Eve a conflict of interest.

Would the guy turn Eve away? Rejection. A whole new meaning to the walk of shame.

"That's cool."

They'd breached the door. The first battle won, but that only left Eve with the rest of the evening to fight through. An early defeat might have sent her home embarrassed, but it would've been far easier than this party was going to be. Carrie grabbed Eve's elbow and drew her inside where it was dark except for a strobe light, and the music was way too loud. Carrie pulled out her cell phone to snap a picture of the two of them, no doubt announcing their status on some social-media site. Eve reminded Carrie not to tag her in the picture—her mom would murder her if she saw Eve in this ho get-up.

Eve's eyes and ears had barely adapted when Carrie dragged her to a clump of guys surrounding a giant trashcan in the corner. One of the guys stirred a green drink with an oar. Eve wondered if it was the same liquid that scarred the Joker.

A boy slurred in Eve's ear, "Swamp Frog."

Eve winced at the surprise invasion of her personal space, but the boy was too drunk to notice.

Carrie handed her a red Dixie cup filled with the green punch that tasted like lemonade. Maybe it would give her superpowers—Party Girl powers.

The wet-breath boy was back in her ear, "Wanna dance?"

Eve shrugged and took another sip. Carrie winked and gave her a gentle nudge toward the dance floor.

Under no illusion that she had any dancing talent, Eve shifted from foot to foot and swung her arms and hips around. Ally always said she was too stiff. Back when Ally used to talk to her. Eve was grateful for the Swamp Frog and the strobe light, which pretty much made every dance move look cool.

The room wasn't big enough for the swarm of moving, sweaty people packed inside. Somebody jostled Eve's elbow, and punch sloshed on her hand and the floor. It occurred to Eve that she'd better chug before more of her precious resource was lost.

Wet Breath ordered some passing cloaked dude to get Eve a refill. "Pledge," he explained as he pulled her close. Like close. Like she could tell he was hard close. Eve searched for Carrie, planning to flash her a nonverbal, "Rescue me." When she finally spotted her in the corner, she wished she hadn't. Tim had arrived, and they were busy grinding into each other, making Eve want to hurl all over again.

The pledge delivered Eve's second drink. Eve chugged it down, forced a smile, and asked for another. Someone bumped her from behind. She peeked over her shoulder to discover, a sloppy, fat drunk boy leering at her. He pushed his body against her back and whispered in her ear, "Tasty sandwich."

Eve's face lit up with shock, and the boy laughed but backed off her behind. Since the pledge hadn't returned, Eve took a sip of Wet Breath's drink, noting that the punch must not have much liquor in it since she couldn't taste it and still felt horribly sober.

The dance floor smelled like a locker room. Eve's leather clothes stuck to her skin. Overcome by heat and sweat, she yelled to Wet Breath, "I'm going outside for some air!"

"Sweet Home Alabama" kicked on. "I love this song!" he said, spit flying.

"You should stay."

"You sure?"

"It's all good."

"What?"

Eve flashed him a lame thumbs-up. Then she weaved through the soft-porn movie set to make her way to the deck. Afraid he might change his mind and follow her, she didn't dare check behind her until she made it outside. The coast was clear.

The muggy Florida air provided little relief, but at least there was a light breeze coming off the ocean. Carrie's hooker boots pinched Eve's feet. Since all the lawn chairs were taken, Eve climbed the rickety railing to perch herself on top. *Whoa!* Not as graceful as she'd have wished. Maybe the liquor was kicking in after all. That's what Eve needed—more Swamp Frog.

Most of the smokers had found their way to the deck. A blast of their secondhand smoke sent her into a coughing fit. When she slid to the left, trying to get out of its stream, her fishnets ripped on a splinter. Crap.

From across the deck, a guy with shaggy hair caught her eye. For the most part, he looked like every other guy there—tan, blonde, and wiry. Eve's dark hair and pale skin made her practically exotic in this surf town. The chest hair creeping from the V in his T-shirt and the stubble on his chin, though, gave him a potency that most college guys lacked.

Don't come over. Don't come over. He was hot and all, but what could they possibly have to talk about? Suddenly, the dance floor seemed much safer.

Like cornered prey, Eve watched him approach. He was carrying two shots garnished with limes (awfully fancy given the shithole in which they found themselves) and a shaker of salt. Must be tequila. Eve hadn't ever had tequila, and rumor said it was nasty, but then there was that song about tequila making clothes fall off. Eve suspected if it had that kind of power guys wouldn't care too much about how it tasted.

"Hey, you want a shot?"

Not really. But tonight she was Party Girl, and Party Girl did the opposite of Eve, so, "I guess." Scrambling to remember what she'd seen in movies about taking this shot, she reached for the shaker of salt.

He plucked it away. "We do it a little different around here."

"Oh?"

"Here, I'll go first." He gathered her hair off her neck.

Eve closed her eyes in relief as the breeze cooled the sheen of sweat. But they flew open when she felt his tongue on her collarbone.

He sprinkled salt on the wet spot and then licked it off.

Eve's eyes widened.

He tossed back the shot. "Open your mouth."

Eve's brain must've been functioning a few steps behind her body because she obeyed.

He stuffed a slice of lime, fruit side out, and then bent to suck it while she held it with her teeth. He flashed her a wolfish grin.

What nice teeth he had.

"Body shot. Your turn." He offered her the side of his neck.

Her mouth went dry.

She needed to pee.

She slid off the railing and stumbled into him.

He smelled of leather, salt, and surf wax. He grabbed her arm to steady her. "You okay?"

"Gotta go," she muttered as she pushed past him. Her head was fuzzy. The punch was working its mojo. She finished off her third cup. *Time for a refill. Must pee first.* Now if only she knew where the bathroom was. She climbed the stairs. The hazy lighting made everything surreal. At the top of the stairs, she opened the first door. Empty, except for the purple bong in the middle of the floor and the stench of incense. And behind door number—*oh wow*—*naked butt. Note to self: knock first.* The third, the bathroom.

The tile floor was caked in black grime from muddy boys' shoes and mildew. The toilet wasn't flushed and spots of piss, both fresh and dried, were splattered on the seat. But Eve wasn't in any position to be picky, so she hovered, and then discovered there was no toilet paper.

She rinsed her hands, no soap, and shook them dryish. She needed to get out of there—the bathroom—the party. All she wanted was a shower.

She marched to the dance floor and found Carrie on a couch lying on a pile of discarded pimp jackets. Tim had his hand under her shirt. Hair tousled and face flushed, Carrie didn't even notice

Eve. She reminded Eve of a contented cat purring with pleasure, and Eve envied her ability to let go, to seize life, to trust. Carrie had everything Eve wanted—fun, confidence, a life, happiness, a normal mom, Tim. Eve fought the temptation to hate her for it, reminding herself that her dysfunction was hardly Carrie's fault. Still, Tim and Carrie wrapped up in each other was a punch in the gut.

Eve's head spun. She staggered backward, bumping into a dancing couple, spilling her drink, and weaving toward the floor.

A strong hand gripped her elbow and pulled her upright. "You okay?" It was the guy from the deck, the wolf who'd marked her with his tongue.

Eve nodded.

"You wanna get out of here? Go somewhere quiet. Get to know each other." He grinned. "I have a room upstairs."

Eve supposed his smile was intended to be flirtatious, but to her, it appeared predatory. She shook her head no, wanting nothing more than to flee the party, to flee this man, to flee Carrie and Tim. Only Carrie and Tim decided that moment to take a breather and noticed Eve lurking nearby.

"Eve, what's going on? You okay?" Tim asked, getting to his feet.

"What? Oh. Fine." Eve leaned against her Wolf, drawing courage from his touch, imagining being wrapped up in his arms—fun, confident, happy, normal. Perhaps the life she wanted was within reach. "We were just headed up."

"Really?" Carrie's eyes practically popped out of her head at the un-Eve-like behavior.

"Really." Eve gave them a Party Girl wink, grabbed the Wolf's hand, followed him up the stairs, and into his den.

Decorated with empty beer cans, dirty clothes, and posters of half-dressed women, the Wolf's den was about what Eve expected—until he turned the overhead light off. Then the room was lit with a black light and the walls came alive with fluorescent caveman art.

"Want to leave your mark?" The Wolf offered her a highlighter.

Eve shook her head, having no interest in leaving behind any record of her presence. She'd agreed to come to his room for one reason, and all she wanted was to get it over with.

"C'mon, it's fun."

"No, thanks."

The corners of his lips turned down, and Eve felt as though she'd disappointed him, upset his seduction ritual. He offered a sip from a jug. "How about some moonshine?"

Eve knew better than to deny him a second time, so she took a swig and nearly spat it out. Her eyes watered in the effort to swallow the liquid fire without gagging.

"Good, huh?"

Eve suspected he was making fun of her, but she nodded in agreement. She took another sip to prove how very cool she was. They took turns sipping from the vile jar. Eve's tongue began to feel thick, and her thoughts dulled, but she hadn't come for the moonshine.

She chewed on her fingernail, not sure how to move this along. Should she start undressing? Recline on the bed? What would Ally do? Ally always knew how to act in any situation. At least she used to. Back when she returned Eve's calls.

Thoughts of Ally had no place here. This experience was awkward enough without adding another person to the room, even if she was only in her head.

"So. . . ." Eve groped for something to say, something clever and sexy, "Do you have a condom?" She clamped her hand over her mouth. That was not what she'd meant to say. She closed her eyes, so she wouldn't have to see him laugh at her.

Only when she opened them a few seconds later, he wasn't laughing. Instead, he was holding up a condom, and he looked delighted.

Eve wished she shared his delight. Eve had dreamed that this super, big moment would be the magical stuff of romance novels. She'd placed losing her virginity high on a pedestal. Maybe that was her whole problem. What if the pedestal was making her frigid? Could getting laid free her of all her hang-ups? Could taking control of her body release her from her mom's domination? Party Girl was going to find out, but she wasn't delighted about it. She was scared, and drunk, and sad.

The Wolf leaned in to kiss her.

She opened her mouth to accept his tongue. What was his real name? He'd told her. Hadn't he? Didn't matter.

His hands stroked her bare shoulders. He pressed into her, and slowly backed her toward the bed. A door slammed somewhere nearby causing Eve to startle, but he didn't seem to notice. Rather he was busy burrowing his head in her cleavage. For several minutes, he fumbled with the back of the bodice, before finally groaning and pulling back. "Don't get me wrong. This thing is hot, but how do you get it off?"

Eve turned, so he could see the lacing on her back better. "It's like a shoelace. Untie the top and then loosen it."

Eve took a deep breath, trying to relax, trying to enjoy the sensation of his fingers on her back. Once the bodice was loosened, he pulled it off and spun her around so he could take in her bare breasts. She fought the urge to cross her arms and hide them.

He fumbled to unbutton his jeans. In seconds, he stood before her naked. Eve stared down at his penis. She'd never seen one in real life. Never seen one erect. She wasn't really clear on how it was going to fit.

"How about you take the skirt off?" he asked.

Eve tried to shimmy it off sexily, but the leather was sticky, making it more difficult than it should have been, and the fact that he was watching her made her nervous. At last, though, she stood wearing only a choker, fishnets, and heels. The Wolf looked like he'd discovered an unlocked hen house.

Eve reached over and took a gulp of the moonshine. In her enthusiasm, some splashed on her chin and dripped onto her breast. The Wolf dove in and licked it off, pushing her onto the bed.

He slid her underwear and tights to her knees, then slid his finger inside her. Eve flinched and then relaxed, reminding herself that she wanted this.

"Do you like it?" he asked while he swirled his finger inside her, and Eve found that she did, sort of. She pressed against his hand, craving more, and he complied—moving his fingers faster and deeper until she was squirming beneath him. They were both breathing hard when he paused to slide on the condom. Eve kicked off her shoes and finished removing her stockings and underwear.

Sheathed now, the Wolf returned, stared down at her with hooded eyes and then he rammed inside her. She gasped, pleasure mingling with pain, but he barely noticed her, caught up in his own need. He pumped into her again and again until at last, he relaxed on top of her.

Eve waited underneath him, wondering when the surge of power would transform her. While she waited for her metamorphosis, she distracted herself by reading the writing on the walls: #GOODTIMES #SODRUNK. CALL BRIDGET. SURF'S UP. YOU'RE AT A CARNIVAL, YOU HAVE COTTON CANDY, HOW CAN YOU BE UNHAPPY?

She waited until he finally rolled off her.

"There's blood everywhere," he remarked. "Are you having your period?"

Eve's face turned the color of the blood smeared across her thighs. "No," she said, holding back tears. She scrambled out of bed. "I gotta go."

"Okay. . . ." he sounded surprised, like this wasn't how things usually went. He'd gotten what he wanted, why did he care if she left?

She squeezed back into the skirt and pulled on the bodice. She couldn't manage to tie the stupid thing though. The Wolf leaned over and helped her. "You could stay." He kissed her neck. Eve forced herself not to pull away. It wasn't this guy's fault. He didn't know.

"No." She struggled with the fishnets, her toes getting caught in holes, then finally gave up and threw them on the floor.

"You want me to walk you home?"

"No," she practically bit his head off. In a calmer voice, she mumbled, "Thanks though."

"Maybe we can get together some other time."

So he could fuck her again? "Yeah sure. That'd be great," Eve tried to force enthusiasm into her voice, tried to act like this was normal, like she was normal.

He handed her his phone. "Here. Why don't you give me your number?"

Eve narrowed her eyes at him. "What's my name?"

"Uh." He had the grace to blush. "We never got around to . . ."

She tossed his phone back at him. "See you around." And she went home to finally take that shower. As if it could wash away this mistake as easily as her blood.

Where is @allysunshinegirl? #bigstuffbrewing #callme

CHAPTER 3

To: ald2@mail.com
From: seams274@mail.com
Date: March 5 2:42 a.m.
Subject: Call me

Dear Ally,

Is everything okay? Are you mad at me? I don't know whether to be worried about you or worried about us, so I guess I'll worry about both. We've never gone more than a week without talking before. It's been over two months! Argh!!! I miss you! Your voicemail box is full—probably all messages from me. I've tried texting you, emailing you, messaging you, tweeting you, Snapchatting you . . . nothing. In a world with so many ways to connect, how can we be so disconnected?

I'm almost desperate enough to call your parents or Aunt Victoria, but we made a pact long ago to keep "us" between us and for now, I'm waiting, but I'm so worried about you. What if you are in trouble and you need help? What if my sounding the alarm is the only way you get the help you need?

I keep telling myself you're probably just busy with your glamorous life in LA. I'm dying to hear about it, so I can live vicariously through you, since I'm sure as hell not living it up here. It feels like I'm stranded in a desert and our friendship has become a mirage—and we thought you were the dramatic one! College, my love life, everything is a disaster. For a million craptacular reasons—and I keep making it worse. I can't seem to pull myself together. Guess I'm the disaster. Maybe you're smart to avoid my fallout.

I've set up this email account, hoping you'll finally feel comfortable answering me on it. My mom doesn't know it exists, it's not connected to any of my devices, and I'm only using it on the school's computers. We should be safe from her paparazzi parenting if that's what you're worried about. Please respond. I need you. I'm a mess—unraveling. Call me. Please. I love you. I miss you. I hope you're okay.

Love,

Eve

P.S. Do you still want me to visit this summer?

CHAPTER 4

End of April

The last time Boop moved, she'd spent days haunting liquor stores. But since the ABC stores now recycle their sturdy boxes with the efficiency of a Yankee, her only reason to head to one was to stock up on bourbon for her weekly mint julep. She was all for recycling, but as her arthritic hands fumbled to build the boxes she'd purchased, she didn't feel especially enthusiastic about environmental friendliness.

In a surge of frustration, Boop tugged on a flap a mite too hard, tearing it half off. She smacked the box, innocent victim of her withered hands and Justine's bullying.

"Careful, Boop," Justine tsked.

Boop glared at her dear daughter. Not for the first time, wishing fifty-eight wasn't too old for a well-deserved licking and eighty wasn't too old to dole one out. She'd have to make do with knocking the box around, so she popped it again for good measure.

Reckoning she was decades past the do-it-yourself stage, Boop had hired movers to pack and ship her belongings. However, when she'd let that detail slip to Justine—let's just say, Justine has trust issues in general, and deep-rooted trust issues with movers specifically. On a practical level, Justine couldn't insist on canceling the movers for the actual moving of boxes, but on the issue of packing, she held firm.

Justine, looking as though she'd just stepped out of a Vineyard Vines catalog, held up a neon orange flamingo birdhouse. It'd been a housewarming gift from her neighbor, Shirley, who, bless her heart, had a hole in her bag of marbles. Like Shirley herself, the birdhouse plucked Boop's nerves. The house, nestled in the bird's body, was perched atop one of the flamingo's legs and toppled over every time the door opened. She'd had to glue it back on half a dozen times. Boop held onto the klutzy mis-colored flamingo though—a reminder that she'd once toppled over every time the door opened too. Wouldn't do to forget where she came from.

"These birdhouses make you seem like a crazy old lady. Your condo's more like a gardening store than a home." Justine's coiffed perfection underscored the flamingo's ridiculousness.

"Honey, I am a crazy old lady. Don't make no difference to me what people think." Boop's eyes swept her collection—all forty-three birdhouses. The one in the middle of her mantle was hands-down her favorite. Eve had built it in shop class back in middle school. Boop still imagined she caught a whiff of sawdust when she got right on up to it. She fancied the one next to it too. That was the one she'd picked up in Nashville three years before. It played "Take Me Home, Country Roads"—when she remembered to replace the batteries.

Thankfully, Justine let it go at that. Maybe she chalked up Boop's strange fetish to the three pet birds she'd lost in as many months. Only it wasn't the birds. None of them had lasted more than ten days; hardly enough time to get attached. No, it was the emptiness that Boop sought to fill, but Justine wouldn't know about that. No one did.

Justine had surprised her that morning by flying down from Richmond to manage the packing. Boop wasn't naïve enough to believe that Justine's motives were altruistic, rather she reckoned that Justine didn't trust her with her future inheritance any more than the movers. In fact, Justine didn't trust her with much, including keeping an eye on Eve. Packing for Boop was the perfect excuse to check in on Eve herself.

Boop expected Eve any moment. Only Eve was blissfully ignorant of her mother's arrival. Boop had tried to warn Eve several times, but Eve hadn't answered her calls. Since Boop was unsure about the ins and outs of leaving messages, she rarely bothered.

A knock on the door sent Justine to her feet and rushing to greet Eve. Justine flung the door open. "Surprise!"

Eve glared at Boop over Justine's shoulder.

"I tried to ring you," Boop said.

Justine gathered Eve into a stiff hug. "I've been helping Boop pack while we waited for you," Justine said, putting an unnecessary emphasis on the "waited" as if Eve were egregiously late. She wasn't.

Eve bit her lip.

With her plucked eyebrows arched, Justine held Eve by her shoulders and gave her a once-over. "You're thinner. Are you getting enough to eat?"

It was true that Eve's jeans hung looser on her hips than usual and perhaps that should be a source of concern, but Boop fretted that this was merely Justine's opening line in a barrage, which would include Eve's perpetual ponytail, chewed up fingernails, depressing black shirts, and pasty complexion. Boop didn't have the stomach for it today. "Thank you kindly for coming, Eve."

Eve nodded at Boop and stuffed her hands in her pockets.

The circles under Eve's eyes troubled Boop. Between all-night study sessions and parties, college life could be exhausting, so it would be understandable if Eve was a hair run down. The catch was that Eve didn't ever mention any parties. The flatness of her gaze, as if Eve had crawled into herself, sent shivers of familiarity down Boop's spine. Even her scent—a barrage of vanilla—spoke of desperation. As if reeking of birthday cake masked . . . what? What was Eve trying to cover-up? Boop shook away the foreboding that threatened to swallow her.

"Eve, why don't you get those plates down from the china cabinet? Careful, they don't even make that pattern anymore." Justine grabbed a stack of newspaper and an empty box. "I can't believe you still get the Leeside newspaper, Boop. Nobody gets newspapers these days, and you get one from a place you haven't lived in for forty years?"

"I like keeping up with everybody. Actually though, I'm thinking about canceling my subscription."

"Seriously? The stuff they put in there cracks me up. Remember the cat that looked like Elvis?" Eve asked.

"Well there's that, but everyone I know's moving from the society pages to the obituaries. It's depressing—more depressing than a friendless mosquito." Boop finished the box she was working on and struggled to her feet. Every muscle in her body had stiffened in the time she'd sat on the floor.

Eve lurched toward her as if to help, but Boop shooed her away, determined to make it to her feet on her own.

Justine's pursed lips whitened as she watched Boop struggle. Once Boop finished straightening and it became clear she wasn't going to fall, Justine turned on Eve, "How are classes going?"

Eve shrugged, eyed the door and then the grandfather clock birdhouse—tick, tick, tick.

"Biology?"

"Fine," Eve mumbled into the cabinet where she'd stuck her head.

After decades of prevaricating, Boop was finely tuned to the nuances of truth, and she'd have bet her senior citizen discount Eve was lying like a coon dog on a hot summer's day.

Justine's frown suggested she wasn't buying it either, so Boop swept in to change the subject. "Your momma's already taken care of my bedroom closet. She's quite the whirlwind."

"I still don't understand why you're moving out. You're only staying with me until your shoulder heals; then where will you go?" Justine asked. Boop's shoulder surgery was scheduled for late May. She planned to stay with Justine while it healed, somewhere in the neighborhood of two to six months.

Boop said, "I don't know where I'm headed afterward, but I've lived here for five years and this place still doesn't feel like home." Nowhere had felt like home in a long while. Didn't seem to matter how far she ran. It was as if she was running on a treadmill and home was the carrot dangling just in front of her.

Boop watched Eve rifle through the drawers of a side table, pulling out honeysuckle-scented candles, a dancing Santa, and a folder of recipes, torn from old *Southern Living* magazines, which Boop would never cook. Scrunching her nose, Eve held up a hand-sized oblong carving. "What's this supposed to be?"

Boop shuddered. When her sister Vicky had learned about Boop and Tommy's impending divorce, she'd given Boop the statuette "to cheer her up." Chocolates, flowers, or a bottle of wine would have scratched that itch, but no . . . her gift had been a statue titled "Cleave." A childhood of Sunday sermons ensured that Boop knew Genesis 2:24 and its dictates that man "shall cleave unto his wife." Nothing like a kick when you're down.

The irony wasn't lost on Boop that the onyx statue, with its bulbous bottom and rounded top, resembled male genitalia, but she was hardly going to acknowledge that. "Either of y'all want it? Be my guest. It's so ugly it'd scare a buzzard off a gut pile."

"Let me see." Justine's long capable fingers grasped the air in Eve's direction.

Eve tossed it to Justine, who caught it, but not without sending Eve a scathing glare, as if to say that the statue's safe landing was no thanks to Eve's flippancy. Justine's fingers explored the small statue, weighing it, measuring, stroking its smoothness in a way that made Boop squirm, given her earlier musings.

"It's heavy. Where'd you get it?" Justine asked.

"From Vicky." Boop slammed the cupboard shut a tad harder than she'd meant. Vicky had a way of inspiring overreactions in Boop. Her name alone was enough to set her off.

"This is real art—not some trinket. How come I've never seen it before?' Justine said. Like a vulture, Justine didn't know when to let something lie.

"Heavens, that thing didn't get hit with the ugly stick. It is the ugly stick." Boop wiped her hands on her sweatpants in a fruitless attempt to the clean off the dust and newspaper print.

"Mom, I want to talk to you about my plans for this summer," Eve said.

"Right. Me, too. I've got some amazing news." Without bothering to ask either Eve or Boop if they wanted any, Justine poured three glasses of iced tea.

"Oh?" Eve nibbled on her pinky nail, seeming nervous about what Justine might consider "amazing news." The small kitchen table could only accommodate two chairs, so Eve sat atop the green step stool. This was usually kept folded between the refrigerator and the wall, and used when Boop couldn't reach stuff in the cabinets, which was pretty much all the time.

It seemed as good a time as any for a break, so Boop took one of the two chairs, expecting Justine to take the other, forgetting that Justine didn't take breaks.

Instead of joining them, Justine returned to packing birdhouses. "I've found you an internship at the hospital, in the emergency room."

Boop would've guessed that Eve couldn't get any paler, but darned if Eve wasn't proving her wrong.

However, Justine was too engrossed in packing the birdhouses to notice, so she prattled on. "It's practically a done deal. You'll have to do an interview when you get to town, and they want you to submit your grades for this semester, but assuming you don't blow it, the internship is yours. The administrator owes Trevor a few favors."

Trevor, Justine's boss, was a real son-of-a-gun. Everyone knew it, including Justine, but Justine also appreciated the weight he could, and did, throw around for her benefit. What Trevor lacked in height, he made up for in sheer magnetism. He reeked of raw energy and manly cologne that was somehow both compelling and off-putting at the same time. Some might call him silver-tongued, but Boop pegged him better—all hat and no cattle. The way Justine talked about Trevor gave Boop the willies, but she kept her opinions to her herself. Justine would take advice from a baboon before she'd take it from Boop, so there was no sense in broaching the subject.

"Aren't you going to say anything?" With her eyebrows arched again in that uppity expression Boop loathed, Justine peered at Eve over a blue beach-shack birdhouse. Eve had given the birdhouse to Boop for her last birthday, excited that the sand around the base actually smelled of ocean salt. Too long had passed since Boop had seen that side of Eve.

"I don't know what to say." The jostling of the ice cubes in Eve's tea betrayed the slight tremble of her hand.

"Thank you would be a great start."

"Thanks, but I'm not sure—"

"Really, Eve? Do you have some other plan for the summer? If you think you're going to binge watch *Project Runway* all summer, you've got another thing coming."

"It's not that—"

"What? C'mon, Eve. If I'd had the opportunities you have . . ." Justine cut her eyes at Boop.

Boop braced herself, but Justine let her off easy this time and instead turned back to Eve. "Don't do this. Don't make me look bad. Don't make Trevor look bad."

Boop let herself imagine going to town on Trevor with a Sharpie, adding a mustache, glasses, and devil horns. When she felt her lips turning up at the corners, she had to pinch her thigh to maintain the proper decorum. Holy Moly! It wouldn't do to have Justine catch her smiling.

"Yes, ma'am," Eve said. Clearly, her chastened granddaughter didn't have the benefit of an imaginary Sharpie.

The screech of Boop's chair scraping back on the tile floor made everyone flinch. "How's Ally?" Boop asked after her great-niece in an obvious attempt to change the subject.

Eve shrugged.

"You haven't mentioned her in a while." Boop's gaze narrowed. Something about Eve's expression was off, like she was trying too hard to look casual. "Don't y'all young people word message one another all the time?"

"Text," Justine corrected.

"What?" Boop asked.

"It's called text messaging," Justine spoke slowly, enunciating each word as if speaking to a dingbat.

Boop could feel her blood pressure rising at Justine's contempt, but she was determined not to have a hissy fit. She forced her tone to remain light. "Is it now?"

Eve broke in, "I don't text all that much. And Ally and I never do . . ." Her eyes narrowed in her mother's direction. "Anymore."

"Don't blame me." Justine crossed her arms over her chest.

"What am I missing here?" Boop asked, swinging her eyes like a badminton birdie between them.

"Well, Boop, not that you would understand this," Justine said, "but I consider it my duty to look after Eve and make sure no predators contact her, so I read her text messages."

"And emails," Eve muttered into the running water while she rinsed everyone's glasses.

"You can't be too careful these days."

"Can't you?" Boop asked. "Careful" wasn't the word to describe Justine, "smothering" might do it. Heck, the woman was like a gag soaked in sweet-smelling chloroform!

Eve jammed the glasses into the dishwasher and slammed it shut. "Anyway, after Mom narced on Ally last year for smoking pot, Ally and I decided we would no longer communicate electronically."

"It's for your own good, for both of you. Her father is running for governor, for heaven's sake. What was she thinking?"

"I know." Eve ducked her head.

"You sound like Vicky," Boop said to Justine. No one in the room doubted that this was meant to be an insult.

However, Justine chose to pretend differently. "You'd do well to sound more like Aunt Victoria."

"You don't know the half of it." Boop wandered around the condo gathering framed photographs off of shelves, tables, and walls.

"What don't I know?"

Refusing to dignify Justine's question with an answer, Boop dumped the armful of photos on the sofa. The waft of dust tickled her nose and inspired her to dig out the Windex. No time like the present.

Justine continued, "'Cause from where I'm standing, Vicky did a hell of a better job at . .. everything than you did. Maybe you should listen to her more often."

Boop picked up a family photo, circa 1970, of her, Tommy, and Justine. Funny how deceptive a photograph could be. The lake was behind them, and you could just make out the front of Tommy's red speedboat. His pride and joy. The colors were browned in a way that all photos from that decade were. Muted colors, muted memories, muted feelings. It had been their last family vacation together, but there was nothing to indicate that in their happy-go-lucky expressions. A smile can hide a million betrayals. "I know you think that. I know why you think that, but you're plumb wrong."

"Enlighten me." Justine came over to take a gander the photograph that Boop was eyeballing. She twisted the newspaper in her hands while she, too, stared at it.

Boop met Justine's eyes. "You know I can't do that."

"Can't? Won't. You are so—" Justine smacked the rolled-up newspaper against her thigh.

"Mom, quit it, would you?" Eve's voice trembled with the effort.

"Eve, it isn't your place to—"

"Now don't take your resentment of me out on the girl." Boop snatched the newspaper from Justine's hand and used it to wrap up the photograph.

"I thought you said she was all grown up?" Justine said.

"Oh, for crying out loud, I declare this conversation complete. My belongings ain't gonna box themselves. Less talking, more packing." Boop stuffed the now concealed photograph into Justine's hands and bent to wrap another.

Boop woke with the roosters Monday morning. She couldn't seem to sleep in to save her life, which was a shame since she didn't have all that much to fill her days. After Justine and Eve had taken care of the bulk of the packing, they'd headed back to their respective homes. As she rolled out of bed and put on her pink terry cloth bathrobe, she couldn't help relishing having the condo to herself. Her stomach rumbled.

Grits with a side of bacon. The mere thought of them got Boop's engines revved, and she headed to the kitchen to whip some up. Since the instant kind didn't taste right, a good thirty minutes passed before the grits were ready. Boop stirred in a dollop of butter, all the while shaking her head as she remembered Justine informing her yesterday that butter wasn't nutritional. Justine had recommended she switch to I Can't Believe It's Not Butter, but as far as Boop was concerned the name said it all. The scent of bacon sizzling on the frying pan made her stomach grumble. A cup of coffee rounded out her morning feast. She sat down to dig in. It was gonna be a good day.

Then the telephone rang. It was only seven in the morning. No one rang with good news at that time of day.

Boop dodged around towers of boxes to answer the phone. She was worried the call had something to do with Eve. Girl hadn't seemed at all right yesterday.

"Hello?"

"Betty . . . how are you?" Only one person called her Betty. Boop's good day was shot to hell in a handbasket.

"In the feather, Vicky. In the feather." Boop's sister fancied herself a lady and insisted that she be addressed as Victoria by her intimates and Mrs. Victoria to the rest of the world. Boop was of the opinion that her sister was too big for her crisp linen britches and reminded her of this by persistently calling her Vicky.

"Mmhmm . . . yes," Vicky said.

Boop could practically hear her biting her tongue. Was she a terrible person for wishing she'd draw blood?

Vicky continued, "I haven't seen you and your sweet granddaughter in a month of Sundays. I'd hoped that Eve might drive you up to Savannah to visit me occasionally."

"Those college kids are busier than mustard trying to ketchup."

"I suppose. However, the semester is ending, and my guest bedrooms are aching for some company. Might y'all come for a spell soon?"

Boop took a deep breath, attempting to inhale calm but really just inhaling the aroma of her coffee. She massaged the handle of her red coffee cup.

"I don't reckon so. Thank you kindly." The grits were getting cold, so Boop took a bite, making sure to smack her lips. Listening to her eat was sure to drive Vicky batty, but that was just a bonus. Boop was hungry, or at least that was what she told herself.

"Now then, what's more important than family?"

"Really, Vicky—" Boop felt a headache coming on, so she yanked the plastic rollers from her hair, hoping to relieve the pressure a bit. Only their absence didn't do anything to quell Vicky's nagging voice. Her dulcet tone was like an electric drill grinding in Boop's ear.

"Really, nothing. We aren't getting any younger," Vicky said.

Boop glared at her knobby hands with their protruding blue veins, liver spots, and wrinkles. Oh, the wrinkles! Boop sometimes imagined she even smelled of decay, or maybe it wasn't her imagination. She wasn't sure she wanted to know. "Maybe you ain't, but I'm right spritely." Spritely like swamp mud.

"Mmhmm. I'm not sure your shoulder would agree."

"Aw, now." Boop stuck her tongue out at the phone.

"I need to chat with you and Eve about a few things." Somehow Vicky made this simple request sound like a royal command. Must be all that time she'd spent married to the senator. She'd aspired to the governor's mansion, but her husband hadn't managed to pull off that feat. Maybe her son, Preston, would.

"I'm all ears," Boop said.

"I'd rather speak with you in person."

In another time, Vicky might have run for governor herself. No doubt she'd have won and would have been a force to be reckoned with. But she hadn't been raised to have such aspirations. In this case, that might be a blessing for the world. Boop asked, "Is that necessary?"

"Yes. No reason to sound as though visiting me is like a trip to the dentist."

"I like my dentist."

"Betty . . ."

"Seriously, it never goes well with you and me, and now you want to drag Eve into our mess?"

"If you weren't so flippant—"

"And you weren't so stuffy—"

"We should be friends."

"That ship done left the dock long ago." Boop's glance strayed out the kitchen window where she could see that the gray mockingbird was back on her balcony pecking at the Spanish moss blanketing her flowerpots. For two weeks, that little thief had visited every morning gathering supplies for her nest.

In a tone that was far too casual for Boop's comfort, Vicky said, "You might want an old photograph that turned up recently. It's awfully precious to trust to the postal service, but if you insist . . ."

"What's the picture of?" Even as she asked it though, Boop knew.

"Davey."

Boop reeled. She never let herself think of him. It hurt too dang much. Her eyes darted around for the comfort of her birdhouses, but they were packed away along with the rest of her life.

She worried her bottom lip. She only had one photograph of Davey. One measly photograph. The rest had turned to ashes when her house had caught fire. Of course, Vicky knew that. No doubt she'd held onto this photograph, so she could play it like a trump card. Boop shivered to imagine what Vicky was planning to ask for in return for the picture. Davey's story had already cost her years, her marriage, and her daughter's respect—everything, though no more than she'd owed. Davey was a debt she could never make right.

The silence on the phone was so heavy Boop thought she might smother. Until finally, she broke it before it broke her. "Let me see about Eve. I'll get back to you."

"You do that. So lovely to speak with you."

Boop hung up the phone and crawled back into bed where she burrowed under the comfort of her lavender-scented sheets.

A Long Time Ago

Everybody who was anybody in Leeside was invited to Susan Cochran's costume party. When the invitation was delivered to their door, there was only one name on it, and it was Boop's. Vicky acted as if she didn't give a hoot, but Boop knew she did. Course Vicky'd stolen Susan's boyfriend Tommy ten months before, so Vicky probably wasn't surprised by her exclusion. Still though, one should never underestimate the power of a snub.

Not about to miss an opportunity to put Boop in her place, Vicky said, "Betty, you've only been invited to get at me. So don't go around thinking you're somebody special. Everybody knows you're a baby, and Daddy won't let you out to play with the big kids anyway."

Boop pounded her feet up the creaky stairs in a fit 'cause Vicky was right on both accounts. Susan was three years older than Boop and knew full well Boop's daddy wouldn't let her attend an evening social event until after her sixteenth birthday. Her daddy was a legend of virtue in Leeside, deeply religious, and civic-minded. Vicky had caught the civic-minded spirit, but both she and Boop had escaped his holy spirit. A childhood spent on their knees hadn't done much to sell the lifestyle.

Holed up pouting in her room, Boop turned to thinking, thinking turned to plotting, and by the time the party came along, Boop had planned to sneak out of her bedroom window without her daddy's leave. The fact that it was a costume party meant that Boop could wear a mask and the busybody chaperones wouldn't even know she was there. All eyes would follow her as she flitted around in her bright yellow and blue butterfly costume. She'd wear a floral perfume to trail her scent behind like pollen. The town would be atwitter for weeks, talking circles around the identity of the mysterious butterfly. Boop would be a legend in her own right.

Outside Boop's second-floor bedroom window was a magnolia tree. As a small child, she'd built houses for fairies among its roots, complete with acorn cap bathtubs, bark tables, and moss-covered rock beds. Years later she used her cousin, Jackie's, Swiss Army knife to carve her initials into the trunk, marking it for her very own. Only a childhood spent dolled up in ruffled dresses and Mary Janes didn't lend itself to much tree climbing, so she'd managed to make it through her whole life so far, without ever climbing her very own tree. And so it was that her virgin tree-climbing experience was to climb down a tree, rather than up one, which is like parachuting out of the first airplane you ever fly in.

Even though Boop was as scared as a long-tailed cat in a room full of rocking chairs, she didn't dilly-dally. Her heart was beating so loud, she thought surely her daddy would catch wind and come running. Thoughts of the whooping she'd get if she got caught only made it pound harder. Boop imagined herself as Tarzan swinging from branch to branch, but reality was that she was as clumsy as a toddler on a tightrope. The rucksack, which she'd stuffed with her mask, yellow dress, and blue gauze wings, kept getting snagged by twigs and jerking every which way. Boop was ready to call it quits, but her knees quaked at the very idea of tempting fate a second time on the rickety branch she'd already conquered once. The ground looked safer.

Once she made it to the trunk, she stopped to rest and tally up the damage. The shoulder seam of her blouse was ripped, her riding pants were smudged, and her right hand was scraped. She'd need to come up with a whopper of an explanation by morning. She blew on her smarting hand. In preparation for her shimmy down the trunk, she eased the troublesome rucksack off her shoulder and was about to drop it to the dirt below when she heard noises—kissing sounds. She peered between the fresh spring leaves and pink flowers, which were just thick enough to both hide her and give her an owl's eye view of the porch. There, cuddling on a swing, were a chaperone-less Vicky and Tommy. Seemed Boop wasn't the only one sneaking around.

Boop froze to take a deep breath and consider her options.

Strategizing didn't come naturally to her like it did to Vicky. Vicky got that talent from their daddy. Daddy said he learned how to think that way in the army, but the only war Vicky had ever served in was the one with Boop, so Boop supposed with Vicky it was more a natural-born talent than a learned one. Even though both girls had been caught with their britches down so to speak, Boop worried Vicky would find some way to turn the whole thing around and hang Boop out to dry, a butterfly lost in Antarctica.

While Boop spied on them, Tommy and Vicky took a smooching break, and Tommy said, "I talked to a recruiter yesterday."

Vicky gasped. "Please, no. Tell me you're teasing."

"Nah, I ain't teasin'. A man's got a duty to his country."

Vicky drew back. "What about your duty to me?"

"Baby, I'm thinking about you—about protecting you, loving you, making the world safe for when we get hitched and have a family. All I do is think about you and making you proud."

"What about college?" Vicky's voice shook. Boop couldn't see her face, but knew Vicky was upset. Tommy had made the most romantic declaration Boop had ever heard, and there was Vicky pulling a Scarlet O'Hara. Boop could just picture her stamping her feet and fiddle-dee-deeing.

"I can finish school when I'm done," said Tommy.

"What if something happens? What if you die?"

"That'll never happen, not when I have you to come home to." Tommy leaned forward to kiss her, but Vicky pushed him and jumped to her feet, smoothing down her emerald green skirt. This was no impromptu dalliance, Vicky was dressed to impress.

"No, I won't do this." She stomped her foot (just as Boop had imagined) and crossed her arms over her chest. "You join the military, you leave me behind, Tommy Wilkes, and I'm not waiting for you. I'm not turning into some old maid because you got to go prove you're a man. You stay right here with me where you belong."

A gnarled knot dug into Boop's backside, and as she shifted to relieve the pressure, the small branch holding her left foot snapped. She grabbed the branch above her head while she sought firmer footing.

"Is that you, Betty? You little snoop. I'll get you for this."

By the time Vicky finished cursing Boop, Tommy was under Boop's feet. "C'mon, Boop. Let go. I'll catch you."

Boop gazed into his dreamy Frank Sinatra blue eyes and knew he would do just that, and so she let go and plummeted into his muscular embrace where his musk of pine and black pepper enveloped her. He grinned down at her, and she simpered, imagined his mouth on her hers.

"What in tarnation were you doing up in that tree?" asked Vicky. No one would call Vicky pretty, not that she was ugly either. Vicky was what you'd call "put together." But at that moment, with her face all flushed and her hair mussed, she was neither pretty nor put together. That made Boop happy.

When Tommy set Boop gently to her feet, she couldn't wipe the goofy grin from her face.

"I believe Boop may have been on her way somewhere." Tommy handed her the rucksack that had fallen to the ground. "A costume party, perhaps?" He raised his right eyebrow. Boop was pretty certain Tommy was aware of the effect his dancing eyebrow had on her—on all the girls at that. She wondered if he practiced it in the mirror. She'd tried it herself but could only manage a squishy-faced grimace.

Boop snatched her bag back.

"I'm going to tell Daddy!" Vicky said.

Boop cleared her throat. "Oh, does Daddy know you've got a gentleman caller then?"

"Yes." Vicky was bluffing.

"Okay then, you tell Daddy I was sneaking out, and I'll tell him you and Tommy were petting on the porch."

"We were not."

"Then Tommy's got someone else's lipstick smeared on?"

Tommy wiped his mouth with the back of his hand, but Vicky's bright red brand was not so easily erased.

"You little—" Vicky said.

"Aw, Victoria, she's just a kid. Let her be." Tommy was no kid, and he made sure everyone knew it, between his straight-as-a-board posture and his deadly grip of a handshake. It's sad, people spend the first half of their lives wishing they were older and the second half wishing they were younger. Always chasing their tails.

Boop's face flushed. "I'm not a kid. I'm fifteen years old, and I even kissed a boy last month."

"Playing post office don't count," Vicky said.

Boop ducked her head.

Tommy nudged up her chin. "It ain't kissing that makes you grown-up."

Boop could smell the minty freshness of his breath. "Then what does?" Boop whispered, wishing he'd lean down and kiss her, knowing full well he wouldn't, couldn't. For Boop, Tommy was a dangling carrot.

"Doing the right thing even when it's hard. Even when it breaks your heart."

Boop knew then he'd go off to the army, knew Vicky'd break off with him, and that very moment Boop swore if he came home—when he came home—she'd mend his broken heart. She'd show them who was grown-up.

CHAPTER 5

May

Eve snapped and posted a picture of her bare feet framed by the shoreline with the comment: THIS IS THE LIFE.

Then she wandered to the water to cool off or maybe drown. No, she wasn't really suicidal. That took too much energy. But if a giant wave swept her away . . . if she drowned in some freak accident . . . she wouldn't mind.

Eve floated on her back and closed her eyes to the glare of the over-bright sun, daring the ocean to do just that.

Comment under Eve's post: So jealous! (27 likes)

The chicken-flavored ramen noodles looked disturbingly normal after stewing in an orange bowl on the suite floor of Eve's dorm for three days. The edges had hardened and darkened, but after a zap in the microwave and a stir, no one would be the wiser. Must be all that salt. Eve glared at the wrapper, half of which was smashed under her biology textbook—1,960 mg of sodium. Yum. The Japanese said salt wards off evil spirits. If only a steady diet of ramen noodles were the antidote to all of Eve's problems.

Her eyes strained to stay open as she read *The Metamorphosis*. Once she finished the page though, they drooped shut against her will.

She rubbed her cheek against the rough, brown fabric covering the sofa. It reeked of vomit and beer. The television droned in the background.

Dribble. Dribble. The infuriating guy upstairs was bouncing his basketball again. At least this time it wasn't two o'clock in the morning. Many months ago, back in the day when she and Carrie had still been buddies, they'd gone up in their pj's to complain. Carrie had gone from mad to flirty the second the tanned bare-chested stud had opened the door. Without Carrie to back her up, Eve had lost her courage and stood there stammering like a gaping fish until finally, she'd blurted out, "You smell like seaweed." Which he did. But still. Ever since, she'd ducked behind corners to avoid the guy, and his basketballs had continued to plague her.

Eve pried her eyes open to search for the place where she'd stopped reading but couldn't find it. So instead of reading, she huddled in her robe, thinking. Well, she'd have liked to call it thinking. Sounded better than the truth—that she was watching the antics of the resident cockroach as it scurried from crumb to crumb. While it hid under furniture between bites, Eve felt a kinship with Kafka the cockroach.

Eve imagined her mom's probable reaction to this scene, to Kafka, and shuddered. After exams, she'd have to face her. That wasn't long to pull her shit together. Otherwise . . . She flipped back a page, hunting for a familiar spot to begin again. Only nothing was familiar. She slammed the book shut and chucked it across the room.

Dribble. Dribble. Eve's cold feet longed for socks, but they were all dirty and the laundry was in her room—easily fifteen feet away. So instead, she contemplated the "gunmetal gray" chipped nail polish on her toes. A morbid name for a morbid color. She'd bought it mostly because she knew her mom would hate it. Since her mom wasn't around to see it, it had felt like a safe act of rebellion. Stupid and pointless, but safe.

It'd only take a few minutes to slap on another layer but getting the bottle on her dresser would ruin her record for the longest couch lounge ever, and Eve liked to think she could win at something.

Carrie and Tim wandered through the suite, whispering. Eve pretended to sleep, relieving them of any obligation to speak to her. A win-win, since their fake attempts at friendship made Eve want to bang her head against Tim's stupid surfboard. Or bang their heads against it—depending on the day.

It occurred to Eve that two days had passed without any food. She wasn't hungry. How long would it take for her to starve? Too long. Carbon monoxide? No car. Hanging? Ow! Slit wrists? Gross. She supposed she'd better eat, but her stock of dried crap had run out, and leaving the dorm to get real food was inconceivable. Eve considered ordering pizza, only that required effort. As if.

Kafka ran off with a Dorito crumb and went back into hiding.

That left the ramen noodles. Dribble. Dribble.

Under normal circumstances, Boop wouldn't dream of invading Eve's space. Her mama'd taught her better than to pop up on someone's doorstep without an invitation. Boop held Eve's right to privacy with the utmost respect. The good Lord knew Eve didn't need one more adult meddling in her affairs, she got enough of that—more than enough, from Justine.

However, these weren't ordinary times. Since Eve had started college down here, she and Boop had had breakfast together every Thursday morning. Only Eve hadn't shown up this morning. Didn't even call to cancel. Didn't answer the phone when Boop rang. Didn't return Boop's message—though Boop wasn't certain she'd left a message. With all the beeps and whatnot, Boop hated leaving messages, but she had this morning. At least she thought so.

Boop spent most of the day fiddling with her garden and trying to talk herself out of worrying and trying not to listen for the telephone to ring—a watched pot and all. Only today it hadn't rung. There were heaps of reasonable explanations, but not one of them rang true. Eve had been off for a while.

When Boop walked into Eve's suite, everything clicked into place lickety-split. That beaten slump, that kicked puppy expression—Boop had faced them in the mirror, herself, many times. She'd seen that matted greasy hair before. And she'd smelled the stench of overripened body odor mixed with old food. She'd seen it, smelled it, lived it. She'd lost eighteen years to it—and now Eve.

What a blind fool she'd been! Boop could've kicked herself for pushing aside the warning signs. She, of all people, knew how possible it was to fake it for a couple of hours every week. Justine was going to roast Boop on a spit for letting it get so far.

"Boop, what are you . . . oh, is it Thursday?"

"Sure is. I see you must've needed a little pick me up. Watching the news always cheers me—what with all the murders and fires." Boop pushed the power button and the television went black. Boop instantly regretted it though, because the room's sudden silence hung like morning fog. She groped for something calming and cheerful to say, but nothing like that sprang to mind. Instead, Boop found herself wanting to throttle the poor girl, so she busied her hands gathering all the used tissues, empty water bottles, and wrappers that littered the floor.

"You don't have to clean up," Eve mumbled. "I don't feel good."

Boop's hands trembled as she dropped the half-drunk Coca-Cola can into the metal trash can. The clang barely registered. Because she couldn't bear to look at Eve, she gazed at the small brown splatter that sprayed the inside lining of the trashcan, wondering if the soda could eat through the plastic lining and how long it would take, and what it did to their insides, and how many other things were eating them from the inside out.

Eve hadn't been feeling well? No, Boop supposed she hadn't at that. Only this was no flu, like she wanted Boop to believe. Maybe Eve was trying to fool herself too.

"Why don't you jump in the shower? That'll fix you right up." If only that were true. "Then we'll hit the road. Go to Whaler's. Get some grub in your belly."

"How about another time when I'm feeling better? I'm not hungry." Eve's stomach growled.

Boop had her now. "We got important matters to discuss. Plans to make. Sorry, sugar, this can't wait."

Eve scrunched her nose. Boop wasn't sure if Eve had caught wind of her own BO or merely wasn't buying Boop's baloney. "What?"

In an attempt to channel Justine's forcefulness, Boop put her hands on her hips. "Not now. Hop in the shower. I'll tell you all about it at Whaler's."

With a sigh, Eve rolled off the couch, stumbled a bit on jellified legs, and disappeared into her room. For a split second, Boop worried she'd been dismissed. But then Eve came out with a basket of beauty supplies and a blue towel. One small step . . .

Boop listened for the shower to turn on and then busied herself stuffing the empty pizza box, cock-eyed, into the trashcan. Her stomach lurched. This couldn't be happening. Not to Eve. Boop was worried she couldn't pull Eve through this. Heck, Boop wasn't sure she'd pull through this herself. Maybe this time she'd become a crazy old lady on the top of a mountain with only a shotgun and a grizzly bear for company. She reckoned she'd make a right good hermit.

As for the important plans, Boop had vomited that out without any clue what important plans they were going to discuss. So in desperation, she considered Vicky's mysterious request and wondered if it couldn't serve multiple agendas—removing Eve from her toxic situation while also protecting her from Justine, and buying Boop time to figure out what was going on with her. Not to mention that Vicky had a picture of Davey.

She folded the musty blanket and laid it back on the couch, thinking she ought to put it in Eve's laundry basket. Only Eve's door was closed, and Boop wasn't sure she could handle what she might find on the other side of it. Shut doors were all too often unappreciated.

She pictured the happy little girl who used to stand under her outside shower rinsing off sand before coming in for a visit. How could that same girl be standing in the shower right now struggling to find the wherewithal to clean herself? A wave of dizziness hit Boop, and she grabbed on to the edge of an armchair for dear life.

It hadn't been all that long ago that Boop had loved wrapping Eve in a beach towel and racing her up the stairs. Eve's breathless laugh would wash over Boop like a sunny day. Then they'd head out to the balcony to finish drying off her bathing suit and chow down on some homemade strawberry ice cream. One bite of ice cream and Eve would start talking. Boop listened to tales of slumber-party pranks, street-game injuries, and mean teachers while she picked the dead leaves off her red geraniums. Afterward, they'd watch the four-lane highway below and count RVs as they chugged along. One afternoon they counted seven. They used to say that when Eve turned sixteen, they'd rent an RV and head across the country together.

Boop had forgotten all that silliness. If only she could reacquaint this Eve with that little girl who found such joy in a bowl of ice cream.

A waft of citrus leaked from the bathroom as Eve shuffled out and slid into her room.

Eve's sigh filled her dorm room. If she could think of any way to get Boop to leave her be, she'd jump on it. Well, not jump—that would take more energy than she could muster. Eve picked a pair of dirty jeans off the floor, hoping they didn't smell too bad, but not bothering to check as it wasn't like she had any that were cleaner. Over a month had passed since the last time she'd done any laundry.

Her computer was on. She leaned over to shut it down but paused when she noticed that she had a message in the email account she'd set up for Ally. Her hand shook as she clicked to open it. Ally . . .

To: seams274@mail.com
From: ald2@mail.com
Date: May 3 4:38 p.m.
Subject: Re: Call me

Dear Eve,

OMG. Whatever you do please do not sic my parents or grand-mother on me!

I'm in big trouble, and I don't know what to do. I can't go into it here. It's not that I don't trust you, but nothing can get back to my parents or, God forbid, my grandmother, and with your mom's history . . .

I'm gonna disappear for a while. I can't think in the land of bleached out dreams and bankrupt souls. Hell, I can't even breathe here for the all the damn smog. I need you to cover for me. Please. That's rich, huh? I'm ignoring your pleas for help and begging you to help me. I wouldn't ask if it weren't important. When my family gets around to wondering where I am, please play it cool. Act like you don't know what they're talking about, like you and I talked the other day, and everything is awesome and normal and I'm just way busy. Please. Buy me as much time as you can before they hunt me down like the vultures they are. I've got to get my shit straight before they pick me apart.

I'm so sorry that everything's awful for you, and that I haven't responded before now. Your best friend sucks. You can't even imagine how much I suck. Or maybe you can and maybe you have. But whatever you think is going on out here, you're wrong.

I love you, Eve. Take care of yourself. Seriously. Don't buy a plane ticket. Maybe getting away to the family beach house would provide some clarity for you. Is that silly, since you live at the beach now? Something about that place, though.

Your Kindred Spirit,

Ally

Eve was overwhelmed by many emotions as she read the email, but it was relief that won out. Ally wasn't dead or kidnapped or anything quite that dire. And, for once Eve had done the right thing by not alerting anyone about Ally's disappearance. And, Ally wasn't mad at her. And, most importantly, if Eve was reading between the lines correctly, then she knew Ally's location. Eve just had to figure out how to get there.

Boop was waiting. With her car.

Boop surveyed the suite. She'd done about all she could without cleaning supplies.

The girls had put some time into fixing up the suite. On the wall next to her was a hand-drawn, life-size refrigerator. Several of the girls had pinned on top marks and other honors. Boop noticed that Eve's school work was conspicuously missing.

A door opened. It wasn't Eve's. Two girls—young women—would Boop ever get used to calling them women?—walked in, clucking like a pair of hens. They didn't notice Boop right off.

"Look who's finally off the couch," the blonde said. Her nose sniffed the air as if she could still smell Eve. Maybe she could.

"Good. Maybe now the rest of us can use the suite," her friend said. "She's so weird."

Only then did they catch sight of Boop. At least they had the courtesy to blush.

"Eve's grandma! We didn't see you."

The nice thing to do would be to pretend Boop didn't know they'd been talking about Eve or to pretend that Boop hadn't heard them. She considered being nice but couldn't seem to find it in her right then. Instead, she wanted to wash their swarmy mouths out with soap. "That much was clear."

"We didn't mean—it's just that . . ." the blonde's voice trailed off.

"It's all right, girls, I understand." It wasn't all right. Boop didn't understand, but it turned out her mama's training was too ingrained for Boop to derive any pleasure from watching them squirm.

"Well, good to see you. We've got to get busy. Exams next week. Study. Study!" They scurried out of the suite, the door slamming shut behind them.

Exams broke many a normal college student, but what would they do to Eve who appeared already broken? Nothing good. Boop needed a plan.

Eve came out wearing her usual uniform of denim and black. Her wan complexion made her eyes appear huge. Between her collarbone, which popped above the neckline of her tank top, and her dungarees, which hung too loosely on her hips, it was obvious she'd lost weight.

"When in Florida, dress like Floridians, huh?" Boop teased.

Only Boop didn't get the smile she'd been aiming for. Instead, Eve stared at her with eyes so dead, Boop shivered.

Forced from her suite, Eve almost gagged when the wave of salt air bore down on her. She wanted nothing more than to return to her hideaway, but Boop's wince stopped her. Evidently, Boop had forgotten her torn rotator cuff when she grabbed hold of the stair railing.

Guilt tugged at Eve. "Sorry."

"Ain't your fault this old lady's body is breaking down."

"It's my fault you're on these stairs."

"Now then, the way I see it, you're worth it."

"Yeah, right." Eve didn't feel like she was worth much these days. She couldn't seem to do anything right, couldn't do much of anything at all.

The heat made Eve's underwear stick to her butt like chewing gum on the sole of a shoe. Eve couldn't wait to be free from the brutal temperatures, the swarming tourists, and her surf-obsessed classmates. Not that going home to Virginia was much better. Not with her mom lying in wait to smother her—Justine was worse than the humidity.

When they reached the bottom stair, Boop let out a long breath.

"Want to rest a minute?" Eve pointed to a stone bench under a palm tree.

"Nah. Car's over yonder. I'd rather sit for a spell in the air conditioning."

The ride to Whaler's was short. Short enough that Eve didn't even mind Boop's driving, which was . . . lacking. Maybe it was that Boop couldn't see over the dashboard quite right. Though you'd think that sitting on a phone book would give her enough of a boost. Eve was glad that Boop was putting a phone book to good use. Otherwise, they seemed like a criminal waste of paper. It never failed to amaze Eve that someone still printed the damn things or that anyone paid to be listed in them. Proof of the power of habit.

Phonebook aside, Boop's poor driving skills were probably age-related. Eve usually drove when they went somewhere together, which said it all, because Eve wasn't much of a driver herself.

The Glen Miller Band playing on Boop's stereo saved Eve from having to talk. Perfect, since her head was busy plotting how to get Boop to let her borrow her car. How much would she need to give away to Boop, and how much could she trust her?

They shuffled along Whaler's winding ramp so they could stop and pet the stray cats that swarmed the place. When they'd first started coming to Whaler's, Eve had tried to name them, but every time they visited different cats showed up. A fat, orange tabby brushed against Eve's legs. No doubt these cats were well fed. Eve wondered what it would be like to live off the handouts of strangers and whether she'd have as much luck as these cats. Given that most people were kinder to animals than their fellow man, it likely wouldn't turn out too well for Eve.

A blast of noise molested Eve when she opened the door. She swung around to flee, but the hostess stopped her.

"Oh, Boop and Eve, so glad to see you. You worried me when you didn't show this morning." Almost everybody was a regular at Whaler's, and the hostess was an institution—a dwarf, maybe a midget—Eve didn't know the difference, but a small lady. Her most memorable feature, though, was her foot-high beehive, which rose from her head like a beacon. Suddenly Eve found she wanted nothing more than to follow her light into the safety of Whalers.

The smell of fried fish made Eve's stomach growl with a mixture of hunger and nausea. Eve didn't want to eat. Too tired to argue though, she ordered anyway—clam chowder, a side salad, and hot chocolate. Boop ordered fried oysters. Gross. The magic of Whaler's was not in the mediocre food.

Eve stared at the life preserver hanging over Boop's head while Boop talked about something—her trip to Kash 'n Karry maybe? Eve tried to grunt appropriately. Her cave-girl lexicon staved Boop off for a remarkably long interlude during which Eve wallowed in a fantasy about life as a stray cat at Whalers—and all the hush puppies she could eat.

But she hadn't agreed to come so that she could sit around day-dreaming about hushpuppies. She had a car to secure and a best friend to save. Since finessing situations wasn't Eve's strong suit and in her current state it was even less so, Eve decided not to dance around the subject and instead burst out. "Can I borrow your car to go to the beach house for a few days?"

Boop's eyes narrowed. "Now that might fit in real nice with my news."

This was unexpected. Eve had dismissed Boop's earlier comment as a bluff to get her out of the dorm. Had she been serious? "Oh?" Eve unfolded the paper napkin in her lap.

"Vicky wants us to come for a visit."

"Us?"

"Sure. Instead of flying back to Virginia, I thought we could drive and stop in on the way."

Eve smoothed the paper napkin on her thighs, struggling to focus on Boop's words. She folded the napkin, again and again, making it smaller and smaller. A road trip with Boop wasn't what she had in mind. Not to mention that Ally would be pissed to have Boop brought into her mysterious mess. Boop looked at her as if she expected some sort of reaction, but Eve didn't have one for her. A road trip? Visiting Aunt Victoria was tempting fate. Where was this coming from? It sounded like torture. "Is this about your fear of flying?"

In the past, Boop had waxed poetic on the trials of flying—from her metallic body part replacements setting off metal detectors and the sardine-like accommodations, to the ear-popping madness. There was no reasoning with her on this particular topic. She grimaced. "You can forget that. No siree, Bob. You and me, we're going on a road trip. Like we used to dream about."

What was she talking about? And then Eve remembered all those childish ramblings. Was Boop on crack? "In an RV?" Eve tried to keep the horror out of her voice, but Boop's flinch suggested she'd failed.

Boop tittered. "Nah, we'll take my car."

The waitress, sporting a grease-stained Whalers tee, arrived with dinner.

Eve swirled a potato around with a spoon and gazed into the white whirlpool forming in her soup, wishing she could spin down it, thinking it seemed a relaxing way to go, like drowning in a creamy hot tub. She needed to get to the beach house but couldn't see how, without going along with Boop's fool plan. Think, Eve, think.

"You gonna eat it already?"

It was so hard to hold on to any of her thoughts in any real way. Eve watched the steam wafting off the thick chowder uninterested in eating it, but couldn't summon the energy to protest, so she sipped her soup. And then she practically gulped it as some repressed instinct rekindled. Clam chowder, chicken noodle, didn't seem to matter the flavor, soup had healing properties that were undervalued by the medical profession. She needed to talk Boop out of coming with her. "But your shoulder . . . your arthritis . . ."

"I'll be fine as long as you do the driving."

The iced tea zipping up Boop's straw entranced Eve.

"Why do you want to visit Aunt Victoria anyway? You usually avoid her."

Boop nudged the basket of saltines toward Eve. "I know, but I'm not getting any younger and neither is she. It might be nice to set things right with her."

Eve stuffed saltines in her mouth, enjoying their melty, salty goodness until they sucked all the moisture from her mouth and left her unable to swallow. Teach her to indulge! She guzzled half her water before she managed to dislodge the mass of soggy cracker from the roof of her mouth.

"Mom will never let this happen."

Boop dipped her hush puppy in the bowl of drawn butter and then licked a drop off her index fingers. That lick was exactly the kind of thing that endeared Boop to Eve. Having grown-up with a "perfect" mom, it was refreshing to be around someone so very human. "You leave your mom to me."

Maybe bringing Boop along wasn't such a terrible idea. Maybe Boop could help. And best of all Eve might finally catch up with Ally. Assuming Eve was right about Ally being at the beach house. And assuming she could get past Aunt Victoria without letting anything about Ally slip.

For the first time in weeks, Eve felt a bit lighter, as if she'd dropped her backpack loaded down with all of her textbooks off a fishing pier. Following Boop's lead, she licked the whipped cream seeping over the edge of her mug of hot chocolate, relishing the scent of chocolatey goodness. "Okay, I'm in." Eve was far from thrilled by Boop's scheme, but if it would get her to Ally, then so be it.

Boop clapped. "Hot dog! So, you ready for your exams?"

And the weight came crashing back as if the sea had spat back her now waterlogged backpack. Exams started in the morning. There wasn't time to catch up even if she tried. Not that she planned to try. She couldn't seem to wrap her head around anything. All she wanted was to crawl under Whaler's deck and curl up in the cool white sand, blissfully surrounded by her soft fur family.

"What's going on with you, honey?" Boop reached across the table and rubbed Eve's hand.

"Nothing. All is good." And it was, sort of. Nothing terrible had happened to her. She had a solid life—her mom and Boop who loved her, her dad Karl, college, food to eat, clothing. Eve had no reason—no right—to be like this. Her mom had given her everything and this was how Eve thanked her? By being a lazy, spoiled, and selfish brat. Eve made herself sick.

"Really?" Boop's eyebrows rose. "Okay, but if you need to talk . . ."

Talk? What would Eve say? She didn't have any real problems to work through. She just sucked. "I'm good. A little stressed out. You know, exams and all." Sounded believable. She ripped a corner off her napkin and rolled it in a little ball between her fingers.

Boop bit her lip. "Any plans this weekend?"

Plans? Like what? Getting smashed at frat parties? Going to the beach with a bunch of girls and trading stories about random hook-ups? Maybe compare our six-packs and talk about how hard it is to stay thin? No thanks. Eve dropped the itty-bitty paper ball on the floor. She didn't have any plans. And she didn't have any friends. She didn't want any. In the end, they just disappointed her. "Nah, studying."

"And Ally? You seeing her any time soon?"

What was with the inquisition? Boop didn't normally pry, but today she was acting more like Justine than was comfortable.

"She's great." Eve's toe tapped a rapid staccato against the table leg. "Thanks for dinner, Boop, but I've gotta get back and study. You think we can get the check?" Eve needed to get away before losing her shit.

"Don't you want dessert?"

"No, thanks." But Eve did want to rip the dessert menu from Boop's hands and stomp all over it as if it were a swarm of fleas.

"Do you mind if I order a—?" Boop lifted her head from the menu to look at Eve. Instead of finishing her sentence, she flagged down the waitress, and a few minutes later they fled.

CHAPTER 6

When Danielle Grusky heard the voices of her husband and his doctor, she paused to listen outside of the hospital room where they couldn't see her. Twenty years her senior, Wyatt had a tendency to handle her like a hothouse orchid, and she had a tendency to soak up his paternalism. However, she was much less fragile than either of them pretended.

As far as she was concerned, his car accident two weeks before had put their little dependency game on hold. Since he'd yet to come around to her way of thinking, she'd had to resort to eavesdropping and snooping.

"At best, you're looking at six months before you're returning to work full-time," the doctor said.

She leaned against the wall as the news sank in. Wyatt ran a one-man PI firm. Six months was a long time to put that on hold.

"You're underestimating me."

The doctored murmured something that she couldn't catch, but Wyatt's response was clear. "Don't tell my wife."

This, she decided, was the perfect note on which to end this nonsense.

"I heard." She stopped at the antibacterial foam receptacle to clean her hands.

"Danielle!" Wyatt sputtered from the hospital bed. The color was returning to his cheeks, but the last two weeks had aged Wyatt. She didn't mind. She thought him distinguished, but when Wyatt was well enough to give the mirror any thought, he'd be horrified by the sagging of his skin and the deepened grooves and the overnight doubling of gray strands.

"Could you give us a few minutes?" she asked the doctor.

He nodded and scurried from the room.

"Don't you worry about it, honey. That idiot—"

She cut him off. "Please stop. I need you to listen."

Wyatt's mouth gaped open.

Danielle felt a twinge of guilt, but she wasn't sure if it was for springing this self-sufficient side of herself on him without warning, or if it was because she'd hidden it from him for so long. "I love you. You've always taken care of me. I know you will again when you're able—and I'll look forward to it. But in the meantime, I'm capable, more than capable, of taking care of us."

"But—"

Unwilling to give herself time to worry about how Wyatt was going to take the new Danielle, she plunged on. "When I was thirteen and my dad died, who do you think took care of things? Don't you dare say, 'Your mother.' You've met my mother."

Wyatt nodded and chuckled. His sense of humor was one of the many things that attracted her to him. In spite of his broken neck, leg, and hand, and the stitches crossing his midriff, the man still found a way to laugh.

"I was a girl then, but I did it. And now I'm a grown-up, and I can surely act like one."

"But—"

"I've gone through your files, so I'm up to speed on all your current cases."

Wyatt's coffee-colored eyes bugged out of his gaunt, bruised face. "You're not saying what I think you're saying, are you? You don't honestly think that puttering around in my office a couple hours a week makes you a PI?"

His questioning was almost mean, but Danielle knew Wyatt, knew the pride he took in his work and knew that such an assumption on her part would be profoundly offensive, so she shrugged off taking any offense herself. "Of course not. I got in touch with Charlie. He says he can get me licensed in two weeks."

"Two weeks? Really, you think you can take over my life's work after two weeks?"

Danielle was aware of her lack of preparation, skills, and investigative instincts. She was under no illusion that her attempt to step in would be seamless, but there wasn't an alternative. "No, but I do think if you call the shots and direct me by phone, then I can be your virtual legs, arms, and eyes. At least enough to finish up the cases you're already working on. The license just makes me legal."

"It's too dangerous." Wyatt bucked against his immobility, causing the hospital bed to shake.

Danielle paused, giving him a minute to calm down before she continued. "Sometimes your job is dangerous, but your current cases—a runaway granddaughter, searching for a birth mother, a lost dog, two mystery shopper clients, and a business background check. I'll be all right."

Wyatt's face was impenetrable. Danielle forced herself to maintain eye contact with this proud man that she adored.

"You've really thought this through."

"I have." She sat down in the armchair next to his bed and crossed her legs, willing her body and her voice to remain calm. Their closeness meant that they fed off each other's emotions. She needed him to feed off her pretended calm. It wouldn't do for him to pick up on the insecurity, fear, and anxiety his accident and her plan had left in its wake.

"Maybe we could hire someone temporarily."

"With the medical bills . . ." she softened her voice, in an attempt to waylay the guilt such a comment might leave.

"You let me worry about—"

"Believe me, I will in about six months. But right now—"

"Dammit, Danielle." He slammed his good hand on the bed railing. The clang of his wedding ring against the metal punctuated his frustration.

Danielle flinched. Wyatt never raised his voice, at least not at her.

He sagged. "I'm sorry."

"I know."

"This sucks."

"Yep."

He closed his eyes. "Okay. If you can get my clients to agree."

"That'll be the easy part." Danielle wouldn't point out that she'd just talked him around—that she always talked him around. She might not know the first thing about being a detective, but she had a knack for knowing the best way to handle people—especially when people didn't realize they were being handled. Not that Wyatt wasn't aware of it on some level, but still . . . some things were better left unsaid.

"Ha!" Wyatt laughed. "You haven't met Victoria Liddel yet."

After a day that passed like a herd of turtles, Boop had only one item left on her to-do list—call Justine.

So, logically, Boop cleaned out her pantry (filling yet another moving box) and then her refrigerator where she found some old squash congealed in bacon fat and apple butter covered in a hairy, blue mold—discoveries and odors she could've done without. Then, because it was imperative, she swept the back patio free of cobwebs, wishing it were that easy to clear them from her mind, where, at her age, the cobwebs had seized control. When she finished on the patio, she dusted the blinds in her bedroom.

Boop couldn't figure how it went wrong, but all that work hadn't made the phone call go away. Since the clothes wouldn't be dry for another ten minutes and Boop was out of distracting chores, she picked up the telephone. Eight o'clock on a Friday night; maybe Justine'd be out dancing or singing karaoke or whatever it was that swinging fifty-eight-year-olds did these days. Who was she fooling?

Justine answered on the second ring. "Hi."

"It's me—Boop."

"I know."

There's no privacy these days.

"What's up? Eve okay?"

Why had she asked that? Did she suspect?

"Fine. Fine." May lightning strike her down. She couldn't lay Eve's struggle on Justine, who'd endured a front row seat to Boop's misery. Boop still hadn't forgiven herself for failing to protect Justine's childhood. Maybe this time she could protect her. Maybe it wasn't too late. She'd promised Justine she'd look after Eve, and by golly, she would, but she hadn't promised full reports.

Somehow, she needed to show Eve that life was worth living, that she was a worthy human being, and to seek out professional help. What Boop needed was a miracle.

"So?" Justine said.

"Eve and I decided we're going to drive up to Virginia instead of flying." Boop leaned against the dryer, letting its heat ease her pain after her day spent in back-breaking labor.

"You what?" The news droned behind Justine's voice. What a way to spend a Friday night. Justine was single and attractive. She needed to get out more.

"We're gonna take a little road trip. Stop by and see Vicky."

"But you hate Aunt Victoria."

"And you exaggerate. She's my sister."

The silence on the other end meant Justine was thinking. Boop pictured her lolling in her recliner. By now she'd have taken off her cosmetics and removed her contacts, replacing them with bifocals. Her bloodshot eyes would speak for the long hours she slaved for Trevor. Boop almost felt sorry for her, until—"No."

"No, what?"

"No, you two aren't doing this."

Boop nibbled on a cheese straw, debating whether she preferred the smell or the taste of its cheddary goodness. The fat and calories didn't make it a figure-flattering choice, but a girl gets to a certain age and it doesn't matter so much anymore. One of the few benefits of getting old. Another one was that it had gotten much easier to get her way. Maybe Boop had finally cottoned onto her daddy's war strategies. "Well now—"

"You've got no business going on a road trip in that crappy car with your bum shoulder."

"The Gray Ghost might be timeworn, but she gets around all right, and Eve's going to drive me around like in *Driving Miss Daisy*."

Justine sighed. "That's hardly reassuring."

"Look, Vicky and I are getting old, and maybe it's time we set things right between us. Eve's willing to chauffeur me. We've both got the time."

"Eve doesn't have time. Remember I got her that internship?"

"It'll just be a couple of days." The dryer buzzed. Boop hauled her clothes out and heaped them on the floor. Might as well settle in.

Justine tapped her fingernails on the telephone. "I'm not going to allow Eve to participate in your reckless plan." Gauntlet thrown.

Time for a new strategy. "If that's what you think is best, then I understand. You know I'd never do anything to interfere with your parenting. I'll figure out a way to manage the trip alone."

"You're a dreadful driver and a hopeless navigator."

"Oh, you do exaggerate." She didn't, but Boop wasn't about to admit as much.

"No, I do not. Do you even know how to work the GPS on your phone?"

"I've gotten around fine for years without such nonsense." Boop piled her unmentionables together. She felt like such a rebel when she stuffed them unfolded and unironed into a drawer. Her mama would've been horrified. Of course, she'd be horrified at the state of Boop's underthings too—giant, dingy colored, and elastic-loosened—maybe Mama had a point. At least they smelled better than they looked. Thank goodness for fabric softener. No one had been privy to her undergarments for quite some time. Nevertheless, Boop ought to take more care of her foundation. Real change started from the inside and worked its way out, which meant her underwear was a real barrier to self-improvement. Boop wondered if she could recruit Eve to help her pick out some modern ones at Victoria's Secret. Eve might get a kick out of that. "I'm not one of those old lady drivers."

Justine's finger tapping stopped. "Really?"

Sarcasm wasn't necessary, but Boop chose to take the high road and ignore it. "No. Once my shoulder's fixed—"

"Yes, I'm sure. In the meantime, for this trip, you need to fly, Mama."

Justine was cracking. She'd stopped calling Boop "Mama" when she'd left home. No ignorant Southern accent for her. Justine spoke all cultured except when she got her knickers in a knot.

"I'm too old for air travel." While the phone hung with a noisy silence, Boop imagined Justine with her eyes closed counting to ten. Such control.

"How ironic."

Boop folded her salmon-colored hand towel, centering the monogram on the bottom. Her fingers traced the letters of her name. She regretted she hadn't dropped Tommy's last name when he'd dropped her—reclaimed her identity. At the time, she'd had good reason not to, but those reasons seemed old-fashioned now. "It's too bad Eve can't join me. Vicky was so looking forward to some time with her. She called me up specifically asking after her, but I'm sure she'll understand."

Justine took a deep breath. "I'm sure she will."

"I mean it's not like you're beholden to her or anything. I mean, not anymore. It's been a long time since she covered the down payment on your townhouse. Oh, and got Karl's DUI dropped. And then there was the time—"

"Fine."

"What was that?"

"You heard me. Go. But I expect both of your phones charged and on at all times. And—"

"Of course." Time to bail out before Justine got going with crazy stipulations. "Oh, my doorbell's ringing. I gotta run. Toodles."

Boop hung up before Justine could object. Then she turned the ringer off and finished folding her laundry. Might need a new brassiere too.

The next afternoon, Eve's long-lost roommate interrupted her nap when she banged into the room with Tim draped all over her. Carrie was sporting a new look these days. She'd bleached her hair, gotten a deep tan, and often wore bikini tops instead of shirts. Tim, too, had adopted the beach-babe look. Eve wished he didn't wear it so well. Their presence felt like an invasion. Admittedly that wasn't fair since it was Carrie's room too, but since Carrie spent the night at Tim's most nights and only stopped by to change her clothes and check her messages, Eve had grown territorial. Maybe Eve should've done a better job of marking her territory. Pee on Carrie's bed or better yet replace one of her essential oils with urine.

"Eve, you're here. I thought you'd be at your English Lit exam."

Eve's heart slammed into her chest. Her eyes darted to the

alarm clock next to her bed. Crap. She'd already slept through the first hour, which meant she only had two hours left. She could still make it. Maybe beg for more time. She raced over to her desk and dug through a stack of papers for a blue book. None. Such a freaking idiot, she'd meant to pick one up that morning. The fact that this professor still insisted on the paper monstrosities was a point of contention. What would happen if Eve turned her exam in on regular old notebook paper? Would he refuse to accept it on principle? Probably. Teachers had this annoying habit of excusing their own hard-ass policies as preparing students for future hard-ass policies. Were they really so misguided that they thought they were doing their students a favor? Or just too weenie to own their dickishness?

"Do you have an extra blue book?" Eve asked Carrie as much as it killed her to ask Carrie for anything.

"Nope." She shook her head as she climbed the ladder to her loft. Once she crawled over the railing, she gestured for Tim to join her. "Tim, do you have any?"

"Nah, man. Sorry."

Eve squeezed her eyes tight damming the tears threatening to spill. No way could Eve make it to the bookstore and still have time to complete enough of the exam to pass. Though to be honest, her last-minute movie binge and cliff-note skimming probably weren't enough to pass under the best of circumstances anyway. She collapsed against the wall and pushed her palms against her closed eyes.

"Eve, you okay?" Tim asked.

Eve slid her hands to her jaw to cup her face. She couldn't answer.

Carrie frowned at her, but stayed silent, having given up her initial attempts to persuade some life back into her. "Tim, I so need your help understanding neurotransmitters."

Eve wanted to gag at the throaty way she'd said neurotransmitters. Neurotransmitters weren't all she was transmitting. Get a room.

Tim cleared his throat and shifted. "In a minute." Turning to Eve he said, "You want me to see if I can scrounge one up for you?"

Eve had spent so long envisioning the two of them as the villains in her tale, she'd forgotten how nice Tim was, forgotten why she'd been interested in him in the first place. But finding her a blue book wouldn't be worth his effort. "Forget it."

She stared at the poster of The Kiss, which Carrie had hung over her bed. Between the poster (hung post-Tim) and the orange-blossom aphrodisiac essential oil she'd opened, could she be any more obvious? Good thing Eve's dad hadn't come to visit. He'd probably have ripped the clichéd poster off the wall. Even great works of art can be ruined by overuse. No fear of that with Karl's artwork or Eve's fashion designs though.

Eve tried not to stare at Tim's tenderness as he brushed the hair from Carrie's eyes. No one had ever touched Eve like that.

"There are three main types of neurotransmitters: amino acids, peptides, and monoamines." Tim's hand rested on Carrie's stomach.

Eve imagined his hands on her, and she trembled. Freak. Lonely, ugly, boring girl who can't get a date, who gets off watching her roommate cuddle with her boyfriend.

Eve knew she should give them some privacy and leave, but she couldn't bear to go—and she couldn't bear to stay.

Carrie giggled. Eve forced her eyes away. She needed a distraction. Her bookcase with its unread textbooks beckoned. After all, she had four more exams to fail. Calculus was next. Eve could hear Carrie's breathing. She snuck a peek. Tim's hand had slipped under Carrie's waistband. Eve flushed. Calculus wasn't going to do it. Eve surveyed the room for something more stimulating than neurotransmitter porn. If only she had her sewing machine, but no, Heathcliff was still in exile at Boop's. Perhaps her sketchbook.

She thumbed through it, lamenting at how far she had fallen behind. She hadn't made any new sketches in months. Without the ability to construct them, it had seemed pointless. The skirt on the third page caught Eve's eye. And then the dress on page seven. But really what was the point of designing anything else? Even if she had her sewing machine, who was going to wear her designs? Eve certainly never would. It'd be like walking around naked. Ally might, but living in LA had probably changed her, accustomed her to more sophisticated designs. Eve wished she didn't have to wait until after exams and a stop in Savannah to rush to Ally. What if Ally needed her now? What if Eve got there too late? If only Eve knew what the hell was going on, then she . . .

Would what? What would that change?

Whatever. She had to keep busy. She couldn't keep ruminating on Ally or spying on Carrie and Tim. A jacket. She'd work on a jacket. Eve liked to start with fabric, as she often found inspiration in the texture or patterns, or even the way it moved, so she dug through her footlocker. Wafts of lavender from moth-deterring satchels intermingled with the orange-blossom oil created a surprisingly pleasant aroma. Near the bottom, she found a promising tweed, but it was a bit rougher than she preferred. Some red velvet caught her eye. Now that might work to offset it. The tweed jacket could be lined and cuffed in red velvet—ooh, and the collar could be red too. Eve pictured herself in the jacket and nothing else, modeling for Tim, and Tim's eyes full of lust.

Carrie and Tim were kissing now. Eve wasn't watching this time, but she knew because she could hear little slurping sounds.

Again, Eve considered leaving. Could she do it? Could she leave? The sound of laughter from the suite made her shudder. No.

She sharpened her pencil. The grind from the electric sharpener must have disturbed their "study date" because when she finished Carrie said, "So you're not going to your exam?"

Eve shrugged, wishing Carrie would mind her own business. She blew lead shavings from the tip of her pencil.

"You'll fail your class."

Eve shrugged again. She didn't lecture Carrie about contraception; what right did Carrie have to lecture her? Eve concentrated on her sketching.

"Your mom is going to kill you."

The sleeve was all wrong. It needed to taper more. Eve erased and attempted the sleeve again, but now it was too short. She scribbled all over it and restarted the jacket on the next page. This time she nailed the sleeve but screwed up the collar.

"Okay, so glutamate is the most common neurotransmitter. The next most prevalent is GABA—it's inhibitory."

Eve tried again. This time she was slow, careful, deliberate, but the lead broke, and her pencil tore across the paper. She ripped the page from her pad, balled it up, and winged it in the general direction of the trashcan by the door. She missed, throwing the ball several feet too high, so that the ball landed on Carrie's rainbow bedspread folded at the end of her loft.

Tim picked it up and smoothed it out.

"Don't!" Eve lurched toward him but was too late.

"I didn't know you designed clothes," he said. "This is cool."

If only he meant it, but Eve could tell he was just saying it to make her feel better.

"Give it back." She snatched the sketch from his hand.

Tim looked hurt, so Carrie rushed to comfort him. "It's Eve's big, dark secret. She doesn't want anyone to know. Eve, I don't know what you're so worried about. No one cares."

She was right, and that knowledge made Eve want to slap her. No one cared. Eve glared at her sketchbook filled with her silly, stupid dream. The urge to run from Carrie and Tim finally overtook the fear of leaving her room, and as she slunk out the door like a naughty dog, she slammed her sketchbook into the trashcan.

CHAPTER 7

The movers were hot—pin-up poster worthy surfer boys. The more Eve tried not to ogle them, the more she did. Unfortunately, they were keenly aware of their assets. Seriously, one of the guys turned to stare at his reflection every time he passed a window. And the other guy, kept flexing unnecessarily. Boop didn't seem to mind though. She was flirting, and these boys were eating it up. Eve wanted to barf.

"Boop, you're paying these guys by the hour. Stop distracting them!" Eve yelled across the dorm parking lot. She was on door duty, which suited her fine. Boop was supposed to be relaxing in the lawn chair in the truck's shade. Only, whenever the guys shoved something in the truck, she'd make an observation about the weather, ask after their mothers, or offer them some Gatorade, etcetera, etcetera, ad nauseam. Loading the truck was taking forever. Eve's skin crawled. She needed to leave, like ten minutes ago.

Eve caught bits and pieces of the boys' scintillating life stories— surfer, college, yadda yadda, money, yadda yadda, time off, yadda yadda, surfing, yadda yadda. Eve didn't pay close attention. She didn't need to, as this was the loser tale of every surfer boy she'd met at school. Life was all about catching the wave, dude. Shaka-brah.

Joey . . . no, Johnny . . . no, his nametag was hidden on his discarded shirt, so it was hardly her fault she couldn't remember it—the mover in chambray shorts carried her footlocker toward the truck.

Her mom's voice rang in her head, "Don't ever trust movers. They steal. Don't put your valuables in a moving truck." Eve didn't know what her mom thought Eve's valuables were, certainly not her sewing supplies, but they were the only thing she would miss if they disappeared. Boop had returned Heathcliff just a few hours before, and Eve knew her time with him was limited. Once her mom got her grades, it was doubtful that Eve would ever see her sewing machine again. She yelled, "Hey, dude, stop." Ugh, she grimaced. Had "dude" really become part of her vocabulary? This place was rubbing off on her like poison ivy.

Chambray Shorts turned to stare at Eve. "What?"

Everyone turned to stare at Eve—the kid walking her pit bull, some guy on his early morning jog, Boop, the proud muscle-shirt wearing mover—everybody was staring. All those eyes. The hairs on her neck sprung up. Her breath quickened. Beads of sweat gathered on her forehead. The flexer continued. "Any day now. This thing's heavy. What's in here, babe?"

Eve winced. How she hated that word—babe. Eve was not a babe. She did not want to be a babe, and she did not want this boy calling her a babe.

"None of your business. Put it in the trunk of the car."

"Whatever." He changed direction to head toward the Gray Ghost.

Eve followed to make sure her sewing machine was still nestled safely within, all the while he muttered something about "please" under his breath. Maybe she'd overreacted a smidge. It was just so hot, and she was so tired, and he was so annoying. "Whatever." *Right back at you, Chambray.* Eve didn't need a new friend. She needed him to get his butt in gear.

Instead, he gawked at the suitcases already filling the trunk, as if the idiot couldn't figure out how to solve this conundrum.

"Just move the suitcases onto the back seat." And hurry it up.

Once the locker was settled in the trunk and Chambray's head was shoved in the backseat arranging the suitcases, Eve opened the foot-locker. Everything appeared okay, but she shuffled the stuff around a little bit anyway, to be sure.

"What's your deal?" Chambray asked as he slammed the back door shut.

Eve took a deep breath, searching for patience. "I don't have a deal. Just do your job." And shut your mouth.

"Be-atch," he said under his breath.

Oh, no, he didn't. Cue mental four-snap wave. Eve really disliked mumblers. Got something to say, then say it. The bomb inside of her threatened to detonate.

Tick.

Tick.

Tick.

Tick.

"Sugar, what's all that stuff?" Boop asked over Eve's shoulder. She'd snuck up behind Eve and was pointing to the open footlocker.

Eve closed it. "Nothing." Then she banged the trunk shut and returned to her post at the door.

Thirty grueling minutes later, the "dudes" left in the truck with most of Boop and Eve's worldly possessions. It had been a taxing morning, first at Boop's then Eve's, and it was gonna be a long day, a long trip, a long . . . Eve threw the car in reverse.

"You eat any breakfast?" Boop asked.

Eve shook her head no.

"I brought some goodies for the road. Want something?"

Eve shook her head no again and stopped at a red light. C'mon, c'mon, she urged the light to change. And . . .

Green. Only the dipwad in front of her didn't seem to notice. Eve punched the horn.

"Honey, you gotta eat. Here, I got pork rinds and Corn Nuts to hold you until lunchtime." Was she kidding? Did anyone really eat pork rinds, or Corn Nuts for that matter?

Eve took a pork rind just to get Boop to back off. It smelled bad, but she stuffed it into her mouth anyway. It tasted kind of good and gross at the same time. She ate another. Something about them . . . Her stomach growled.

Boop propped the bag between Eve's stomach and the steering wheel.

Eve ate another. Bacon-flavored crack. Yeah, that was it. She couldn't help herself—she needed more pork rinds. And then more. By the time they pulled onto I-95, she'd eaten the whole bag. Eve licked her finger and rubbed it in the creases on the bottom of the package, sweeping up the crumbs. Delish.

Finally satisfied, Eve leaned back against the headrest, but her ponytail pushed her head forward at an annoying angle, so she yanked the rubber band from her hair and sighed in relief. *St Augustine, ready or not, here we come.*

Eve hadn't spoken in the twenty-three minutes since they'd hit the road. Boop hadn't an inkling what to do. She'd been pleased to watch Eve scarf down those pork rinds, and her hair sure was pretty draped over her shoulders instead of in that godforsaken ponytail.

But Eve's silence made Boop antsy. This wasn't how Boop had pictured their trip. She'd imagined them riding in a convertible, the wind blowing, their hair aflutter, big band blasting, and their eyes sparkling with laughter . . . silly, old woman. Boop didn't own a convertible, and as for the rest? She should've known better.

Boop considered asking if the cat had caught Eve's tongue, but a tired cliché seemed too trite at the moment, even for Boop. The poor dear was so pale. What had set off her depression? Boop ached to know. Only, worried that questions might come off as judgmental, she was afraid to ask any.

Like a Ferris wheel on a busy night at the carnival, her thoughts circled. She wanted to tell Eve that she loved her, but what if Boop's love added to her burden rather than eased it? There was such a thing as too much love.

She flipped on the radio in search of a nifty tune that might simmer down her thoughts, but the commercials blaring on the three stations she checked only made her edgier. With gritted teeth, she turned off the dang thang.

She was tempted to take Eve by the shoulders and shake some sense into her. Maybe not while she was driving though. And what if taking the hard line pushed her away? She shook off images of Vicky and Justine.

Maybe if Boop told Eve that she'd passed some time in that there sinkhole herself? But she didn't want to relive all those years she'd lost, all that pain. What if talking about it brought it all back? What she wanted was to pretend that she'd never felt that hollow, had never seen her own ghost staring back in the mirror. So she said nothing. The afternoon air sat on them like a wet blanket. She could hardly breathe. She hadn't been strong enough to carry her own weight before. What made her believe she'd be strong enough for Eve now?

Boop glanced over at her. The little lamb was so pale.

Clearly, Eve needed her. It seemed Boop didn't have the luxury of deciding whether or not she was strong enough.

"Na-na-na-na, na-na-na-na. Hey, hey, hey, goodbye," Eve sang in a whisper.

"You sure do hate that place, don't you?" Boop asked.

Eve frowned.

Now Boop'd done it, said the wrong thing. She hadn't the faintest idea how to navigate Eve. Boop stared out the window, watching the palm trees flash by. This was going to be a long trip.

But then Eve cleared her throat and said, "No. I hate who I am there."

This was it—Boop's opening. All she had to do was take it. She steeled herself. "So why the sudden interest in the beach house?" Boop was chicken-shit. Unable to meet Eve's eyes, she continued to stare out the window.

"I don't know. You looking forward to catching up with Aunt Victoria?"

Boop's eyes narrowed and swung back to Eve. Eve's uneven tone hinted that Boop wasn't the only one in evasion mode.

"Yeah, like a root canal." Boop grimaced at the foul taste in her mouth, the result of either the thought of Vicky or pork rind aftertaste.

"We don't have to go. No one is holding a gun to your head."

Boop scrounged inside her white leather purse for a Tic Tac. Bingo! "Just 'cause you can't see the gun, don't mean it ain't there." Boop tossed three into her mouth.

"I know what you mean."

Boop imagined she did at that. "Tic Tac?"

Eve shook her head.

"I half expected your mama to insist on joining our little jaunt."

"Something to be grateful for anyway. Can you imagine?"

"Oh, I surely can." Boop put her hands on her hips. "Eve, slow down. We don't want a ticket. That would destroy your driving record, not to mention what it would do to our insurance rates. Eve, you're following that car too closely. Back off. Eve, we're down to a quarter tank of gas. We need to stop and get some more. We don't want to run out. No, not there. They don't have good gas. Boop, why don't you take a nap? You'd better save up your strength." Boop cackled at her hilarity. And darned if Eve didn't start laughing too. Hearing the sound of her joy made Boop happier than a camel on Wednesday. So giddy, that she found herself in the throes of an unladylike snort, which only made Eve laugh all the harder. Eve was laughing so hard that Boop could see her shoulders shaking, so much, in fact, that Boop worried about her driving ability.

Eve must've had a similar thought because right about then she pulled onto the shoulder. Boop tried to gather herself together, but she couldn't seem to stop giggling, that is until she noticed Eve crying. Sobbing and laughing at the same time. She sounded as crazy as a loon.

Boop rubbed the arm Eve had braced to the steering wheel. It took every ounce of Boop's willpower not to shush her, not to tell her everything was gonna be okay, hand her a handkerchief and suggest she dry those pretty green eyes. It's excruciating to watch someone you love in pain. Boop's throat was so tight it was hard to swallow, and a sharp pain stabbed at her chest like a knife to her heart. But silencing Eve's grief would have been for Boop's benefit, not Eve's. Boop grew up being told that a Southern Belle should always smile and act like a lady; that big girls don't cry. To heck with that. Boxing it up would eat away your insides. Every girl needs a good cry now and again. It washes out her heart.

Boop must've sat there for fifteen minutes before a case of the hiccups finally gifted Eve with sobriety. Poor dear looked like she'd been rode wet and hung out to dry. "Why don't I take over the chauffeuring for a while, sugar? You look about done in."

"I'd rather keep driving if you don't mind. I need the distraction."

Boop opened her mouth to share some deep thought, but instead her stomach growled louder than a NASCAR race.

Eve shot her a faint smile. "Maybe we could stop to eat soon. Where do you want to go?" Eve eased onto the highway.

"How about Wendy's? I sure do miss those commercials."

"What commercials?"

"You know the ones with the old lady hollering 'Where's the beef?'"

"No idea."

Huh? Boop could have sworn it'd only been a few years since those commercials had aired. Funny how the older she got, the more her memory jumbled together things that happened yesterday— almost lost, with things that had happened decades ago—still as fresh as a garden harvest.

Boop snuck a peek at Eve and was rewarded with a glimmer of a smile. Maybe this trip wasn't a calamity after all. Boop didn't kid herself that one good cry would make everything better, but it was a start.

Hours later, Boop's bony elbow jabbing Eve in the ribs cut short her contemplation of the motel lobby's ear-wax yellow wallpaper and snot-green carpet.

"Ow! What?" For an old lady, she packed quite a wallop. Eve rubbed her injured side.

Boop tilted her head toward the desk clerk who was on the phone with what appeared to be an irate guest.

"What am I supposed to be looking at?" Eve asked.

"He's cute," Boop whispered.

Eve supposed so; "cute" in a buttoned-up, grandma-pleasing kind of way, but she was too tired for this nonsense. "So?"

The desk clerk hung up the phone. "Can I help you, ladies?"

Eve stared at her feet as if avoiding his gaze would render her invisible. Her face was tight with dried tears, and she was sure her eyes were still puffy. She wasn't a pretty crier.

"You might could," Boop said. "Any rooms available?"

Eve crossed her fingers. This motel might be a dump, but they'd already passed three with illuminated No VACANCY signs. She dreaded spending the rest of the afternoon searching for a bed.

"It's your lucky day. I've got one room."

Eve could feel him checking her out. Probably wondering if she was an escapee from the loony bin. She took the ponytail holder from her wrist, pulled her hair back into its rightful spot, and resisted the urge to check for hair bumps because there was hardly any point.

"We'll take it. I'm Boop, and this is my granddaughter, Eve." She dragged Eve forward as if presenting the dessert tray. If he was smart, he'd check the expiration date.

"Jeff. Nice to meet y'all. Now if I can just get a bit of info from y'all, I'll get y'all all set." He smirked, no doubt laughing at Boop's desperate attempt to find Eve a beau.

Once he finished entering Boop into the system, she said, "So, Jeff, you're a happening young man."

Oh, no she hadn't! Eve couldn't believe this was happening.

Jeff blushed.

Boop continued, "See, I'm an old lady, and I'm plum tuckered out. But Eve here is young and bursting with energy. I sure do hate for her to be stuck in a motel room with her sleepy grandma. You got any suggestions?"

This couldn't be happening. Eve's hands shook. She squeezed her eyes shut to block out the black spots that danced around the edges of her vision. She was about to burst, but it wasn't with energy.

"I get off in an hour. I could—" Jeff said.

Eve didn't think she could take his sympathy. "No!" she said.

He cringed.

Digging for some semblance of normalcy, Eve took a deep breath and tried again. "No. I'm fine. Really. Thanks though." There now, that should do it, dead in the water. Eve was going to kill Boop.

"Yeah. Sure." Jeff dismissed Eve and turned to Boop. "So, I'll need a credit card to hold your room."

Eve interrupted, "Boop, if you need me, I'm gonna go look at those brochures." She wandered off and leaned her shoulder against the wall with her back to them, trying to strike a nonchalant pose while she thumbed through the brochures.

THE XIMENEZ-FATIO HOUSE ,WHERE EVERY ROOM HAS A STORY

Eve almost wished they were on a real road trip and had time to play tourist. But Ally was waiting, and the trip already had enough built-in delays.

CASTILLO DE SAN MARCOS—AMERICA BEGINS HERE

Ideally, they'd get an early start tomorrow, stop by Aunt Victoria's for a visit, and make it to the beach house by nightfall.

MISSION OF NOMBRE DE DIOS, THE SHRINE GIFT SHOP: TAKE A PART OF HISTORY HOME WITH YOU

Only if today had been any indication, Boop was only able to stand the discomfort of riding in the car for a couple of hours before she called for mercy. This trip was likely to be slower than Eve hoped.

THE FOUNTAIN OF YOUTH ARCHEOLOGICAL PARK

Eve glanced over at Boop. With her head bent over the credit card slip, Eve could see the gray roots peeking from her dyed-blonde hair. Her knobby knuckled fingers struggled to sign her name to the bottom of the slip. Boop was old. If only the very idea of a fountain of youth wasn't ridiculous.

Boop finished up with Jeff and joined Eve by the brochures.

"Vicky isn't expecting us until the day after tomorrow."

What?

"We have time to do something in the morning. You see any-thing good?"

They'd lose another day. Eve handed her the fountain brochure.

"I'm game."

Clearly, she should've asked more about Boop's timetable. Especially since Boop didn't know about Eve's. "How long are we staying with Aunt Victoria?"

"One or two nights."

"Oh."

"You sound disappointed."

"It's just that I was hoping to get to the beach sooner."

Boop lifted her chin. "Why the hurry?"

"No reason." Eve looked down at the floor, worried that Boop could see through her skirting.

Justine: Everything okay? Where are you?

Eve: Fine. Outside of St. Augustine

Justine: Are you having fun?

Eve: Awesome

Justine: Tell me more.

Eve: Cute boy works in hotel. Going with him later to hear band

Justine: Be careful. He's a stranger.

Eve: I have Boop with me

Justine: Good, but if he is a serial killer, she won't be that helpful.

Eve: Serial killer? Drama much?

Justine: You never know. Even if he is nice, how will this work out?

Eve: How does what work out?

Justine: A long-distance relationship. You will have plenty of time for boys after you are done with medical school.

Eve: Medical school?

Justine: Ha. Ha. Just be careful.

Eve: Okay. Good night

Justine: Love you. Good night.

CHAPTER 8

The next morning, after guzzling four cups of coffee, Eve was as ready as she'd ever be to take on the Fountain of Youth. She spent the drive over reminding herself to be pleasant. Boop didn't deserve any of Eve's moody crap.

The canopy of live oaks lining Magnolia Avenue as they approached the fountain was a promising start to the morning.

They stepped through the entrance into a beautifully landscaped park and a trio of peacocks greeted them. A tour guide wandered by in period costume—a Spanish explorer with a red jacket and a blue hat. A horrible get-up in the Florida heat, but pretty impressive. Eve wondered if she could design something modern inspired by it, but even as the idea struck—she shot it down as stupid.

"Guess we start in there." Eve pointed to the spring house where an employee waited, poised to take their ticket.

As they wandered through the kitschy life-size dioramas portraying the history of the site, they learned there was no proof that Ponce de Leon ever searched for the Fountain of Youth or that he'd ever even been to this particular fountain. In fact, it wasn't even discovered until after his death. So basically, some lady found a spring, claimed it was the one Ponce had been looking for (when in fact he probably wasn't searching for it all), put up a sign, and started charging admission.

"There's not even a spring?" Eve glanced at the dripping rocks where the tour guide gestured they could get their sample from the fountain.

"The spring dried up when the water table dropped, but it's the same water. Only we pump it now," he explained.

"Right." She shook her head at the whole charade. And yet there she was waiting to take her turn to drink from the famous "fountain."

Eve snapped a picture and captioned it: THE FOUNTAIN OF YOUTH, WHERE HOPE SPRINGS ETERNAL. She showed the screen to Boop before hitting post.

"So you're feeling a mite better?" Boop asked.

Eve shrugged. "Maybe. But don't read too much into any of my posts."

Boop frowned.

"That's how social media works. Everybody shares their perfect lives and then gushes all over their fake friends and hates all over strangers," Eve explained. She tapped her foot impatiently at the slow-moving line.

"That sounds exhausting. Why in tarnation do you play along?"

Eve watched the giggling couple in front of them filling their cups, so caught up in real life that they didn't even notice the restless line behind them. "When I get to control the message and people like me—for a few minutes, anyway—it makes me feel good." The couple sealed the youthful sip of water with a kiss. "Pathetic, huh?"

"You don't have to be perfect for me." Boop stepped closer to the fountain. It was almost their turn. "I love you just the way you are."

"You don't even know me, not really." Until Boop knew about her fashion-designing dreams, then she couldn't really know Eve. Eve wanted to bring Boop into her secret. She wanted to trust her . . . soon.

She and Boop reached for their paper cups at the same time. Their hands touched. The comparison was startling. Eve's were smooth, even toned, and capable. Boop's though—the paper-thin skin almost crackled it was so dry, and several liver spots marked the passage of time. Her gnarled fingers resembled tree roots as they fumbled in the simple act of grabbing a cup.

"Forever young," they toasted.

Boop would die. Not today or tomorrow even, but certainly more of her life was behind her than in front. And one day, Eve would have to deal with her absence. The knot in Eve's stomach tightened.

Eve tossed back her sample and scrunched her nose. Eternal life tasted like sulfur and brass. "Did it work?" she asked Boop. Hope and stupidity—same thing.

Boop kicked a little Charleston action. "Like magic." She let out a belly laugh.

Eve didn't respond. Her failure to catch the laugh cue wrapped around them in an awkward silence until Eve cleared her throat. "Do you hate it?"

"The water's not good, but 'hate' is a strong word. In fact, I reckon we should get bottles for Justine and Vicky at the gift shop on our way out."

"No, not the water. Do you hate getting old?" The sunlight blinded them as they stepped out of the spring house. Eve slid on her sunglasses and did a double take at seeing the peacocks again. Beautiful. Random, but beautiful.

"You mean, do I curse this jalopy of a body? Is it depressing to see my skin shriveled like a prune? Then yes. But, it's not all bad."

"Oh?" Boop was having surgery soon. Surgery could be dangerous for old people. Boop hadn't indicated that, but still Eve worried.

"The way I figure it, I've traded my body for my soul. It's a good deal."

Eve took advantage of the privacy behind her sunglasses to stare at Boop, wondering about her story. Eve wasn't the only one with trust issues. Eve was scared to question Boop. Scared Boop wouldn't tell her, scared she would. "Why can't you have both?"

Boop pointed to the left where a white peacock spread its fancy plumage. "Don't know. Maybe you can. Me—I spent my youth chasing after approval. It was only after I lost everything that I figured out life wasn't about chasing."

"What is it about then?" Dying? Seemed that was the only guarantee. Had to at least be in Boop's line of sight these days. Eve envied her that freedom.

"It's about being."

The Spanish moss on the small palm tree behind Boop framed her head like a curly gray wig.

"Being what?" she asked.

"You."

Eve rolled her eyes, glad though that her sunglasses hid her rudeness.

They headed toward the faux Timucua village, dodging creepily friendly squirrels along the way. Eve took a deep breath and let it out slowly. In an effort to lighten the conversation, she said in her drollest tone, "Maybe I should ask my mom who I am."

This time it was Boop who missed the laugh cue. Instead, she frowned. "Justine doesn't know you, not the inside you."

"I was being sarcastic. Like a joke about how Mom thinks she knows everything."

The peacock's caw startled Eve. That thing was loud. Another answered.

"What do you think those birds are going on about?" Eve didn't want to discuss her mom, or herself, for that matter.

Only Boop wasn't biting. "Your mama, she means well. Only . . ."

Eve sighed, resigned to getting the whole conversation over with. "Only what?"

"You gotta live your life, not the one she never lived."

"It's not like that." It wasn't. Mom just wanted what was best for Eve. She loved her. She'd done everything for her. Sure, she could be overbearing, but she was always right. Eve stifled a yawn.

Boop stared at the reed-filled sanctuary and answered with silence.

Eve watched her, as if in doing so she might find the young girl inside Boop. Maybe they were lost in the same place.

Justine: Your stuff arrived.

Eve: That was fast

Justine: You could be here now too. I'll unpack your stuff this weekend.

Eve: I'll do it when I get home. Just shove everything in my closet

Justine: Fine. Savannah tomorrow?

Eve: Yep

Justine: Tell Aunt Victoria hi.

Eve: OK

Justine: I would say tell Boop to go easy on her, but Aunt Victoria can take care of herself.

Eve: Yep

Justine: Always liked her.

Eve: Me too

Justine: How is Boop?

Eve: Fine

Justine: And the boy last night?

Eve: Fine

Justine: What did you do today?

Eve: Went to the Fountain of Youth

Justine: How was it?

Eve: Touristy

Justine: Texting with you is like pulling teeth. You remind me of your grandfather.

Eve: Was he quiet?

Justine: Most of the time. Wish you had met him.

Eve: Me too. Constance was nice though

Justine: Nice? More like a homewrecker. Any plans for the evening?

Eve: Dinner

Justine: Okay. Don't forget to eat some fruits and veggies. Traveling can be rough on your stomach.

Eve: Sure

Justine: Love you.

Eve: Love you too

Eve sat across the booth from Boop at O'Toole's Pub looking quite fetching. The shirt Boop had bought her earlier that afternoon while Eve napped fit perfectly. Boop was pleased as punch for a few hours reprieve from staring at the usual tank top. Afraid to overwhelm her, Boop had bought her a sleeveless black shirt with a gray lace overlay. Boop had laid on her delight in picking out such a becoming gift real thick too. By the time she was done, Eve could hardly have refused to wear it. Boop had even talked her into putting on a touch of lip gloss—okay, worn her down might be a better description. Either way, she was wearing it. Baby steps, and after a most productive after-noon at the mall, Boop had a few more tricks up her sleeve.

Given that their waiter Hank was quite the fox, Boop was even more pleased with herself than usual. Hank couldn't seem to keep his eyes to himself, but Eve was so buried in the menu she didn't notice. Boop nudged her under the table.

Eve glared at her, but Boop stayed strong in her mission, raised her eyebrows and tilted her head toward him as he left to fetch them some peanuts and water.

"Stop it," Eve hissed.

Didn't she know girls her age were supposed to be boy crazy? "What?" she feigned innocence.

Eve's eyes narrowed.

"Honey, do you like boys?" Boop asked. "I know there's some girls that don't. Can't say I understand it, but if you're like that, I'll . . . I'll worry, pray, well sure, and . . . start looking for cute girls."

"You are insane." Eve stared up into the heavens as if she was seeking deliverance. "Who has this conversation with her grand-mother?" Then Eve lowered her gaze from the heavens to Boop. "No, I'm not a lesbian." She smacked her lips and rubbed on a knot in the wooden table.

"Ladies." Hank set down the peanuts, his eyes twinkled as he if might've caught wind of their little chat. "Now then, you ready to order drinks? Can I get you an appetizer?"

"Mmmmhmmm," Boop said. "You got Milwaukee's Best on tap?"

"Sure do."

"We'll have two then, and some buffalo wild wings, extra spicy."

Hank didn't blink, but Eve's eyes widened.

Silly girl, did she really think Hank was going to call out an old lady for buying alcohol for a minor? And heck, Boop doubted Hank would mind if the pretty girl got tipsy.

He said, "Sure thing. That's how I prefer my wings too." He winked at Eve as if they were sharing an inside joke, but she responded with a puzzled frown. Boop wanted to smack her in the forehead. She and Justine had failed this poor girl.

After Hank left, Eve said, "I don't like beer."

"So what? Honey, you need to loosen up. You're so tight you squeak." Boop shucked a peanut. "Hank was flirting with you, and you just sat there."

"Flirting? What are you talking about?"

Some country music warbling about breaking hearts provided background music. Boop enjoyed the irony. "Didn't you notice when he winked at you?"

"So you're saying that wasn't because he had something stuck in his eye?"

"Seriously?"

"I don't get boys. They make me nervous. I don't know what to say to them." Eve tugged at the hem of her shirt. "Not that it matters. They don't ever talk to me anyway."

"Could be the cold fish vibe you send out."

"Fish?"

"Never-you-mind that. You're pretty enough and smart enough, and kind enough to catch any boy out there."

"Could've fooled me." She tossed an empty peanut shell on the ground along with the hundreds that already carpeted the restaurant. "Why the obsessing over my love life?"

Or lack thereof. "I'm not obsessed."

"If you say so."

Was she right? Was Boop obsessed? Nah, she merely wanted Eve to recognize that other people admired her. Maybe then she might start admiring herself a little. Humility is good and all, but Eve was downright self-abasing.

Hank returned with their beers and wings. "I brought you some extra blue cheese." He smiled at Eve, who shot Boop a panicked look.

"Get on with it now," Boop mouthed.

Eve cleared her throat and croaked, "Thanks."

"Y'all ready to order?"

"I'll have the brisket with a side of potato salad. Eve?"

"Uh. What do you recommend?"

"Most girls order the house salad, but I prefer a girl with an appetite. The chicken fried steak rocks."

"Okay, I'll have that," Eve grinned, "and a side salad."

Hank laughed.

Eve blushed.

"All righty then, I'll have it out to you in a minute." The peanuts crunched under his feet as he walked away.

"Now that wasn't so bad."

Eve closed her eyes. "It was awful."

"You just need some practice is all."

"No, I need lessons."

"Butter my butt and call me a biscuit! Look no further."

"This ought to be good." Eve crossed her arms over her chest.

"I'll assume you meant that in all sincerity."

"You know what they say about assuming."

"I do not," Boop said in her most imperious, Vicky-like tone. Eve's chuckle almost broke her straight-man act, but Boop was a mountain. "Flirting lessons: let's begin. Boys want to talk to pretty girls, but they're intimidated. Your job, then, is to signal your interest, like those peacocks this morning. Boost their manhood."

Eve raised her eyebrows and burst out laughing.

It was Boop's turn to blush. She hadn't meant it like that and was grateful that all Eve said was, "Like the peacocks. Right."

It was probably too late to teach Eve about respecting her elders. She'd probably point out that elders needed to act respectable first, and Lord knew, Boop was done playing that game. "However, you must let them chase you."

"Well, of course." Eve batted her eyelashes and simpered. She could mock it all she wanted, but it worked.

Hank returned with their dinners. "How long you ladies in town?"

He gazed at Eve as he spoke, but certain Eve would remain mute, Boop answered, "Depends."

Only Eve surprised Boop and answered at the same time, "Just passing through."

"We got a band coming in later tonight. You should come back. They're awesome."

Eve said, "I don't think—"

Boop cut her off, "We might do that."

An old man at a table across the restaurant waved Hank over, so he reluctantly left.

Eve said, "I don't want to come back to this peanut-littered death trap to hear some local-yokel band play honky-tonk crap."

After admitting her vulnerability only minutes before, Boop knew Eve wielded this attitude like a shield. Even so, Boop struggled not to bite back. Instead, she said, "So getting a boy's attention is a simple three-step dance."

"Dancing lessons too? Lucky me."

Boop flinched at the venom in Eve's tone. Was Boop pushing her too hard? So be it. In for the penny, in for the pound. When Eve acted like a regular boy-crazy nineteen-year-old (though Boop would settle for thirteen), then she'd back off.

"Allow me to demonstrate." Boop scanned the pub, searching for a candidate. Maybe at her age "victim" was a better word. Boop couldn't believe she was going to attempt to pick up a man. It'd been forty years since she'd batted her eyelashes, and she didn't have nearly the assets she'd had back then. There was a decent chance, a better than decent chance, she'd fall flat on her face and embarrass herself. Boop supposed she'd sunk lower at some point in her life, but she was hard-pressed to remember such an occasion. The old man who'd called Hank over was a decent candidate. No wedding ring. Shoot—Boop would never lay eyes on him again— might as well.

"Step one. Stare at the boy until he catches you staring and then quickly turn away." Boop ogled her prey, watched as he slurped on his chili and wiped a stray bean from his chin with the back of his hand. He was a little slow on the uptake, but eventually he pulled away from the Braves game and turned his head to meet her eye. Boop, however, returned her attention to Eve. "Step two, repeat. Only this time when he catches your eye, you flash a shy smile and then look away. Pretend you're embarrassed."

"Who's pretending?"

Again, Boop stared at the old man, nose hairs and all. This time around he was quicker on the uptake. Boop simpered, trying not to think about how foolish she must come across, and then ducked her head. "Step three. You do it again, but this time you hold the stare, toast your drink, and take a sip."

And so Boop did, and to her relief the old man came shuffling over. "Good evening, can I buy you girls a drink?"

Eve was trying so hard not to laugh, she looked like she was about to explode.

"Oh dear, aren't you a doll? I think we're okay though." Boop gestured to their nearly full beers on the table. "I hope I wasn't staring, but you look familiar. Have we met before?"

"Why no, ma'am. I don't think so. Philip Candor's the name."

"You remind me of somebody. Paul Newman maybe." *Paul Newman my foot,* Boop thought. Now, how was she going to get rid of this fella?

"He reminds me of Grandpa."

"You think so? Your grandpa'll be here in a few minutes. We can do a side-by-side comparison."

Poor Philip seemed confused. Boop felt a twinge of guilt for toying with him. Time to wrap this up. "Philip, it was so lovely to meet you. I'll be sure to tell my husband you took care of us when he wasn't here. You're such a fine gentleman."

"Any time." Sweet Philip drifted away.

Eve snorted. "I can't believe that worked."

"This old girl's still got it." Maybe Boop did still have it, but she wasn't interested. She hadn't been interested in anyone since Tommy. Not that she'd been pining for him. More like when he left the sex part of her up and died. Love's a roller coaster, and Boop was too old to take another ride.

A Long Time Ago

Tommy burst into the bedroom, his hair mussed like a bird's nest, his cheeks flushed, and his eyes glassy. He was drunker than Cooter Brown. Bourbon, from the smell of him.

"We need to talk," he said.

Boop glanced at the clock on her bedside table—half past seven. So much for working late, more like happy hour.

She propped her pillow on the headboard and leaned back. Goose pimples prickled her arms. Tommy never came into her bedroom, and they never talked. She crossed her arms to cover her lacey neckline and braced herself. "Go on."

"I—" He ran his hands through his thinning hair and then threw his shoulders back. "I'm leaving you."

"You left me fifteen years ago."

"I didn't go anywhere. I've been right here waiting for you. Only my girl never came back."

Boop's throat tightened. She would not cry in front of him.

"I'm filing for a divorce," he said.

A divorce? People like them did not get divorced, not in Leeside anyhow. Divorce was such a nasty word. He'd never go through with it. "Ha! You don't have the guts."

"You can say I was having an affair and file for a divorce. I'll take the blame."

How noble. Boop may have spent years dreaming about getting a divorce from Tommy, but darned if she'd let him dictate the terms. Logic had nothing to do with it. "Your la-de-da reputation will be in shreds. You'll be nothing."

"Maybe you should worry about your own reputation instead of mine." He cocked his right eyebrow.

Did he think Boop gave a hoot about her reputation? All she wanted to do was roll over and die. Only she wasn't brave enough to do it herself. How pathetic was that? Too many Sundays listening to the preacher hammer on about sin. If she wasn't already in hell, then hell must be a dreadful place. "I'm already nothing."

Tommy bowed his head. His shoulders shuddered. If Boop hadn't known better, she'd have said he was trying not to cry. When he finally looked up, his eyes had pinkened and the fine lines on his brow deepened. He cleared his throat. "I thought after Davey died, you'd come around, but it's been seven years. I've tried to be patient."

And he had been. Tommy'd been more patient than most men. The poor man had a loony wife and an unruly daughter. He didn't deserve this. That's what all those biddies at church said anyway.

He glowered at her. "Boop, this isn't a marriage."

"No, it ain't." More like a death march. Boop couldn't maintain eye contact. Instead, she stared at the drapes. He was right. She'd failed this marriage. She'd failed him. She'd failed Davey. She'd failed Justine.

"And I've met someone else."

Boop closed her eyes. She wasn't some bobble-headed idiot. She knew he'd dallied over the years, although they'd had an unspoken agreement to pretend otherwise. "Do you mean to tell me this floozy is worth destroying your reputation? The very same reputation you traded in our son for?"

"It wasn't like that . . . we couldn't care for him, he wasn't—"

"What? A person? He wasn't your son? What wasn't he exactly?" Boop seethed with hatred for this man that she'd once loved with the passion of a teenager. Divorce would be a blessing. Only neither of them deserved the release. Their marriage was their penance.

He stared at his feet. "Let's not rehash this."

He was right. What was the point? Boop got out of bed and wandered over to her vanity. She sat and picked up her brush, then watched her hair smooth in the mirror. Her mama used to tell her to brush her hair a hundred strokes every night. One stroke. This was probably the first time she'd brushed her hair in three days. Two strokes. Was that right? Three strokes. Yes, she'd taken Justine to Leggett's to get some new platform shoes. Four strokes. Ridiculous shoes that would break Justine's ankle. Five strokes. Boop watched her hand tremble in the mirror as if it belonged to someone else. Six strokes. One hundred was a lot. She slammed the brush down, pinched her cheeks, and said in the calmest voice she could muster, "Who's the Jezebel?"

"Constance is a very nice woman. In fact, she's Justine's drama teacher."

"Justine!" Boop spun around to glare at him. "Have you given any thought about what this will do to her?"

Tommy's eyes widened. "To her? How about for her? How about giving her a mother figure who actually mothers her?"

"That whore is not her mother. You keep her away from my Justine, or I'll . . ." He'd already taken away one child. He would not steal Justine away from Boop too. Somehow Boop would find the strength to fight like she should've done for Davey.

"You'll what? Sic your sister on me?"

"Asshole." Wishing she'd been born a man, Boop stood and

squeezed her hands by her side. What she wouldn't give to smash her fist in his smug face. Instead, she was left with a different sort of ammunition. More potent, but less gratifying. "No, I'll tell the world about Davey, about what you did—"

"What we did."

Boop deflated and belly-flopped back on the bed. She kicked her feet at the truth and unfairness of it. And then she rolled over, snatched *Love Story* from her nightstand, and pegged it at him. "Get out!" The book hit the door closing behind him and thudded onto the floor.

CHAPTER 9

The air conditioner in the Gray Ghost had two settings: Cold as a Witch's Tit and Off. Boop usually kept a sweater handy but with all the hubbub of packing, it had slipped her mind. So when Eve popped into the service station to prepay for their gas, Boop swung round to the trunk in search of her yellow cardigan. She stopped to admire Eve's backside as Eve wandered away. The black flowy skirt and peasant blouse looked so feminine on her that Boop had to pat herself on the back for talking Eve into wearing them.

Earlier this morning back at the motel, Eve had given her an opening when she'd complimented Boop's white slacks and pale-yellow silk blouse. Boop had said, "We're off to see Mrs. Mayor. I can hardly show up looking like a pauper, now can I?"

Eve, still in a giant T-shirt and tacky Valentine pajama shorts, had frowned.

"And honey, if she gets on you 'bout your clothes, you let me know. I'll put a stop to it."

"Boop, Aunt Victoria isn't going to say anything."

"Not outright, but she'll get a dig in. You mark my words." Boop lined the bottom of her suitcase with shoes, exploring the possibility that she might've overpacked a touch.

Eve flicked off the television and rolled out of bed for the first time that morning. "If she does, let it go. I don't care. I don't want you two fighting over me."

"I'll try to be on my good behavior." Boop made a show of packing yesterday's shopping bag.

Eve bit her lip. "Okay, I'll wear something you've stashed in that bag of yours if you promise you won't say another word about my clothes for the rest of the trip."

"I didn't say nothing."

Eve arched her eyebrows.

Boop decided against suggesting she shape them brows up a little.

"Stop trying to change me."

"I ain't trying to change you. I'm trying to find you." Boop tossed her the skirt, blouse, and sandals from the shopping bag.

"It's gonna take more than some fancy clothes."

"You're right. But 'Look good, feel good.' I always say." Boop zipped up her suitcase and gave herself a once-over in the mirror. She'd do.

Eve put on her new outfit. "But these costumes," she gestured down her body, "don't make me feel good."

"How do they make you feel?"

Eve walked over to the bathroom. At first, Boop thought she was going to ignore her question, but before she slammed the door, she answered, "Exposed."

Now that was a conundrum. Boop wanted to build her up, not tear her down. Would she have to do the latter before she could manage the former?

Boop still didn't have an answer to that quandary, but Eve sure did look pretty. Boop opened the trunk.

Turned out the sweater was at the very bottom of her stack. She rifled through the pile, leaving disarray behind her. Finally, she surrendered and, instead, plucked the garments out one by one, shaking them flat with her right hand, and then gathering them by their hangers with her left.

Once she'd unearthed the sweater, she couldn't help but spot some navy-blue linen caught in Eve's footlocker. She'd not planned to pry into Eve's personal effects, and she remembered how protective Eve had been of the footlocker, but Boop didn't give it enough thought. She whipped open the trunk to shift the fabric out of harm's way. Boop didn't know what she'd expected to discover inside, but it wasn't the sewing machine, a dress form, various fabrics, and a few sketchbooks. Boop didn't get it.

Boop's shoulder ached from the weight of her hanging clothes, so she set them on her seat to rest for a spell. With only the innocent intention of stuffing the fabric inside and shutting the footlocker up tight, Boop returned to it. However, when she touched the linen, she thought about how easily linen wrinkles. So rather than tucking it back in, she decided to refold it.

She was surprised to discover the fabric was not just fabric. It was actually a wraparound jacket, with butterflies embroidered along the neckline and closure. It was so divine, she couldn't resist trying it on. Since it was a little too big, she rolled the sleeves and admired the candy-apple green lining that now showed on the cuff. After she tied the belt, which was navy on one side and green on the other, she wandered over to the side-view mirror to take a gander at the full effect.

"Where y'all headed?" said an old lady through the window of the car next to them.

"Savannah, visiting my sister."

"Oh, you're gonna love it."

Clearly, she didn't know Vicky.

"I just left there after visiting with my daughter. She's got a new grandbaby. That's five great grandkids I got now. You want to see pictures?" The woman had already opened the door and stepped out with a small photo album in hand. The gas station attendant who was filling the woman's tank smiled good-naturedly at Boop. She had the feeling he'd already had the pleasure of a look-see.

"Sure." Boop graciously accepted the album, being sure to "ooh" and "aah" appropriately as she flipped through.

"I sure do love that jacket you're wearing. Where on earth did you find such a gem?"

Boop stared at the trunk and considered the sketchbooks and the lock. Ding-ding. "Why, I think my granddaughter might've designed it."

Eve left the gas station convenience store with a Red Bull, hoping it would cut through the fog she couldn't seem to shake. In her current state, it was uncertain they'd be safe with her behind the wheel. Inside the plastic bag that hung from her wrist were a Yoo-hoo and a MoonPie for Boop. Maybe Boop's excitement over the unexpected treats would wear off on Eve.

The car blocked Boop from sight, but Eve could make out the ridiculous pink feathered Derby hat of some stranger Boop had befriended. Boop adored picking up strays.

Eve twisted off the gas cap and set it on top of the car. She'd had enough practice at making herself invisible that she dared hope she might pump the gas without either of them noticing her and dragging her into a pointless conversation about the weather. Eve never understood why people found it necessary to point out how hot it was. Duh. If only people with nothing to say would shut up. She lifted the nozzle from the pump and stuck it into the tank.

"Is that your granddaughter?" the Derby hat said.

Alas, Eve's hopes were crushed. Eve gave a weak smile and a half-hearted wave, praying that would suffice. It didn't. As she lifted up the 87 lever and squeezed the trigger, she could see the hat bobbing toward the back of the car. Only when the stranger popped into view, did Eve notice that the trunk was open.

"Honey, did you make your grandma's jacket?"

What? Out of the corner of her eye, Eve caught movement near the front of the car. She turned. Boop was wearing Eve's jacket. Eve noted that the shoulders needed taking in and she'd need to hem it an inch or two. The cuffs were larger than Eve had intended, but Eve kind of preferred them big.

Then Eve's eyes narrowed. What the hell? What was Boop doing wearing her jacket?

The open trunk. Eve clasped the key dangling from her neck. How had Boop—? Eve must've left the footlocker unlocked after checking behind the mover. Such a dumb ass.

The Derby hat said, "So honey, did you or didn't you?"

"I did," Eve's voice came out a whisper. Her face turned scarlet, and she hung her head. The pump clicked off, and Eve released the trigger. The gas fumes made her stomach churn, and Eve reeled.

"My daughter owns a boutique on Broughton Street in Savannah. I've got a good eye, and I know she'd love to get her hands on that jacket. You got more stuff?"

Eve shrugged, hung the nozzle back on the pump, and tore off the receipt. The Derby hat was crazy.

"Her shop's called Papayas, and her name's Delilah Grace Scott. You tell her I sent y'all. I'm Tilly by the way."

Eve slunk around to the driver's seat like a zombie. Was this a prank? Tilly's daughter would laugh Eve and her jacket out of her shop or, even worse, reject her in that syrupy sweet way only a Southern woman can. Make Eve feel like a four-year-old. Nope. Wouldn't catch Eve dead at Papayas.

Eve was nobody's fool. Boop was lucky Eve wasn't flipping out. Eve could hear Boop outside the car gushing all over Tilly and her Derby hat as if trying to make up for Eve's supposed rudeness.

The trunk slammed shut, and Boop slid into the passenger seat and tossed Eve a puzzled glance.

Could Boop be that obtuse? She'd invaded Eve's privacy,

"borrowed" her jacket, and outed her to a complete Derby-hat wearing stranger. Now Boop was puzzled about Eve's non-reaction to Derby hat's suggestion? What did Boop think? That Eve would fall for this nonsense? Was Eve supposed to be thrilled that a complete stranger felt so sorry for her that she was sending Eve on a fool's errand?

"I reckon you got caught with your pants down just now," Boop said.

"That was mortifying. You had no right." Eve started the engine and gazed out the windshield. Who was this woman beside her? It was as if an invasion of the body snatchers had swapped Boop for Eve's mom. Eve's eyes burned.

In a soft voice, Boop said, "I'm sorry." Eve could hear her fumbling around and muttering about knots. Her arthritis was probably making untying the belt difficult. "I'll take it off."

"Don't bother. You can have it." Eve gripped the steering wheel tightly and pulled onto the entrance ramp.

"Really?"

Boop sounded so psyched that for a minute Eve believed she actually liked the jacket and wasn't just pretending to make her feel better. Then Eve thought again. Don't be a fool. "Whatever."

They sat in silence. The monotony of the road calmed Eve until she loosened her grip. "But I need to take it in for you, so it fits right. And don't go telling people I made it."

"Why ever not?"

"I don't need people feeling sorry for me." Eve jerked into the fast lane.

"What are you prattling on about? Why would anyone feel sorry for you?"

Eve shrugged. "Can we stop talking about it?"

"In a minute, but first . . . a total stranger just complimented this here jacket. Not only that, she suggested her own daughter might want to sell it in her boutique. She didn't feel sorry for you." And in a lower tone, she continued, "Especially after you acted like such a nincompoop."

However, Boop might have meant it, it was difficult for Eve to feel insulted by such a silly word. A smile threatened, but she squashed it before Boop could imagine she was off the hook. "Tilly's old and wears Derby hats, not exactly a fashionista."

"We'll see."

"Oh, no. No way we're going near that shop." Eve's heart swelled as she imagined her designs on mannequins in a shop window. How cool would that be?

"If you're sure."

Daydreams were for children. "I'm sure." She might be a nincompoop, but Eve was nobody's fool.

CHAPTER 10

Vicky might don the pearls of a sophisticated lady, but the faint-blue ceiling of her porch told a different tale. Vicky insisted it was merely a decorative preference. Still, to Boop it spoke of an underlying superstition that was decidedly uncultured. Boop couldn't rightly tell how effective the paint was at warding off evil spirits; mostly 'cause she couldn't decide if Vicky herself was an evil spirit.

When Eve thumped the pineapple door knocker, Boop flinched in surprise at the crash of the brass. Then she about had a heart attack when Vicky herself opened the door. Must've given the help the day off. She ushered them inside.

The aroma—a blend of cedar and must—took Boop back to her childhood. Even after all these years, it made her miss Mama and Daddy. How Vicky could stand living in a house filled with their old hand-me-downs, Boop did not know.

Vicky escorted them to her sitting room where their mama's pink Haviland china was set for tea. Framed in the doorway, with the shadows falling the way they did, Vicky still looked remarkably like the larger-than-life bride who stared down from her portrait over the fireplace. Vicky'd aged like a fine Kentucky bourbon. No small investment on her part, although how much of that investment had been financial and how much of it effort would forever remain a point of contention between Vicky and Boop. Whatever the case, Vicky's skin was more like silk after a day's wear than like Boop's cottony wrinkles.

As always, a string of pearls choked Vicky's slender neck, held in place as tightly as her self-restraint. Both envious and grateful, Boop self-consciously stroked her own unadorned chicken neck.

Vicky tinkled the silver bell on the piecrust table. Then she sat down on the wingback chair, leaving the settee for Eve and Boop to share. The mere names of all that fancified furniture gave Boop a headache.

"Betty, what a charming jacket."

Boop tensed in expectation of her backhand. She'd chosen the white slacks and sandals because she knew her failure to follow the dictates of the calendar would stick in Vicky's craw. Vicky'd be sure to compliment them, putting a hair more emphasis on the word "white" than necessary since her sister was the kind of la-de-da lady who would never dream of wearing white before Memorial Day. These sorts of shenanigans were Boop's only chance of staying sane during their spell in Savannah, as she had an uneasy feeling that whatever bee Vicky had in her bonnet about Ally was gonna stir up a hornet's nest.

Only there was no follow-up dig. To her complete and utter shock, there were no veiled remarks about wearing white, checking calendars, or being raised in a barn. Nothing. Who was this woman?

A plump woman in a maid's uniform entered pushing a tea cart laden with sweet tea, itty-bitty pimento cheese sandwiches, and pralines. Now this was standard Vicky.

"Thank you kindly, Greta."

Greta might've been a shadow for all the response she gave.

Vicky said, "So Eve, let's get down to business. Tell me about school."

"It's fine." Eve appeared to be absorbed in watching the ice cubes in her tea melt.

Vicky arched her eyebrows at Boop.

Boop frowned.

"You enjoying your classes?"

Eve shrugged.

"What'd you study this year?"

"The usual—English, math, science, stuff." Eve popped a sandwich in her mouth.

"I used to adore history classes. What about you, Eve?"

She shrugged.

Vicky grimaced at Boop. "And Betty, how's your little road trip going so far?"

The condescension dripping from the word "little" made Boop as happy as a dead pig in sunshine—now this was the Vicky she knew and loathed. Boop was tempted to say fine and shrug, but she took pity on both of them and answered, "Hunky dory. We thoroughly enjoyed St. Augustine yesterday."

"Oh, then you must've taken the legacy tour of Flagler College. Wasn't it lovely?"

"Actually, we passed the morning tooling around the Fountain of Youth Archeological Park." Boop sat on her hands to keep from applauding, while Eve reached for a second sandwich. A healthy appetite was a promising sign. And . . . Eve eating seconds without the hostess's prompting would throw off Vicky's game. Then again, Vicky was acting awfully agreeable for some as yet undisclosed reason.

"Why?" Vicky asked, her voice sharp as a tack.

Not that agreeable, then.

Boop opened her mouth prepared to shoot off a biting retort, when Eve, who must've caught her eyes narrowing, cut Boop off with, "My idea."

"I see. And how was it?"

Eve looked tuckered out. Part of Boop wanted to tuck her into bed for an afternoon nap. But another part suggested she let Vicky have a go at her. Vicky's social expectations had often riled Boop up enough to charge her battery. Maybe Vicky'd light some spark within Eve. Boop couldn't think of anything she'd enjoy more than watching that fireworks show. Shame that it was about as likely as winning the lottery.

"We had fun." A real smile spread across Eve's face.

"I see. And tell me about your plans for the summer."

Eve's smile froze like a clown's. She shrugged again.

Those shrugs were setting off Boop's nerves. Vicky turned to Boop as if expecting Boop to speak for Eve, so she did. "She has an internship at the hospital. She's real good at science."

Eve blanched.

"Do you enjoy science?" Vicky asked Eve.

"Not really."

"What do you like?"

Eve shrugged.

Boop was dying to show off Eve's designing skills and boast about her new jacket, but having already pushed her luck, she held her tongue. This conversation was turning into a downright fiasco, in spite of the fact that both Vicky and Boop were working hard at it. And while Vicky's discomfort amused Boop, it didn't overshadow Eve's. In another rescue attempt, Boop said, "Your home looks lovely."

The house had been an eyesore when Vicky'd bought it—smashed windows, rotting wood, peeling paint, lead pipes. She'd busied herself for years restoring the old bird. Not that she dirtied her hands in the restoration, but the coordinating of contractors and applications for Certificates of Appropriateness were their own kind of labor.

"Thank you kindly." Vicky glowed with pride.

Catching flies with honey, Boop was on a roll now. "How's your family?"

Vicky's three boys, who were younger than Justine, had settled in Savannah and were constant fodder for Vicky's self-congratulations.

Especially Ally's father, whose political aspirations were the stuff of Vicky's dreams.

"Jamie's gotten a promotion at the hospital, and his youngest will graduate from Country Day in the spring. Robert's getting remarried. Nice girl, but bless her heart . . ." Her voice dropped to a whisper. "She's from New Jersey."

Boop thought she heard a snort from Eve but didn't dare turn to face her as Boop wasn't sure she could contain her own bubble of laughter, which threatened to spill all over Vicky. "Oh, my," Boop said with mock seriousness. "Then you've got some work cut out for you."

"Indeed." She sipped her tea. Vicky hadn't had a bite to eat and wouldn't either. She didn't approve of eating in public, thought it uncouth. Granted she'd probably stuffed her face before their arrival, but that was neither here nor there. She asked Eve, "Have you spoken with Ally lately?"

Eve paled but nodded slowly.

"I'm worried about her."

"Worried?" Boop noshed on a praline relishing its melty goodness.

Vicky shooed away Boop's question, focusing instead on Eve. "She won't respond to her parents or me. I hired a private investigator, a local man in LA. He said she's moved out of her apartment. He's asked around, but no one seems to know where she's gone."

"She's fine."

Vicky set down her glass of tea and stood up. "What's going on?"

"Nothing." Eve chewed on her fingernail. Her refusal to meet Vicky's eye spoke volumes.

Boop was torn between a desire to protect Eve from Vicky and to find out what was going on with Ally, because there was no doubt that something was up, and that Eve knew more than she was saying.

"Eve, that's insufficient." Vicky took a menacing step toward Eve. How exactly the old lady pulled off menacing Boop wasn't sure.

Eve met Vicky's eye. "She's safe. She's not in danger. Just give her some time."

"For what? Where is she?"

Eve crossed her arms over her chest. "I'm not at liberty to say."

Boop couldn't believe what she was seeing. After years of watching Eve cower under Justine's manipulation, this backbone was most unexpected.

"Eve, I'm her grandmother, and I have a right to know." Tears welled in Vicky's eyes. A new tactic.

"Ally will tell you when she's ready."

"If she's in trouble . . . I love her. I want to help." Vicky's voice trembled such that Boop almost believed her.

"Then back off. Please. Give her space."

"I can't. Too much rides on the next few months. I need to run damage control while I still can."

Ah, and so now they were getting to the truth of the situation. The election. It was always about an election with Vicky.

"Eve, where is she?"

"Safe." Eve's darting eyes were not comforting.

"Fine." Vicky's eyes narrowed. "I know she's pregnant."

"She's what?" Eve gasped. "All Ally told me was she was going to disappear for a while and to keep everyone off the scent as long as I could."

"Stupid girl."

Boop sputtered praline to the floor. "Don't call Eve 'stupid.'"

Vicky glared at the crumbs and lifted her hand imperiously. "I was referring to Ally, but on second thought . . . Eve, you should've called me."

A pale Eve staggered to her feet. "Excuse me." Even her lips were pale.

Boop worried Eve was going to faint. "Do you want me—?"

"No!"

Boop flinched.

Eve grabbed the back of a chair and steadied herself, and then said in a more even tone. "I want to be alone."

Boop wasn't sure that was a good idea.

Eve's whispered, "Please," suggested she'd cottoned onto Boop's doubts.

Vicky tinkled the bell again. Greta appeared so quickly she must've been looming behind the door. Did Vicky realize she had an eavesdropper on her hands? "Greta, please escort Eve and her luggage to the Rose Room."

The silence that descended between Boop and Vicky in Eve's absence reminded Boop of a waiting room at a hospital. They strained to listen to the fading shuffle of Eve and Greta, and the clunking of their luggage as they made their way up the stairs.

Once assured they were out of earshot, Vicky said, "Eve's lying."

"What?"

"She knows exactly where Ally is and what's going on with her."

Considering Eve's sudden hankering to go to the family beach house, Boop too, suspected Eve knew exactly where Ally·was. She fought to keep her face blank.

"I'm certain of it," Vicky said.

"Perhaps. Now then, I believe you have a photograph for me."

"Same old Betty."

"What the dickens is that supposed to mean?"

"Personally, I find it more graceful to ease into conversations."

"I'm sure you do. However, I find it more effective to say what I mean and mean what I say."

A sneer flashed across Vicky's face before she was able to close her eyes and breathe in ladylike serenity. "There's more. Ally's baby— he's like Davey."

Boop's head roared.

Vicky lifted the top of the Davenport and pulled out a

yellowed photograph. Her hands trembled—whether from age or emotion Boop wasn't sure. "I kept it all these years. I miss him too."

Boop both ached to see the photograph and dreaded it something awful. A sharp pain kicked at her chest like a bucking bronco. A heart attack? Didn't matter. Davey. Boop bit down on her knuckles. And Ally . . . Boop bled for her. "How bad is it?"

"Can't tell till the baby's born."

"Right. Silly question. The father?"

Vicky threw her hands in the air. "Nothing confirmed. The PI found the medical information in Ally's trash. The father wasn't listed. Boop, I've never asked you for anything—"

Boop scoffed, "That's 'cause you demanded it."

Vicky waved the picture of Davey as if dangling a durned carrot. "Will you find out from Eve where Ally is? Then tell Ally about Davey? You could stop by as part of your road trip. I'm sure seeing Eve would do Ally some good too."

No. This was too much. She couldn't talk about Davey. Not to Eve. Not now. Not for Vicky. Not for Ally. Boop loved them, but no. "This secret. It was your idea. It's too late. The truth would break too many hearts." Justine's. Eve's. Boop's.

"Please? Do you want me to beg? I'll do it. I'll beg."

Boop held up her hand as if it had the power to stop the onslaught of Vicky's words. Boop needed this like a hole in the head. "I can't. I'm sorry. I'm not strong enough."

Vicky grabbed Boop's chin. "That's a lie. You are strong. You are not the same woman you were back then. Sure, you took a tumble, but you got back up. Everybody falls down, it's only the strong who can get back up. You did that."

A strangled sound bubbled from Boop's throat like a pot of boiling black-eyed peas. She wrenched her face from Vicky's grasp. "You think I woke up one day and found strength? It wasn't like that. It wasn't a simple case of mind over matter. I'm not you. I don't worship the god of the stiff upper lip. I can't."

Vicky rose and marched to the window.

Boop worried she would make a mess of things with Ally. No words of Boop's could fix this. She had no answers, and she couldn't bear such responsibility, not again.

With her back to Boop, Vicky said, "She's going to have to make a decision." She turned. Her steel gray eyes bore into Boop. "Whether or not to keep him."

"Oh God!"

Boop couldn't bear to consider Ally's dilemma. Her mind snapped shut while she observed Vicky gazing at the picture of Davey; it was as though Boop wasn't really there. Vicky pursed her lips and then with her usual intimidating briskness, marched to Boop's side and thrust the photograph at her. Davey jarred Boop from her detachment.

Vicky continued, "She might listen to you. I'd hate for her to go through the nightmare you did. If the father is who I suspect, then he isn't suitable at all. So unfortunate. Perhaps if she'd come to me in the beginning, someone suitable could've been found."

Davey was round about five in the photograph. He squinted in the sunshine. His was the face of Boop's every fantasy and the one that haunted her every nightmare. She sniffed in a vain attempt not to start bawling, but tears were already running down her cheeks like a runaway river.

Vicky continued, "And adoption for a baby like that, well let's just say I don't deal in fantasies. Which means we are left with only distasteful options. Termination, as abhorrent as I find it, seems the kindest option."

Boop gaped at Vicky.

"Think about it. Quickly. And quietly. With the election, Ally must be very careful."

Of course, the election. Vicky would be worried about the scandal.

They'd been so wrapped up in their conversation they hadn't heard Eve coming down the stairs. Both women were surprised to discover her standing in the doorway. Boop stuffed the photograph into her pocketbook, praying Eve hadn't noticed it. Boop pulled out a handkerchief to dab her face and blow her nose.

"Sorry to interrupt," Eve said.

Boop searched Eve's face for an indication of how long she'd been standing there and how much she'd heard, but Eve was difficult to read—thoughtful, confused, tired.

"I came down for a . . ." her voice trailed off, "glass of water."

Vicky rang her little bell and the invisible eavesdropping Greta appeared with a glass of water already in hand. Boop's secret was no longer safe.

She didn't know how to live without it.

Even though Justine's back was to Trevor's office door, and her white-noise pumping earbuds blocked his sounds, Justine knew Trevor was behind her because the hairs on her arms were tingling. So rather than being startled when his fingers slid the buds from her ears, her body tensed for entirely different reasons. Reasons that had no place at work.

Her eyes slid to his family portrait on the bookcase across from her desk—reasons that had no place anywhere really. Only her body couldn't seem to accept his marriage or his "bossness" and was constantly making room for his slightest touch.

"You finished the slides I need for the presentation tomorrow?" Trevor asked.

Justine spun her seat so she could face him. "Yes, in the drive."

"I'm gonna need you to stay late tonight to go over them." He wiggled his heavy eyebrows suggestively. Justine had once recommended that he get them waxed, but that hadn't gone over well, so she'd set herself on learning to like their bushiness. She'd almost accomplished this task by focusing on his amazing blue eyes rather than the caterpillars above them.

He continued, "Eve ready to start her internship next week?"

"She's so excited, nervous too. Thanks for getting her this opportunity."

"Tell her I'm counting on her. If the undergrad pilot program goes well, and if we expand the internship program—that might mean a promotion for me and raise for you, my little assistant. Assuming, of course, you keep doing such a bang-up job." He winked and then laid his hand on her arm before wandering back into his office.

Justine shifted uncomfortably in her seat, as she pushed away the confusion left in the wake of Trevor's presence. Latching on to the first distraction that came to mind, she logged in to Eve's student portal for the third time that day to see if any grades had been posted. All thoughts of Trevor vanished upon discovering that Eve's grades had indeed been posted. They were terrible. They must be someone else's. What incompetent fool had screwed this up?

Her face flushed and lips pursed, Justine found Bess's number in her contacts and called. She let out a disgusted snort when she got voicemail. That woman was always avoiding her calls. "This is Eve Prince's mother again. Hope you're doing well. I wanted to give you a heads up that some incompetent lackey has posted the wrong grades for Eve. After our last conversation, I'd hoped that you were looking after her a little better. Please have them corrected ASAP."

Justine ended the call, proud to have taken care of that for Eve, but when her eyes met Trevor's wife's in the photograph, every sliver of pride disappeared . . . she was a horrible person.

But at least she was a damn good mom.

A Long Time Ago

"Mama, please can I go to the picnic with you and Aunt Victoria?" Justine clung to Boop's skirt.

"No, sugar. Not this week." Boop crouched and hugged her tight. She longed to take Justine with them, or at least explain why she couldn't, but their secret couldn't be trusted with a five-year-old. Justine wasn't old enough to understand anyway. All Boop could do was hope the intensity of her hug would be enough reassurance.

"Next week? Please. I'll be good." Justine put on her best puppy dog face and near 'bout broke Boop's heart.

"Maybe so," Boop whispered, staring at a splash of dried egg on the tile floor, knowing that next weekend they'd leave her behind again.

"Why do you get her hopes up? No, sweet child. This outing isn't for little girls." Vicky petted Justine's head.

"I'm a big girl. Please, Mama."

Boop's lips trembled. She so wanted to cave and share the burden. What was wrong with her? What kind of monster would even consider unloading this on a five-year-old?

"Go on, why don't you?" Tommy grumbled from behind the newspaper. "Stop dragging it out."

"Okay." Boop peeled Justine's arms off like a banana.

"I don't understand why you continue to participate in this pointless exercise," Tommy said.

"It ain't pointless." Boop's eyes burned.

"It's tearing you apart. Hell, it's tearing our family apart."

Justine backed toward the hallway, preparing to flee should a squabble break out, as it too often did.

"That's your choice. You could always come with me," Boop said.

"I can't." He ducked his chin. "It ain't right. Look what it's done to you."

"No more'n I deserve."

Vicky interceded. "That's enough. Undoubtedly, you and Betty have some issues to work out, but not in front of me and especially not in front of the child."

Tommy turned on Vicky then. "Victoria, you enable this nonsense, you know."

"You can thank me another time." Vicky grabbed Boop with one hand and the picnic basket with the other.

"I won't," Tommy shot back.

"No, don't expect you will either. More fool you." Vicky headed to the door, hauling Boop along beside her. "C'mon, Betty, let's go now." Vicky turned and smiled at Justine. "We'll bring you back a treat, okay?"

Boop prayed Justine's forgiveness could be that easily bought.

Justine: Call me.

Justine: Now.

Justine: Where are you?

Eve: What's up?

Justine: I don't want to text. I'm calling you.

Eve: Can't talk now

Justine: Why not?

Eve: Lots of people around. Reporters and stuff

Justine: Fine. Grades posted. There's been a mistake.

Eve: Probably not

Justine: It says you're on academic probation.

Eve: Yeah

Justine: I left a message with Bess.

Eve: Why?

Justine: To get this straightened out.

Eve: It isn't a mistake

Eve: You there?

Eve: Mom?

Justine: What's going on with you?

Eve: IDK

Justine: English, please.

Eve: I don't know

Justine: How can you not know? Is school too hard? Do you need a tutor? Are you partying too much? Is there a boy?

Eve: No. I don't know

Justine: You don't know?

Justine: That's not good enough.

Eve: It's all I got

Justine: Wait.

Justine: Eve?

Justine: Damn it.

CHAPTER 11

B y this point, Eve had practically memorized the crazy email Ally had sent her, and she spent the evening replaying it over and over again searching for clues that might suggest Ally was pregnant. It was impossible to believe that such a major crisis had occurred in Ally's life and that she hadn't found a way to tell Eve. Even Eve's attempts at sleep were plagued by Ally's words. In desperation, Eve snuck some Benadryl from the medicine cabinet.

In spite of her attempt to medicate the problem away, Eve still didn't sleep well. The antique bed in the Rose Room was cursed with a mattress so ancient Eve had been tempted to search underneath it for a pea. Worse than the mattress though, Aunt Victoria didn't have air conditioning. Even with the windows open, there was little respite as the air was so still the curtains didn't even ripple.

The next morning Broughton Street was alive with shoppers. Aunt Victoria and Boop were acting civil to each other, which was an improvement. However, the best part of window shopping was that it distracted them from pestering Eve, who was suffering from a Benadryl hangover and the same questions were still buzzing around in her head.

She tagged along behind the two sisters, speaking when spoken to, but mostly lost in her thoughts. They wandered in and out of shops. Aunt Victoria bought a porcelain sugar bowl. Boop, still wearing Eve's jacket, bought some brightly colored earrings to match it.

What had Eve interrupted between them yesterday? The photograph Aunt Victoria had handed Boop had upset Boop, and she sure hadn't wanted Eve to see it. They were keeping secrets. Was it a secret lover?

When they entered the fourth or fifth shop, a stylish woman perched on a ladder changing a light bulb said, "Welcome to Papayas. If you need any help, give me a holler."

The word "Papayas" seeped into Eve's thoughts and her body tensed. Papayas—why did that sound so familiar? The rainbow sherbet striped walls sure didn't ring any bells.

Probably her imagination. The awesome selection of clothes in the store distracted Eve from the niggling feeling. The cocktail dress by the cash register was especially drool-worthy. Its designer had meshed together lace and sequins in a surprising way that was both old-school and modern. The indigo fabric was electric. None of it should have gone together, but somehow it managed to go perfectly. Eve would've remembered a dress like that and a place like this. She'd never been to Papayas before. Papayas?

"Any chance you're Delilah Grace Scott?" Boop asked.

The memory flooded back—the gas station and the Derby hat with her stinking Papayas.

"Why, yes." Delilah Grace finished tightening the screw on the stained-glass light cover and climbed down the ladder. How she managed to do it so gracefully in a sundress, Eve would never understand. An amazing sundress too, though it was her chain belt that stole the show. Eve already detested Delilah Grace, with her perfect look and her perfect store.

Eve caught her own reflection in a full-length mirror and

grimaced at her blandness. Her stomach knotted. She backed toward the door.

"We met your mama yesterday. She suggested we stop by," Boop said.

Aunt Victoria threw puzzled glances at each of them. Eve leaned against the door. The glass cooled her sweaty neck. She shivered.

"Did she now?" Delilah Grace looked Boop up and down. "Oh, so you're the lady with the jacket. Mama rang last night and told me all about y'all."

Eve closed her eyes and counted each labored breath—1, 2, 3, 4 . . .

Delilah Grace fingered Boop's jacket—Eve's jacket. Delilah Grace frowned. "It's—"

Eve pushed through the door, blinked in the bright sunlight, and then took off. She had no clue how far she ran. She dodged pedestrians and turned corners to avoid stopping for lights. She ran until she found her breath—which sounded totally nuts since running usually has the opposite effect. Eve's muscles burned, and the effort pushed thoughts from her head. She felt free, alive.

Since she wasn't sporting buns of steel or anything, eventually she had to slow to a walk. Only, the lazy pace let her thoughts return. She couldn't go back to that Papayas place. She couldn't face Delilah Grace Scott. That cocktail dress was a slap in the face to the designer Eve could never be. She never wanted to see it again. Colonial Park Cemetery, where a few barbarians picnicked on graves, loomed on her left.

Boop and Aunt Victoria were probably wigging out. Boop deserved it after that stunt. However, Aunt Victoria did not.

As Eve passed St. John's Cathedral, she continued to weigh her options. Part of her wanted to find a bus station and roll out. The devil inside her laughed at the idea of Boop stranded at Aunt Victoria's. She loved that evil guy sometimes.

The smell of hyacinth overwhelmed her. She had to face them, but she didn't have to talk to Boop. She couldn't trust what she'd say if she did.

Since by then Eve was closer to Aunt Victoria's house than the shopping area, she decided to wait for the old ladies at home.

Let Boop sweat it for a change.

Turned out Eve was the one who ended up sweating it. By the time a cab pulled up with the two ladies, she'd bitten six of her fingernails to the quick. Her original plan had been to watch from the window. However, when she noticed a bandage covering Boop's cheekbone and the ice pack she held to her temple, she rushed outside. "Oh my God. What happened?"

"Nothing," Boop said. Aunt Victoria offered her arm for Boop to lean on as they climbed the stairs. Boop's elbow was bandaged too.

Aunt Victoria pursed her lips. "No, it's not nothing. When you pulled your little disappearing act, Boop took off after you and tripped over a loose cobblestone."

Eve's mouth fell open. Boop had chased her? She hadn't even thought that was a possibility . . . but of course she did. Boop was always there. Eve opened the door for them.

Eve though? Fight or flight? She'd fly away, every time.

All Eve had needed to do was tell Delilah Grace Scott that she wasn't interested in selling her designs. Therefore, she didn't need to hear her opinions on her jacket. Thank you very much. And she could've said it just like that—all polite and official. But no, she'd run like some weird, awkward eleven-year-old.

Boop sat down on the bench in the foyer to rest. "I'm fit as a fiddle. Don't tell your mama, you hear."

Aunt Victoria put her hands on her hips and frowned at Eve. "She's lucky to walk away with only a few bumps and bruises."

"I'm so sorry."

"It's not your fault, honey," said Boop.

Aunt Victoria's "hmmm" lips made it clear she thought differently. She was right. And if Boop was smart, she'd run as fast and as far from Eve as she could, no matter how many cobblestones were in her path.

Justine: Why aren't you answering your phone?

Eve: I don't want to talk

Justine: I am worried about you.

Eve: I am fine

Justine: Your grades aren't. We need to talk.

Eve: What's to talk about? I suck we agree

Justine: We need to get you off of academic probation.

Eve: Why?

Justine: Maybe Trevor can pull some strings. Though I am embarrassed to tell him about this fiasco.

Eve: Forget it

Justine: What?

Eve: Stop meddling I hate college!!!!

Justine: Don't be so dramatic.

Eve: I'm not going back there!

Justine: Ha. Ha.

Eve: No joke

Justine: You have to go to college. It opens up doors.

Eve: It is not a free pass to a better life. It is a scam, like a timeshare

Justine: You are too young and immature to know what is best. Trust me. Have I ever led you wrong? What about medical school?

Eve: I don't want to be a doctor. I have never wanted to be a doctor that is your dream not mine. Why don't you go to medical school?

Justine: I'm too old. Don't turn this conversation into something about me. This is about you throwing away your life.

Eve: I'm not throwing away my life

Justine: Then what is your plan?

Eve: IDK

Justine: Exactly.

Eve: I am not going back in the fall you can't make me

Justine: If you don't go back to school, I cut you off.

Eve: ?

Justine: No money, no house, no clothes, no phone. On your own. Not my daughter.

Eve: Fine I will move in with Karl

Justine: Ha.

Eve: I don't have anything left to say to you

Justine: I have plenty left to say.

Eve: I AM OUT

CHAPTER 12

A glance at the mirror on the sun visor confirmed that Boop looked run ragged, but that had nothing on how rotten she felt. Even the dang seatbelt was an instrument of torture. It took her all not to let on to Eve how sore she was. Boop figured that girl was hauling around enough guilt without Boop's clumsiness adding to it. Between Vicky's Ally bomb and Boop's injury, the trip had been nothing short of a disaster so far, but at least Boop had gotten that picture of Davey. She was torn about what to do about Eve. Did Eve know more about Ally than she was letting on? If she didn't, should Boop tell Eve part two of Ally's predicament? That conversation, though, might lead to questions Boop didn't want to answer.

They couldn't get out of Savannah fast enough. Boop gave a silent rebel yell as they crossed the muddy river. They were headed to Sunset Beach, where Boop had a sinking suspicion they'd find Ally. That was gonna open up a whole can of worms, but Boop was glad they had more time together before Justine got hold of Eve.

"We've got to set some ground rules," Eve said.

"Darned if you don't sound like your mama."

"And you're acting like her. The motel clerk, the clothes, the flirting lessons, Papayas. I'm sorry I'm not good enough for you."

Boop blanched. "Not good enough? For me? Oh, sugar, I'm the one who's sorry. You are all that and then some." Boop studied the

Spanish moss drooping from the trees as they zipped down the road. That stuff gave her the willies. "Only you haven't seemed real happy of late, and I got to thinkin'—"

"Then quit thinking," Eve said. "You don't get it. Nobody gets it."

Boop didn't get it? If only that were so. Boop worried that sharing her pain would only add to Eve's. Same with the Ally situation. Worse. Boop's failure hadn't done any good back then, and it wouldn't do any now. She didn't think she could bear for Eve to be filled with contempt for her, even if it was well-deserved contempt. "I'm sorry."

The sky was darkening at an alarming rate. A storm was blowing in. Goose pimples broke out on Boop's arms. The wind picked up something fierce, and the trees rolled over their leaves toward the heavens. She didn't care for storms, but at least they were in a car. She'd heard cars were the safest place in a storm—something about rubber tires and cages. Admittedly, it didn't feel all that safe in the car. If one of them trees came crashing down on top of them, their car could go slipping and sliding into another car and crash through the guardrail or . . .

"Wonder how Karl's doing?" Eve asked.

"Heaven only knows." Boop gripped her seat belt so tight her hands ached.

"Maybe we could stop by on our way to the beach."

Over Boop's dead body. "I'm sure he'd love that," like a shot in the foot, "but his place is out in the boonies and over yonder a spell."

The raindrops splatting on the windshield were bigger than Boop's stomach after Thanksgiving dinner. This didn't bode well, as she didn't think the wipers were up to withstanding the coming deluge.

"He's only ninety minutes off the highway."

Justine would have a conniption fit if she found out. "Your mama—"

"Screw Mom. I'm tired of her treating us like we're stupid children."

The rumble of thunder made the car shake like a bowl full of Jello. "That right?" The Gray Ghost didn't have airbags. Not that Boop was convinced them things were a good idea—she'd heard they break people's ribs. Still, she didn't have any use for flying through the windshield either. She reckoned airbags were useful, but at a price.

In her experience, dealing with Karl came at a price too. He was about as useless as a screen door on a submarine. "Karl might not even be home and since he don't have no phone—"

"I guess you're right. It was a dumb idea." Eve frowned.

"No, it's a sweet idea, but it ain't real practical." The man sure did dill Boop's pickles, but she had better sense than to go spouting off about Karl to Eve.

"Remember when I was eleven and stayed with him for a week over the summer? You and Mom were nervous wrecks about the whole thing."

Boop could feel a headache rolling in. "I remember."

"He taught me how to fish."

"I'm right partial to fishing." Boop loved how you could just set and wait. Either they bit or they didn't, and since she had a market near her place, it didn't matter much either way.

"I'm not. But I loved spending time with him. Don't get to these days."

When the rain— or was that hail?— hammered at the car, Boop fought the urge to cover her head. She didn't wanna seem foolish. Lightning lit up the sky like firecrackers. Something mewed. At first, she couldn't figure out what was making such a ruckus. Then she realized it was her, and she shut her trap. She closed her eyes and tried to daydream of rainbows and pussy willows, but the blasted rain was too dang loud.

Eve swung onto the shoulder of the highway and flicked on her flashers. "I guess we'll have to wait it out."

What had Eve been yammering about? Karl. Might've forgot that on purpose. Though Boop supposed that Eve needing her daddy right about now wasn't that peculiar, and it was about time that man did something right by her. Karl did pull himself together upon occasion. Mayhap a visit wouldn't be a disaster of hurricane proportions. "To heck with practicality and to heck with Justine. Let's go."

"Are you serious?" Eve's eyes sparkled like lightning bugs.

"Mmmmhmmm." Not a lick of sunshine breaking through those clouds.

"You okay?"

"Right as rain," Boop declared, her voice drippy with sarcasm.

"Boop, it's just a storm. You're gonna be fine. You know that, right?"

What Eve didn't realize is that some storms don't blow away with the wind. The rain pelted down so hard Boop couldn't see through the windshield. She bit her lip to keep from yelping, feeling much like a lame deer waiting on hunting season.

Eve's voice interrupted Boop's worry wheel, "What was all that with Aunt Victoria yesterday?"

"Oh, nothing." Considering Ally's plight might distract Boop from this storm, but Boop far preferred the storm. When Eve turned her back so it rested against her door and faced Boop directly, Boop knew she wasn't gonna wiggle out of this easily.

Eve said, "Didn't look like nothing."

"Vicky wanted me to lend a hand with Ally." *Conversation closed. Now quit your meddling, child.*

"Why you?" Eve rubbed her arms and stared past Boop.

Ain't this girl ever heard what curiosity did to the cat? Boop didn't need another secret on her soul. Damn Vicky for asking this of her.

"Are you gonna help Ally?"

Boop felt she didn't have nothing to offer nobody. She was already knee deep in screwing up with Eve. "Don't think so." Rain was slowing. Hallelujah!

"Why not?"

Boop sighed. "I'm not the best person to help her even if we knew where she was." Did Eve trust her enough to take the bait and confirm Ally's location?

"Wonder why Aunt Victoria thought you were?"

Because Vicky ain't never understood how it is to live under the weight of regret and guilt. "Rain's let up, let's move on."

"Fine." Eve turned on the ignition.

Karl better batten down the hatches.

Danielle wasn't used to getting up to an alarm clock, but Mrs. Liddel had insisted that her "personal private investigator" arrive by eight, so that Danielle wouldn't miss Boop and Eve when they left after breakfast. They hadn't left until ten, leaving Danielle with nothing to do but suck down the thermos of coffee she'd brought. And now she needed to pee.

Boop and Eve had stopped at a gas station, so the possibility of relief was in sight, but for two small problems. One, Danielle didn't want them to see her and if she got out of the car she risked being spotted. And two, Danielle considered gas station bathrooms castles of horror.

Danielle recognized her chance when Boop and Eve stepped into the convenience store. Since the bathroom was on the outside of the building, theoretically Danielle could make use of it before the women came out of the store.

The pressure on her bladder couldn't be denied any longer. She reached into the glove compartment for a pair of surgical gloves, and then squeezed her inner thighs together to squirm out of the rented pickup truck. She slid the gloves on before she touched the germ-slathered doorknob, willed herself to start breathing through her nose (even though the smell was repugnant—those nose hairs might be her last hope against the assault of germs), and slid on her sunglasses so the tint would hide some level of the grime. When she threw open the door, she was relieved to discover no line. Presented with three empty stalls, she checked each one to determine which was the least offensive and settled on the handicapped one.

She'd just finished when she heard the bathroom door open. She peeked through the stall crack. It was Eve. Damn. Now she'd have to wait it out in the stall until Eve closed herself in another stall.

Only Eve didn't. Instead, she stood staring at herself in the mirror. Her lips turned down. Danielle wondered what she saw that garnered such a tragic expression. Danielle, herself, saw a beautiful, sad girl, but she suspected that Eve's vision was different; darker. Not literally darker, since Danielle was the weirdo wearing sunglasses, but emotionally darker.

Eve's face fell further, and tears pooled in her eyes.

Danielle turned away from the nakedness of Eve's grief to afford her some privacy, but her purse bumped the stall.

"Oh!" Eve gave a startled yelp, apparently only now realizing she wasn't alone.

Instinctively, Danielle's eyes returned to the crack. Eve was staring toward her. As though the surprise of seeing someone had broken whatever thread was holding Eve together, her body undulated in a deep sob.

In the face of such rawness, Danielle's chest tightened. The weight of Wyatt's injuries and her new job bore down on her. The walls closed in. She fought the urge to cry. She had to get out there now, even if that meant blowing her cover. She threw open the door, took a deep breath, and tried to pull her shit together.

Their eyes locked. Pain acknowledged pain. Kindred spirits.

Danielle stepped out of the stall. She wanted nothing more than to flee from the bathroom, and she ought to do that very thing. But good sense didn't always win out. She couldn't ignore their connection, couldn't let Eve's pain go unacknowledged. "You okay?"

Eve shrugged, but her shoulders shook less. She was slowing down.

"Can I get you something? A bottle of water maybe? Your grandma?"

Eve shook her head.

"Hang in there." Danielle was talking to herself as much as Eve. She moved toward the door.

Her gloved hand was on the door when Eve said, "How'd you know I was with my grandma?"

Shit. Danielle pulled the door open and mumbled, "I saw you get out of the car together."

"But—"

Danielle didn't hear whatever else Eve was going to say because she was racing across the parking lot to hide in her truck.

Boop: Hello

Justine: You're texting?

Boop: Yes. Eve showed me how. These little keys are annoying.

Justine: Is Eve okay? What's up?

Boop: I want to talk to you, and I don't want Eve to overhear.

Justine: Is she still pouting then?

Boop: Not exactly.

Justine: I just checked Find My Phone, and you aren't at the beach.

Boop: We got sidetracked.

Justine: Are you lost? I knew you two shouldn't be allowed to do this on your own.

Boop: Visiting Karl.

Justine: Damn. Why?

Boop: Eve wants to.

Justine: Stop her.

Boop: Just popping in.

Justine: Is Eve okay? I know she's not. What is up with her?

Boop: She is struggling a bit.

Justine: A bit?

Boop: A lot.

Justine: Boop.

Boop: She is depressed.

Justine: About what?

Boop: I don't know.

Justine: Find out.

Boop: Trying.

Justine: How long has this been going on? Why didn't you tell me sooner?

Boop: I was hoping I wouldn't have to.

Justine: You were supposed to keep an eye on her.

Boop: That is what I'm doing. What do you think this trip is about?

Justine: Dammit. You should have told me.

Boop: I didn't want to worry you.

Justine: You had no right. That is my little girl. How we deal with this is my decision, not yours. Definitely not yours.

Boop: No, it is her decision.

Justine: She is in no condition to make any sound decisions and you aren't any better.

Boop: We are holding our own. Thank you.

Justine: I'm coming.

Boop: Don't!

Justine: She is my daughter.

Boop: You will make it worse.

Justine: How dare you!

Boop: The last thing she needs is you breathing down her neck.

Justine: What's your AMAZING plan?

Boop: I do not have one.

Justine: Not reassuring.

Boop: Was not meant to be.

Justine: Stop mollycoddling her. I'm going to come out there.

Boop: Back off.

Justine: You do not know what she needs.

Boop: I suspect I know more about what she needs than anyone else.

Justine: She's so sensitive and vulnerable. I've protected her for her whole life.

Boop: I know.

Justine: I don't have the patience for this.

Boop: I gave you reason enough to feel that way.

Justine: You should have told me.

Boop: Maybe

Justine: I'm glad you're with her.

Boop: Really?

Justine: At least you get it. I'd get mad at her. She's going to be okay right?

Boop: I hope so.

Justine: Tell her to call when you get to the beach cottage.

Boop: OK

A Long Time Ago

Justine rolled into town once in a blue moon. She never bothered to call beforehand, just showed up with a holey duffle bag. Boop had bought her a decent set of luggage for her last birthday, but as far as Boop knew she never bothered with it. Usually, Boop's house was a mere bed and breakfast for Justine, who spent her visits partying with old high school friends and then sleeping off the consequences the following day.

For several reasons, Boop chose not to call Justine out for her behavior. The most pressing was that Boop was grateful for any crumbs Justine might throw her way, knowing that Justine was capable of cutting her out of her life like she'd done for the bulk of her twenties. But also, because Boop reckoned that Justine's immaturity was a reflection on her own failure as a mother. It seemed unfair to hold Justine accountable when Boop had done such a poor job raising her.

Justine's out-of-character invitation to join her in checking out a new coffee shop in a neighboring town raised Boop's hopes. Was it possible that after all this time Justine was going to forgive her and allow them to have a real relationship?

The coffee shop was a bit of a disappointment. The décor was minimal—white walls, a few homemade tapestries, concrete floor painted black. Boop's fig and pig tart was fine, but hardly as delicious as the combo had sounded. The coffee was hot and good, but Boop was content with her Maxwell House, so it was hardly worth the trip. Except for Justine.

Justine didn't seem all that interested in evaluating her surroundings. Rather, she struck Boop as preoccupied. Maybe she was just too hungover to care. She stirred a sugar cube into her coffee. "So . . . I have some news."

"Oh?" Boop braced herself. What was it now? Fired again? Eviction notice? New loser boyfriend? Justine's news was never good, though sometimes it disguised itself that way.

"I'm pregnant."

Boop choked on her coffee. "How did that happen?"

Justine raised her eyebrows.

Boop blushed. "I don't mean . . ."

"Now I know why Daddy divorced you."

Boop ducked her chin. Justine had no idea.

"But to answer your question. I ran into Karl."

Boop cringed at his very name. Handsome, reckless, Karl had been Justine's high school boyfriend and then on-again, off-again lover. As far as Boop could tell, he'd used her like a Kleenex and thrown her away again and again. The first time had broken Justine in a way that Boop didn't think had ever healed. And now that man's tentacles had gotten another hold. This wouldn't end well. "Prince? Again? C'mon, Justine. When are you going to learn to stop falling for his pretty face?"

"He's more than that."

"What?"

"How about the father of my child?" Justine snarled, reminding Boop of a cornered cat.

Perhaps a different tactic was called for. "Are you sure about this?"

"I'm not a total slut, I know who the father is." Justine's neck flushed.

In an attempt to buy time, so she might gather her thoughts and handle Justine better, Boop took several sips of her coffee before saying, "That wasn't what I meant. I meant are you sure you're ready to be a mother?"

"I'm thirty-eight years old." Justine waited as if expecting Boop to argue. When Boop didn't respond, she continued, "Can't be that hard. Just lock myself in my bedroom for eighteen years, and my baby will raise itself."

Boop stared down at the wood grains of the table. Their swirl reminiscent of blowing sand. Her eyes stung. "Justine, you haven't held down a job for more than a year. You haven't had a relationship that lasted more than four months—unless you count Karl," who Boop didn't. "You go out drinking several times a week."

"Judge much?"

Boop dragged her eyes from the table to Justine. "I'm not judging you. I haven't earned that right. I get it. But this isn't about me. This is about the fate of a child and about whether or not you're ready to be a mother."

"It's a little late to worry about that, isn't it?"

"Not necessarily. There's adoption and . . ." Boop forced herself to maintain eye contact "well . . . you could terminate the pregnancy."

Justine's face paled. "You think so little of my ability to be a mother that abortion is preferable to me raising a child?"

"No. I didn't mean—"

"I'm not going to sit here and take this. I thought you'd be happy for me, but I should've known. I'll show you." Justine stood up. "I'll be the best mother ever. All I have to do is the opposite of everything you did—easy."

Boop shivered. "Justine, I'm sorry."

"No. Forget it. It's too late." Justine propped her hands on her hips.

"Please. I can help." Boop wrapped her stiff, cold hands around her warm mug.

"I don't want your help." Justine's voice bounced over the room. Heads swung toward them.

"You can't do this alone."

"I have Karl." Justine's chest heaved under her crossed arms.

Even though she knew she was screwing this up, Boop couldn't seem to stop herself. "Really? Have you ever really had Karl?"

Justine looked as if she'd been slapped. "You don't know anything about Karl . . . about us."

"Fine." Boop stood too and forced a smile. "So when is the baby due?"

"Forget it." Justine slammed out of the coffee shop.

Boop gathered up their dirty dishes and, with her shoulders hunched, walked them over to the dirty dish tub. Conversation among the other patrons resumed, but Boop barely noticed. She was going to be a grandmother and, whether Justine knew it or not, that changed everything.

CHAPTER 13

The fact that Karl's VW bug sat in front of his trailer didn't mean he was home, since that piece of crap broke down more than it ran. Eve crossed her fingers that they hadn't driven all this way for nothing.

As Eve got out of the car, she kept her eyes away from Boop for two reasons: 1) the crushing guilt Eve felt every time she saw her injuries, and 2) she didn't want to see her reaction to the trailer's overgrown weeds and peeling paint. Karl had more important things to focus his attention on—like his art, but Boop wouldn't understand. She and Justine never tried to understand Karl. They were too busy judging him.

From her visit last summer, Eve knew the cracked doorbell didn't ring, so she knocked.

She could hear shuffling inside, but no one came to the door. The longer it took him to come to the door, the more her stomach ached. Why wasn't he coming?

Finally, a shirtless Karl flung open the door. "Eve!" His eyes still had the cloudiness of sleep, but he sounded pleased. At least, until he noticed Boop. Then in a more subdued tone, he said, "And Boop, too. What are you—I mean—I wasn't expecting you." He furrowed his brow. "Was I?"

Karl wasn't good at keeping track of calendars and stuff. Her mom acted as though it was a major shortcoming, but Eve found it endearing. "No, I wanted to surprise you."

"Oh." Karl stood in the doorway, staring at them while this sunk in. He wasn't smiling. Maybe this had been a bad idea. They shouldn't have come. They were probably interrupting something important.

Boop, more impatient than usual, said, "You gonna invite us in?" She didn't even wait for an answer but nudged past him. "Holy Moly!" she said when she caught sight of the inside.

Granted, the crusty dishes, fruit flies, and the pyramid of empty beer cans were totally gross, but Boop could've shown more couth than that.

"I wasn't expecting company." Karl gestured to Boop's injuries. "Bar brawl?"

"You should see the other guy," Boop deadpanned.

"Why don't you let us help you clean up?" Eve said, wanting to make up for bothering him.

"Don't mind if you do." Karl put on a stained wife beater he found balled up on the couch and stuck his stringy gray hair in a man bun. Poor guy needed someone to take care of him.

Boop crossed her arms. "No siree! I ain't touching nothing in this place."

Eve rolled her eyes and then dug under the kitchen sink for a garbage bag.

"I'm working on my best piece yet. Mixing mediums with wax and paint. Sometimes I let things go a little around here when I'm in the flow. I gotta catch the muse when I can." Karl made himself comfortable on the recliner he and Eve had bought at Goodwill last summer (after she finally talked him into tossing the one he'd had since she was born, and which Eve had been pretty sure was infested with fleas).

"Can I see it?" Eve kept her eyes focused on picking up empty wrappers because she knew he would say no, and she didn't want him to see how disappointed she was when he did. It might make him feel bad.

"You know I can't."

She shouldn't have asked. Karl was private about his work. She kicked herself for putting him in that position. Karl had explained many times that other people's reactions to his work killed his mojo.

"How's your mom? Charming, as usual?" he asked.

"Charming? Not so much."

"Won't get an argument from me. Woman's a ball buster."

Boop made some noise in the back of her throat, pretending to be offended.

Karl and Eve ignored her. "I knew you'd understand," Eve said. After putting a full bag of trash by the door, she went to get another empty one.

"While you're in there, want to grab me a Coke?" Karl said.

"Sure." Eve did as he bade.

"What's she got you all worked up about?" He popped the tab and took a sip. "Y'all want one?"

Boop's, "No thanks," was loaded with condemnation. Somehow, she said without saying that she wouldn't dream of putting anything from his trailer to her lips. Eve couldn't figure out how she managed to convey so much with so few words. Maybe Boop and Aunt Victoria had more in common than either of them would admit.

If only to make up for Boop, Eve accepted the Coke. After taking a sip, she said, "You got it all wrong. She's the one freaking out about my grades."

He scoffed. "Neither one of us were good students, and we turned out all right."

"One of you did anyway," Boop said, still standing in the middle of the room with her arms crossed.

Eve couldn't help thinking Boop should've waited in the car.

With Boop all banged up though, Eve hadn't found the nerve to suggest it, especially given that Boop's state was Eve's fault.

However, Karl had heard enough. "You know, Boop, maybe you're the one with your priorities out of whack. Man's drive for materialism is a vain attempt to fill the empty spaces in our soul. But art . . . now art does fill the soul."

Eve wished she was that wise.

"Too bad a full soul don't pay no bills, or clean your house apparently," Boop said.

"We've never agreed on much."

As entertaining as it was, Eve interrupted their little tiff. "What should I do about Mom?"

"You're nineteen. Tell her to stuff it." He finished his soda and handed Eve the can to throw away. Poor guy looked wiped. He'd been pushing himself too hard.

"Will you help me?"

"Course. I got your back."

Eve felt better than she had in months. Karl would fix this. Fix her. "Then I can move in with you?"

His expression could only be described as horror filled. "Hold on there. What?"

Didn't he want her?

"Here?" he said.

"I could help you with the chores. Just until I figure everything out." Eve bore down on some dried egg stuck to the counter.

"I only have one bedroom."

"I can sleep on the couch." *Please, Karl. Please.* The egg gave way.

"It's fine for you to visit, but not—"

"Just for a few months?" Eve's voice cracked. Her eyes burned as she contemplated the now sparkling clean counter, an oasis in the shithole.

"Months?"

Silence fell.

Boop said, "Eve, running away like a kicked puppy ain't the answer."

"You should talk." Eve turned her anger on Boop. Who was she to act so high and mighty? She was running away from whatever Aunt Victoria was after her about.

"Your grandma's right," he said.

"But you said you'd help," Eve whispered.

"I meant I'd talk to her for you, or, even better, I could coach you on what to say. Give you some advice. Something like that." He stood up and started to pace, a much easier task now that she'd filled two trash bags with his crap.

"But I thought. . . ." Eve was embarrassed by how pathetic she sounded. She examined the thong on her flip-flops.

"It wouldn't work. My art . . . you know . . ." He cleared his throat. "Listen. I've got an appointment downtown. Sorry to run out on you. Y'all make yourselves at home." He locked the door to his studio as if he was worried they'd snoop. Eve was overcome with a desire to kick down his precious door and burn his stupid paintings.

"How long you planning to stay?" he asked.

He really was leaving.

"Late afternoon," Boop answered for them.

"Yeah. I won't be back by then. It was wonderful seeing you though." He slid on his moccasins.

"What kind of appointment you got?" Boop asked, not bothering to hide the fact that she didn't believe him.

"Um. Doctor. Yep."

"For several hours?" Boop was too cynical.

Eve was certain he would stay if he could. "Karl, are you okay? Is something wrong?"

"I'm fine, honey, only a check-up. You seen my keys?"

She pointed to the coffee table.

"You telling us you're gonna be at the doctor all day?" Boop sounded pissed.

"Real thorough, my doctor is."

Maybe he was lying.

"MmmHmm."

Did Boop think it was helpful for Eve to know that her father didn't love her?

"I love you. You know that right? You're my best girl." His goodbye hug was awkward, probably Eve's fault. "It was great seeing you. So glad you dropped by. Lock the door behind you when you leave."

Then he was gone. Eve gaped at the door.

"Eve—"

"Don't say a word." Eve had no interest in hearing Boop's platitudes. Boop had done enough.

"I beg your pardon?"

So maybe Eve'd been a little rude, but she refused to apologize. "Not now." Eve kicked his shorts at the studio wall.

"You know he loves you more than anyone else."

"Could've fooled me." Eve didn't get it—didn't get what she'd ever done to Karl. How could her own father not love her? Was she that hideous? She ripped open one of the trash bags she'd so kindly filled and dumped its contents back on the floor.

"Karl's the fool."

No. That was Eve. For years she'd stuck up for him. Her mom's warnings had fallen on deaf ears, but Justine had been right all along. She was always right, and Eve was always wrong. "How come I got stuck with a mom who loves me too much, and a father who doesn't love me enough?" Eve stared at Boop as if Boop might have a suitable answer; as if there was a suitable answer.

Boop's eyes welled. She gathered Eve in her uninjured arm and led her to the couch.

"I thought if he . . . then I. . . ." Eve choked. Then they drowned together in a flash flood of tears.

Justine: How was Karl?

Eve looked up from her mom's text. "Really, Boop? You told my mom we were going to Karl's? What are you, a spy?"

"I didn't know it was supposed to be a big ol' secret."

Eve sighed. "I guess it wasn't."

"You gonna text her back?" Boop asked from the driver's seat. After Eve's big cry, Boop had insisted that Eve take some recovery time before driving again.

"Later. I don't want to deal with her now." Eve slid her phone onto the dash and stared out the window. The car's windows were dirty from the earlier rain. She'd have to wash Boop's car for her when they finally got to Richmond. No sense in dealing with it before, since the ocean air wouldn't do it any favors. She stared mindlessly into the side-view mirror. The truck behind them looked familiar. She swung around in her seat to look through the back of the car. "Boop, you recognize that pickup behind us?"

"Nah."

"I'm pretty sure I saw it when we stopped for gas earlier."

"Maybe so, but this road might as well be a pickup truck parade."

"But I think I met the lady driving that one in the bathroom."

Boop squinted her eyes at the rearview mirror. "Small world."

"But Boop, we stopped for gas a while ago, and then went to Karl's. What are the chances that we'd be on the same road at the same time again?"

Boop changed lanes. A minute later the pickup truck did too. Boop slowed to an old-lady pace. The pickup did too. "Sweetheart, I do believe you're right. Damn that Vicky."

"She sicced her PI on us."

"Seems so." Boop abruptly swung into the exit lane and floored it. The lady in the pickup truck followed.

"Go, Boop!"

And Boop did. She drove like the NASCAR drivers she'd spent many a Sunday afternoon watching. "Yeehaw!" she yelled as the car bounced over a particularly bumpy patch. From the dash, Eve's phone dropped to the floor.

Squeezing her eyes shut, Eve hung on to her seatbelt for dear life—not sure her bat-shit crazy grandma wasn't about to get them killed. Her heart raced, as the car flung her left, then right, then left again. Building nausea forced Eve to open her eyes again, just in time to see Boop running a red light and two cars slamming on their brakes to avoid crashing into them. Eve squealed.

Boop laughed and turned onto an unmarked road that weaved all over the place.

The pickup truck had disappeared from the side-view mirror. Eve turned in her seat, looking all around the Gray Ghost. Nothing. No pickup. No anything except trees. Trees and more trees. "For God's sake, slow down!"

Boop eased on the brakes. "She gone?"

"Yeah. Where are we?"

"Don't know."

Eve picked her phone up. The screen was black and cracked. She poked at the buttons. "Useless. Where's your phone?'

"Mmm. In my purse, but I forgot to charge it last night, so it died while we were at Karl's." The car hit a pothole, making Boop flinch.

"What are we gonna do?"

"I got a road atlas in the pocket behind my seat." The bat-shit crazy lady was gone, and the grandma left behind just sounded tired and old.

Eve reached over and grabbed it. The Southeast. Circa 2000.

Eve opened the atlas. This would not be a good time for Eve to lose her shit, but the maps weren't detailed enough, and Eve had next to no experience using an atlas. Not that she was about to admit her ignorance to Boop, but it might as well be hieroglyphics for all Eve could make out of it. She clenched her fists to stop her hands from ripping the stupid map into pieces and pegging it out the window.

"Eve, what do I do?" Boop asked, her tone somewhere between panic and pissed.

Eve could've done without her getting snippy. "I don't know."

"Take a gander at the map then!"

No shit, Sherlock. "I'm looking at the map, but I can't figure out where we are on it." Eve hadn't seen a street sign in over half an hour.

"So we're lost." Boop's voice was all panic now.

Breathe in sanity, breathe out hysterics. In sanity . . . out hysterics. Think of a practical solution. "We should ask someone for directions."

"Who do you suggest I ask—Bambi?" Boop asked.

Eve glared at the country road that seemed bent on taking them nowhere. This trip was a total nightmare. They never should've come. "If you'd let me drive—"

"Don't blame me for this pickle. I got us away from the bad lady. Last thing we needed was you chickening out."

Boop wanted to play the blame game? Let's play. Eve glanced at Boop's battered face and bandaged arm, pushing away the guilt. "And what about you? You flinch every time the car hits a damn pothole. You're hardly in any condition to drive either." Eve had just cussed at her grandma. Worst granddaughter ever.

"This road ain't fit for traveling."

The trees on either side of the car closed in. If a car came from the other direction, Eve didn't think they'd both fit. Luckily, they hadn't seen another car in ages, except for the rusted old heap in the pasture they'd passed a while ago. A clue as to the fate of the last travelers to pass this way? "I'm not even sure it is a road."

As they puttered along, the paved road (though it was generous to call it that) gave way to dirt. Eve checked the gas gauge. Quarter of a tank. They weren't in trouble yet. Every road goes somewhere, right?

Boop asked, "How long 'fore it gets dark?"

"An hour, I guess." Not that Eve could see the sun through all the trees.

"I can't drive at night."

Eve had forgotten Boop was night blind. Seemed Eve was going to get her turn in the driver's seat again after all, but she didn't have any interest in driving in the dark either. Driving these winding roads with no streetlights was not appealing. It wasn't difficult to imagine the Gray Ghost wrapped around a tree with Boop and Eve dead inside. And while that held a certain appeal . . . "I'll drive after sunset." Between the two of them, they had a better shot with Eve in the driver's seat.

When they reached another fork in the road, Boop chose the left.

It hadn't escaped Eve's notice that this clusterfuck was all her fault. If she hadn't pushed to visit Karl, then they wouldn't be here now, wherever "here" was. "We should've gotten a hotel room, or better yet, not visited Karl. As usual, Mom was right about him." A branch scraped against the side of the car, doing who knows what to the paint job.

Boop said, "Shoot—Karl or no Karl—Vicky's the one to blame for this. And for the record, your mama makes her share of mistakes too."

"Does she?" Aside from the significant error of getting knocked up, Eve couldn't think of a single one. "I think it's all the turning around you're doing that's gotten us in this mess." Eve tried to sound like she was teasing, and she was, but she kind of meant it too, and Boop knew it.

"I thank you not to blame me, Ms. Navigator."

Eve glanced out the windshield, wishing she were home when what to wandering eyes should appear, but— "There's a clearing up ahead!"

Boop sped up. In minutes they zoomed into the clearing, and Boop slammed on the brakes. "Where the dickens are we?"

Nowhere. Well, it used to be somewhere, but now it was nowhere. A dozen or so run-down wooden buildings lined up on either side of them. A church, a few houses, a store with what appeared to be the remnants of an artificial Christmas tree still in the window. The sun had reached the horizon and was glowing orange. They had maybe forty minutes until it was dark, and they were stuck in a ghost town.

Right where Eve belonged.

Drunk with danger and stupidity, she threw open the car door and lurched to her feet.

"Where you heading? You lost your mind?" Boop followed her out of the car.

Yep. Eve wandered over to the house closest to them.

Boop trailed behind muttering to herself, but Eve didn't care. She just wanted to get away from the car, from Karl, from life.

The paint on the house had all but peeled off, and the glass was long gone from its windows. On the porch, which was surprisingly intact (not that Eve was about to walk on it), sat two giant collapsing cardboard boxes with hundreds of socks tumbling out.

"That make any sense to you?" Eve pointed to the socks.

"Not a lick."

"All righty then." They moved to the next building where the color contrast between the rust of the tin roof and the ivy covering it was strikingly beautiful. Beauty wrought even more so among the neglect.

"You ready to hit the road? It's getting dark."

Eve was tall enough to spy through the window and reported,

"No furniture. Floor's covered with pine needles. Fireplace. Walls are slats of wood with holes all over the place. No socks. Not much to see."

"Except ghosts." They continued to wander down the main street.

Eve shivered as they stepped into a cemetery. With only seven tombstones, "cemetery" was probably not the right word. One of the headstones was covered in moss and impossible to read, and the others had weathered so much the inscriptions had all but worn away—dead and forgotten.

Eve bent to pick a dandelion. "Sometimes I believe you're the only person keeping me from slipping over the edge." Eve closed her eyes and blew the white wisps of the dandelion into oblivion, wishing her heart didn't hurt so badly.

"Nah, you're hanging on all by yourself."

"Thanks a lot."

"You're looking at it all wrong. You gotta stop giving away credit for the good stuff and taking on the blame for the bad stuff."

"I don't do that." *Usually . . . Okay, sometimes.*

"You sure about that?"

All the time. Eve did that all the time.

Boop took her hand. "If only I had the power to wish you happy."

"My fairy godmother."

"Bippidy, boppity, Boop! That's me."

Eve snorted.

Caught in her own thoughts, Boop gazed off in the distance. "Sock mystery solved, folks." Boop pointed at a big building down the street.

Bewildered Eve scanned the area trying to figure out what Boop was referencing.

"A mill. What do you wanna bet it manufactured socks?"

"Oh." Were they still on socks?

"Eve, we've got to make like a tree."

Dusk was settling in, but Eve wasn't ready to leave. "Do you hear that?"

"What?"

"This way." Eve moved into the trees behind the graves, following the sound of lapping water.

"Eve, I don't wanna get lost in the woods now."

"We're already lost in the woods." Eve continued walking as if driven by some supernatural force. Some might call it curiosity, but as it'd been months since she'd had that sensation, and they were in a ghost town, it felt more appropriate to attribute her compulsion to the supernatural.

"But we were safely in a car before!" Boop hollered after her.

"Just a little farther. I promise." A short hike later, they arrived at a creek where she discovered a tiny footbridge.

By the time Boop'd caught up, she was huffing and puffing. Eve expected her to be mad, maybe even wanted her to be, but Boop only said, "There's something carved on that there post." She stepped closer to read. "Culver Creek. Guess that's what this here waterway is."

The creek was shallow. Hardly warranted a bridge or a name, but perhaps at one time there had been more to it. Eve scooped up a handful of the clear water to take a sip. "Tastes better than that Fountain of Youth stuff."

"I bet."

Eve drank in a deep breath, enjoying the scent of the honeysuckle lining the creek. "Holy . . . did you say, 'Culver Creek'?"

"Sure did. Why do you look like the cat that swallowed the canary?"

"'Cause Culver Creek's on the map." Sometimes you have to run away to get found.

"Hot diggity dog! Let's skedaddle."

They turned back toward the town. "Not sure I want to."

"You taken a liking to ghost towns?" Boop trailed her hand over the top of a tombstone as they passed through the cemetery again.

The sun was gone, but the earth still shimmered in its fading light. Eve said, "Everything's so easy here. It is what it is." A rusty fire shed. A lavender bush. A gravestone.

"Don't kid yourself. You stay here long enough, you'll discover this town's got its share of ghosts."

"I don't believe in ghosts." The car was caked with dirt and pollen—so much that Eve couldn't tell how badly the paint had been scratched by the trees. While Boop fiddled in her purse for the keys, Eve wiped her finger along the hood, marveling at how dirty it made her finger and how clean the car was in its wake. Her finger moved of its own volition, and she watched as it scribbled. "Eve was here," which didn't make a ton of sense since Eve was taking the car with her.

"Maybe ghosts ain't the right word," Boop said, as she unlocked the car door.

"What then?"

"It's the secrets that haunt you."

Eve's mind flashed to Boop's secret photograph.

A Long Time Ago

Boop slept through giving birth, as was common in those days. When she awoke, she was introduced to her beautiful baby girl. They named her Justine, and as far as Boop was concerned all was right in the world of her new little family.

Only, later that afternoon, as she drifted in and out of sleep, she overheard Tommy and Dr. Clarkson whispering in the corner.

"And Boop won't remember anything about the other one?" Tommy asked.

"She was sedated. She never knew there were twins."

"Good, because I wouldn't want her to have to deal with this. It's hard enough—" Tommy's voice broke in a sob.

Boop hadn't shaken the effects of the anesthesia, and their words squashed her like an elephant, so it wasn't until the next morning when a nurse brought Justine for a visit that Boop demanded to see her other child.

"Mrs. Wilkes, there is no other child. This is your baby."

"Do not lie to me!" Boop shrieked.

The nurse ran off, and Boop reckoned that without Justine snuggled up to her chest, she'd have fallen to pieces.

Boop never did find out whether the nurse had been in on the shenanigans or whether she had merely thought Boop was a candidate for the asylum. An hour later, Dr. Clarkson returned with Tommy. She'd never seen Tommy that shade of gray before. In spite of her protests, they passed Justine off to a different nurse and plopped Boop in a wheelchair for "a little respite in the sunshine."

When they arrived in the garden, Tommy and Dr. Clarkson sat on a bench and faced her. She tightened the blanket around her and cursed that they'd chosen a garden in the dead of winter for their chat. Biting cold and dead bushes weren't much of a setting for a "respite." They only wanted privacy that the maternity ward with its twenty-odd beds did not afford.

"Mrs. Wilkes, I hear you've been asking some strange questions," Dr. Clarkson said.

"They ain't strange. I had two babies yesterday, and you're keeping one of 'em from me." Boop wasn't entirely convinced she hadn't dreamed or misunderstood the conversation she'd overheard. However, if they were plotting to bamboozle her, this wasn't the time to indicate doubt.

Fear lodged in the pit of Boop's stomach at the glances the two men exchanged. She clasped Tommy's hand for reassurance, but his cold, stiff fingers provided little of that. "Tommy, I heard you and the doctor. . . ."

He wouldn't meet her eyes. What in tarnation was going on?

"Please."

Tears streamed down Tommy's face, but he didn't say anything— couldn't say anything she reckoned.

She turned back to the doctor, who was staring at Tommy as if waiting on some sort of permission. He must've gotten it 'cause he cleared his throat. "You bore twins yesterday. Your baby girl appears to be healthy, but your baby boy—"

"I have a son?"

The doctor flinched. "He has some abnormalities."

"Then fix 'em," Boop responded.

"They aren't treatable…" The doctor continued to drone on about medical hoo-ha that Boop couldn't make heads or tails out of.

She shook her head briskly to dislodge the muffling roar, and she watched Tommy as he let go of her hand to cradle his head on the back of the bench. His sob racked through Boop's body, but her own body sat dry and frozen like a tundra. "You're wrong."

"I wish I were."

"Let me see him." She'd prove them wrong. Prove he was perfect in every way.

"He's gone," Tommy gasped.

"What do you mean gone?" A sob finally spilled from her belly. "He's dead?"

The doctor pursed his lips. "No. We simply sent him to an institution that can adequately care for him."

"I want to hold my son." Boop hugged her abdomen and rocked.

"That's not possible."

"I want to hold my son," she whispered.

"I'm so sorry." With the doctor's expression of compassion,

understanding of the situation slammed into her and the seams that had bound together the fabric of her soul ripped apart.

They found their way out of the labyrinth of back roads in less than fifteen minutes. Several hours passed with Eve in the driver's seat and Boop resting next to her. Boop had been quiet since a brief pit stop when she'd rummaged through her suitcase for several Advil. Eve was glad for the silence. Small talk was exhausting, especially with so much left unsaid. Not that Eve wanted a heart-to-heart while she drove down the highway at night. Her giddiness disappeared with the miles, as reality crept back in.

The silence and monotony of following the white lines allowed her mind to wander. The last thing she wanted to do was think about how much she'd let everyone down. It was no wonder Karl had run out on her. Eve didn't even want to be around herself. She was falling apart and there was no rational explanation. If Boop had realized what a mess Eve was, she'd never have concocted this trip. Eve had ruined Boop's trip. She'd ruined everything.

She wanted to crawl into bed. Every fiber of her body ached with exhaustion, but she wasn't sleepy. The hamster running around in her head prodded her awake, chanting "Loser, loser, loser," leaving her yearning for the reprieve of sleep.

Sunset Beach 9 Miles, the sign announced. Almost at the beach cottage. Full speed ahead.

Hoping the wind would blow away her thoughts, she rolled down the window. It was kind of working until she heard the sirens and saw the blue lights. Her heart skipped. She glanced at the odometer. Only a little over. She eased down on the brake, praying the cop was after someone else, but the cop pulled up on her rear, leaving no doubt who his target was. Why?

"I reckon you better pull over." So Boop hadn't been sleeping.

Eve swung onto the shoulder and came to a halt. Her hands trembled on the steering wheel while she waited for the cop to approach.

"Evening, ladies. I'm Officer Kalani. Any chance you're Eve and Boop?"

"Yeah." Eve didn't have a much experience with the law, but it struck her as odd that he knew their names. Even if he'd gotten Boop's from the license plate—her real name was Betty—and he'd called her Boop, and how could he possibly know Eve's name? She glanced up at him and drew in a sharp breath. Hot damn! This guy looked like a soap opera star.

"Are you okay? Where have you been?"

What was going on? Why was he interrogating them? "Excuse me."

Her tone must have been pissier than she'd meant because Boop leaned over her and chimed in. "What she means is we've been wandering around lost all over your fine state on our way to Sunset Beach. "

"Awesome spot. I surf over there sometimes."

Seriously, another surfer. It was beginning to feel like a Surfer Apocalypse. She rolled her eyes at Boop, who ignored Eve as she was too busy ogling the surfer cop.

"Someone filed a missing person report on you. A Justine—"

"I declare," Boop simpered. Didn't she know she was too old to simper?

"That's it. I hate her." Her mom was insane.

Boop leaned over Eve, probably to soak in more of his hotness. "You can see we ain't missing, Officer Kalani. Your name sounds Hawaiian. Nice place. Never been there myself, but my husband was stationed there before we were married. I saw loads of pictures. So lovely. Maybe I should add Hawaii to my bucket list. What do you think? After Scotland, or before? I guess it might depend on the time of year?"

"Yeah, so. . . ."

Eve stifled a giggle at his confusion. Well played, Boop.

"You said you 'surf'? My husband learned to surf while he was there."

"Really?" said Officer Kalani.

Eve hadn't known that about her grandfather.

"You seem like a real nice boy. My granddaughter here, now she's a nice girl too." Boop elbowed Eve.

Not this again.

Boop continued, "Thanks for doing such a bang-up job keeping the roads safe."

Officer Kalani glanced from Boop to Eve. Eve grew warm under his stare and glued her eyes to her lap in the hope that he wouldn't notice her discomfort. Why couldn't she have been gorgeous like Ally? "Can we go?" Her words were sharper than she intended.

Eve could feel his eyes on her, wanting something from her, an apology probably. Boop nudged her, but she couldn't do it. She couldn't even look at him because if she did, she'd fall to pieces. "Look, it's been a long day, and I'm exhausted. I just want to get to the beach cottage. My mom is crazy. You can see that we're perfectly fine. Can't we just go?"

"Not yet. I'll need your driver's license and registration."

"Seriously? This is ridiculous."

While Boop dug through the glove compartment for the registration and Eve slid her license from her wallet, Officer Kalani whistled a tune. It grated on Eve's nerves. They handed over their documentation, and he stepped away to his car to do whatever it was that cops did in their car.

Thinking he was out of earshot, Eve said, "Stupid surfer."

"What was that?" he called over his shoulder.

Shit. "Nothing," Eve said.

He walked back to the car. "Did you call me a stupid surfer?"

After the craptacular day she'd already endured, she couldn't take anymore. "What if I did?"

Boop gasped.

"I ought to give you a ticket."

Eve's head was on fire. "What for? Your ego too fragile for honesty?"

"How about for being a bitch?" He turned to Boop. "Sorry, ma'am."

"You go right ahead, son. She knows better."

He spun away to his car. In the heavy silence that fell in his wake, Eve struggled to pull herself together. By the time he'd returned with her license and registration, she had. Mostly.

"What's your deal with surfers anyway?" His anger seemed to have diffused some, only a little pissiness came through.

Eve shrugged, knowing he didn't want to hear her real answer, and lacking the energy to come up with a more politically correct one. Better to keep her mouth shut.

He, however, couldn't seem to let it lie. "No, really. Ex-boyfriend?"

"No!" What the hell, the damage had already been done. How much worse could it get? She said, "Surfers are so . . . shallow. I can't stand all that 'hang ten', 'catch the wave' crap."

He crossed his arms and raised his eyebrows. "Have you ever surfed?"

"No." As if.

"Maybe you should try it before you knock it."

"You should teach her," Boop suggested.

Again? Had Boop learned nothing from her other embarrassing attempts to matchmake? "No thanks."

His eyes narrowed. "You scared?"

"Hardly." Yes, of him—not surfing. Surfing was lame.

"Great. Then meet me by the Third Street beach access tomorrow at one."

Eve itched to slap the cocky grin from his face.

"She'll be there with bells on," Boop answered for her.

Eve sputtered.

"Perfect. And call your mom—she's worried." Before Eve could muster a rejection of this plan, he walked away, whistling again.

Was this a date? No, it was merely a surfing lesson for the sole purpose of stroking this guy's ego, so he could prove he was better than her. No way Eve would go. Boop couldn't make her. Officer Kalani had driven away before Eve found her words again.

CHAPTER 14

Eve's excitement over seeing Ally overtook her anxiety, and she took the stairs of the beach house three at a time. The lack of a car underneath the house didn't worry Eve since Ally could be Ubering everywhere. She'd probably Uberred from the Wilmington airport. The locked door was a bit more troubling since the family was pretty lackadaisical about locking the door when they were in residence. But still, Eve was certain that Ally was waiting within.

Eve knocked on the glass door, but Ally still hadn't answered by the time Boop labored her way to the top of the stairs. Boop pulled the key out of her purse, unlocked the door, and immediately plugged in her dead phone.

Maybe Ally had gone out, but the living room and kitchen had the sterile air of an empty cottage last seen by housekeepers. Still though, Ally could've asked them to clean today and left the cottage to get out of their way, and that would explain the locked door, as the housekeepers would've locked it upon leaving, even if Ally wouldn't have. Eve headed to the back of the house to the room where she and Ally usually bunked. Only, it too was empty.

Given that Ally was there alone, maybe she'd decided to take the master bedroom. Eve started up the stairs.

"I don't reckon she's here," Boop said gently.

But Eve didn't answer, she barely heard her. She flung open

the door to the master bedroom. The blue and peach checked quilt was spread over the bed with such smooth perfection that it was obviously the work of a professional rather than Eve's messy best friend. The lack of luggage and the empty drawers confirmed Ally hadn't claimed the room. A quick survey of the other two bedrooms proved that Ally was not in the house. Eve sat down on the corner of the queen bed in the last bedroom and stared at the sea-green wall.

Boop stood in the doorway.

Ally hadn't left her a secret message in the email. Eve was just as in the dark as everyone else. Ally had rejected her; rejected their friendship.

"Eve?"

"I thought Ally was here." Her voice sounded dead even to her own ears. "She's not."

Boop walked over to rub Eve's back. "Don't appear so."

Boop's cell rang.

"That's probably your mama."

Eve shrugged.

"Don't you think we should tell her we're okay?"

"I'm sure the cops already took care of that."

"She ain't going to go away quietly."

"The last thing I want to do is talk to her. Will you?"

"Sugar, we both know that won't appease her. She wants to talk to you."

"I'll text her then."

Boop's raised eyebrows expressed her wordless skepticism.

Eve: It's Eve. I borrowed Boop's phone but can't talk

Justine: You at the beach house?

Eve: Yeah

Justine: I am upset. Where have you been? I have been worried sick.

Eve: Lost cell service then dead phone. I can't believe you called the cops. Mortifying!

Eve was not about to confess that her phone was broken.

Justine: Too bad. Your own fault for going off route.

Eve: Stop

Justine: Fine. Your summer school classes are conflicting with your internship.

Eve: No problem

Justine: How's that?

Eve: I'm not taking classes or doing an internship

Justine: Beg your pardon?

Eve: You should

Justine: I don't think you appreciate the strings I pulled to get you this internship. Summer school is your fault.

Eve: You probably thought you could even pick out my classes for me.

Justine: I spoke to Trevor and Bess. I know what you need.

Eve: For medical school?

Justine: Exactly. You aren't making this easy.

Eve: I don't want to go to medical school.

Justine: What do you want?

The ability to answer that question would be a great start. Sure, she could rattle off an easy list—fashion-designing fame, Ally back, a boyfriend, a different mom. But the deeper nuances of this question were lost on Eve, and it seemed to her that contentment was lost within those nuances.

Justine: Awfully quiet. I'm going to register you to retake the biology and calculus classes you failed. Does that suit you, princess?

Eve: No

Justine: What do you suggest then?

Eve: Figure drawing and textiles

Justine: How about I just throw away my money?

Eve: Why do you hate art?

Justine: I love art.

Eve: You always criticize Karl's art

Justine: I was criticizing Karl, not his art.

Eve: Semantics

Justine: Your father's art is nonsense. He doesn't do anything with it—doesn't study it, doesn't sell it. He doesn't even show it to anyone anymore.

Eve: Anymore?

Justine: When you were a baby, he tried to get galleries to show his work. They weren't interested. Karl gave up. He stopped painting for a few years.

Eve: I didn't know that

Justine: He started painting again after I sent him packing.

Eve: After he abandoned us, you mean?

Justine: Semantics. He refused to subject himself to the "judgment of peasants."

Eve: He's protecting his muse

Justine: He's a coward. Are you still sticking up for him?

Eve: Bad habit

Justine: Karl sacrificed his life for art. Then refused to make something of himself as an artist. It's pathetic.

Eve: Is he good?

Justine: He was. Very but unschooled. The galleries told him they saw tremendous raw talent and suggested he take classes or find a mentor.

Eve: He never did?

Justine: I don't hate art, but I also don't want to pay good money for you to take college classes for fun. College is about setting up a career, not playing with crayons and finger paints.

The beach cottage used to have kids' art supplies. Eve hadn't used them in years, wasn't certain they were still there. But, suddenly struck by a desire to reconnect with her inner child, she went in search of them. Art had been more fun before she'd known enough to critique it. The more skills she'd gained, the harsher her judgment had grown. The irony of her confidence decreasing as her talent grew didn't escape her. Her search met success when she found a stash of crayons and some paper in the loft.

She grabbed a blue crayon and a piece of paper and went to town scribbling a giant mess. It felt so awesome, she took another piece and scribbled all over, this time changing colors periodically.

The ping of another text message interrupted her flow.

Justine: You still there?

Eve: Yeah

Justine: I think I should join you at the beach house. We have a lot to talk about and texting is insufficient.

Eve: No.

Justine: At least let's talk on the phone.

Eve: I won't answer I don't want to talk to you

Justine: This is stupid. You shouldn't be alone.

Eve: Boop is here

Justine: Like that's doing any good.

Eve: I can't think with you here

Justine: You don't seem to be thinking without me there

Eve: Sorry I'm such a disappointment

Justine: Don't be a drama queen.

Eve: Leave me alone. Enjoy your perfect life without your fuck-up daughter that's what you always wanted

Justine: That's enough!

Eve: For once we're in agreement

Eve tossed Boop's phone on the sofa and returned to scribbling.

A Long Time Ago

After two weeks of trying to persuade Tommy to take her to visit Davey, Boop gave up and roped Vicky into bringing her. Up until that point, she'd convinced herself that Tommy and the doctor were mistaken, but his features were undeniable. There was no cure for her baby.

She and Vicky were halfway home before Boop had sobbed herself dry.

"So, Tommy was right," Vicky said.

Boop stared unseeing out the passenger window. "Seems so."

"Now you know, and y'all can move on."

Boop swung her head to wonder at this woman who so matter-of-factly dismissed Boop's son. "What do you mean by that?"

"Enjoy Justine and forget about this unfortunate situation."

"I don't reckon I can do that." Boop would never forget about Davey. What kind of mother could even think of such a thing?

"I suspect if you pretend long enough, eventually it'll be as if it never happened."

"But it did."

Vicky patted her arm. "Don't worry, honey. My lips are sealed."

Boop wondered what she'd done wrong. Boop knew Davey's problems were all her fault. She wasn't certain where she'd gone astray, only that she had. She deserved whatever she had coming. "Go right ahead and shout it from the rooftops as far as I'm concerned."

"That's ill-advised."

"You agree with Tommy then?"

"Betty, if people find out, you'll be the talk of the town."

"I won't sacrifice my baby for the sake of my reputation."

"And Tommy's reputation? It's hardly upstanding for a banker to have a baby like Davey. Nobody would trust him with their money."

"Tommy could get another job." Even as she said it though, Boop knew Vicky was right. Tommy's career would be shot to hell in a handbasket if people found out about Davey.

"And Justine—having him as a twin brother will be social suicide. You'll ruin her."

"People aren't that small-minded." Some people were though. They both knew it. A sharp pain stabbed behind Boop's eyes. "Did you see that place? I can't leave him there."

"Betty, the doctors say Davey may never walk, never talk, never read, never write—he'll never know what a hell hole that place is. You aren't equipped to care for him. You can't bring him home."

Boop couldn't stand another second of Vicky's holier-than-thou lecture. "You act as though you're so worried about my family, but the truth is you're more worried about Zachary's political aspirations. Always looking out for number one, right, Vicky?"

Vicky stopped to let the Summerfield family cross the street. "I don't deny keeping it a secret is in my best interest too, but that doesn't negate my other arguments. I'll thank you not to use that tone."

Boop had been daft to think Vicky would take her side. Boop started to cry again. "I can't forget about him. I can't leave him there."

"You don't have a choice, not really."

It was thoughts of Justine that finally won Boop over. Whatever Boop had done, whatever she deserved, Justine was innocent, and flaunting Davey would only ruin her life too. "Then I'll visit him every week."

"Tommy's not going to support that."

"To hell with Tommy." What kind of man denies his only son?

"You gonna drive all this way yourself then?"

Tommy and Boop only had one vehicle. Though she could drive it, she rarely did. To Vicky's point, an hour drive was more than Boop could handle safely. "Nah, you're gonna drive me." Only four people knew about Davey—Boop, Tommy, the doctor, and Vicky—Vicky was Boop's only option.

"I beg your pardon?"

"You want this to stay a secret, right? You want to remain fresh from the damage it might do to your precious reputation, then you will drive me to visit my son."

"You wouldn't dare." Vicky pulled up in front of Boop's house.

"Try me."

Vicky and Boop stared each other down. Vicky was the first to look away. "You win."

"Every Sunday afternoon."

"Every?" she sucked in a deep breath. "Fine."

CHAPTER 15

Victoria had little respect for her mealy-mouthed great-niece, and Eve's failure to lead her to Ally did nothing to further endear her. However, as Victoria hung up the phone, she wondered if she'd underestimated Eve. Victoria couldn't reconcile Ally's shadowlike best friend with the girl who'd had the nerve to defy her and Justine, with the savvy to lose the private investigator that Victoria had tailing her, and the recklessness to mouth off to a police officer. Victoria though was especially pleased by that last one, as it was this misconduct discussed over a police scanner that resulted in the PI picking back up on their trail.

A laugh from the other side of Victoria's closed office door alerted her that her son had returned to campaign headquarters. His race for governor was coming along swimmingly, and Victoria would do what she had to in order to ensure that nothing derailed it. This meant keeping him in the dark about Ally's state. No doubt, he'd rush in all pro-life and force her to have the child, but Vicky knew what having Davey had done to Boop. She wouldn't stand by and watch Ally's dreams wither and die. No, as distasteful as it was—a secret abortion was Ally's only hope. They were running out of time though.

Victoria glanced at the door handle to confirm that the door was locked and then pulled a file labeled DAVEY from her desk drawer.

Two months ago, she'd relocated it from her home office to campaign headquarters when she'd grown suspicious that her maid, Greta, had snooping tendencies. She ought to fire the woman but was afraid of what Greta had already gleaned. Victoria had learned long ago to keep her enemies close. Campaign headquarters was much safer, as the staff here were too intimidated by her to trifle with her belongings.

Inside the file were dozens of yellowed photographs of Davey, some with Boop, some without. Victoria's favorite was one of Davey sitting on a tire swing with Boop and Victoria on either side—old Joe Morton must've taken that one. It was the only Davey photo with both Victoria and Boop. Victoria had kept Boop ignorant of the secret Davey stash, knowing such memorabilia would only serve as an albatross for Boop.

Victoria doubted Boop would do as she'd bade and steer Ally in the right direction. This file of documents and photographs proved Davey's existence and could be used as leverage against Boop if need be. Victoria felt a twinge of guilt at the thought of blackmailing her sister, and potentially hurting Eve and Justine in the process, but the governorship—and Ally, of course—came first. Boop had come a long way from the yellow-bellied wraith that had spent over a decade hiding in her bedroom. Victoria felt certain Boop could find her footing again. And Justine was much too much like Victoria for Victoria to waste worry on her. And Eve, well Eve, well . . . Victoria's plan was better served with Eve trapped under Justine's thumb and too busy with her own reckoning to interfere with Victoria's plans for Ally. After all, she'd given Eve a chance to play on Victoria's team, to show some family loyalty. Eve had refused. Sometimes sacrifices had to be made for the greater good.

Victoria slid the folder back into the desk drawer and then pulled out another. This one marked ALLY. She rifled past the private investigator's reports looking for the brochure she'd tucked in the day before. Her hand stilled when she found it—a medical clinic in

London—known for its discretion in providing international pregnancy terminations.

Only hours before, she'd gotten an email from a brother of a friend of a friend with a confirmation that she'd secured Ally an audition in the West End. She would use that as either a lure to get Ally to London, or as a reward to Ally for putting her family first.

She dialed the number on the clinic brochure and secured Ally's appointment.

Now if only that piss-poor PI could manage to find her granddaughter, she could get this matter all cleared up.

When twelve forty-five rolled around, Boop still hadn't returned from her errand. Eve had spent the last several hours trying to watch TV. However, she was unable to quiet the self-berating voice screaming in her head—reckless, irresponsible, stupid, pushy, ugly, negligent, inconsiderate, disappointing, crazy, loser—so she left the cottage hoping fresh air and a swim would shut up her tormented thoughts.

East Main Street was still—gotta love off-season at the beach. After a few minutes' walk, she found herself at the Third Street beach access. She hadn't consciously decided to meet Officer Kalani. Since she ended up at the spot he'd suggested, though, she figured she might as well stay.

As the clock ticked on, she figured Officer Kalani wasn't going to show. Why would he? He'd probably been joking, or maybe standing her up was his idea of revenge for her attitude.

Shoot, she didn't want to learn to surf anyway. She hugged her knees to her chest, thinking she ought to leave.

"Eve?" At the top of the boardwalk steps stood Officer Kalani with a surfboard tucked under one arm and a backpack slung over the other shoulder. He'd come. And he was even hotter in his bathing suit and tight shirt.

"You're late, Officer," she said, but instantly wanted to kick herself for starting the conversation on the wrong foot. Why was she such a bitch?

"Sorry. I got hung up. And call me Zed." He set down his surf-board. "I wasn't sure you'd show."

"Neither was I." She slapped her hand over mouth.

He smiled. "I'm glad you did."

She scrambled to her feet, hoping he wouldn't notice her blush.

"Are you ready for this?" he asked.

"No." As someone with no interest in surfing and who felt a repugnance toward surfers, it was unclear why she was there. "Surfing's not my thing."

"I double-dog dare you," he said.

"What are you? Nine?"

His dark, brown dreamy eyes narrowed. "Triple-dog dare?"

She laughed. "Now there's an offer I can't refuse."

He reached into his backpack and tugged out another shirt. "I brought you this rash guard. It'll help you stay warmer in the water." He tossed it her way. She scrambled to catch it, but it fell to the sand, clumsy oaf that she was.

Whose was it?—his sister's, friend's, girlfriend's . . . wife's? Eve glanced at his hand and was relieved to see a naked ring finger, though that didn't necessarily mean anything. Not that it mattered if he was married. This was a surfing lesson, not a date, and she would be smart to keep that straight in her head. "Thanks." She pulled the shirt over her head, glad for more coverage. She felt exposed in a bathing suit, even a one piece.

"Let's practice on the sand first." He crouched at the end of the board to demonstrate. "Hold the sides here and pull yourself on."

Then it was Eve's turn. Easy-peasy.

He said, "Great. Now move your arms a little, like chicken wings."

She mimicked him. "I feel stupid."

"You look stupid."

She flinched at the sucker punch.

"Kidding. You're beautiful."

Her embarrassing blush was back. She stared down at the blue Hawaiian flower painted on his board, hoping he wouldn't notice. Guys like Zed didn't need girls like her to stroke their egos. Why did she even care what he thought about her? Beautiful? He was a liar.

He kneeled next to the surfboard. "Slide up a little more, so your toes are touching the tail."

She slid, wishing she had a towel or something covering her butt.

"Okay, now lift your chin and chest."

She lifted, exposing the curve of her too small boobs—grateful again for the shirt.

"Perfect. Ready to try it in the water."

She frowned at him. "You want me to surf lying down?"

"Yeah, that way you can get the feel of moving with the board before you have to do the hard part." Hard part? C'mon, how hard could it be? If those idiots she went to school with could do it, surely Eve could.

"Okay." She followed him to the water but stopped as her feet splashed into its icy wetness. She took a few hesitant steps waiting for her feet to adjust, but Zed plowed right in.

"C'mon," he called over his shoulder.

Why had she come? She took a few more steps, imagining herself wrapped in a blanket curled on the couch binge-watching Netflix. Not wading closer to Zed.

He was waist deep now and grinning at her. She tried not to think about how hot he was. What was he doing with her? She hadn't even been nice to him. She jumped a small wave, wincing as the water hit her belly button, and caught up with him.

"Watch me paddle out. You can do it next time."

Seemed easy enough.

"You'll want a straight foamy wave." He pointed toward the horizon.

The light glinting off the water was too much even on this overcast afternoon, forcing Eve to squint since she'd left her sunglasses, useless, on her beach towel.

"Here comes one. I'll show you." After paddling for a few seconds, he pulled himself onto the board like they'd done on the sand, lifted his chest, and was gone.

Once he finished his ride, he shook his head like a wet dog and then waded back out to Eve. "Your turn. Give me your foot." He put the leash around her ankle and then held the board steady. "Climb on, wait, wait, and go, paddle . . . relax."

Eve sped along the surface, riding the wave to the shore. Her blood raced, and her head cleared. Only the ride was much too short.

He waved her back out, and she practiced twice more.

After the third time, he met her at the shore. "You did awesome. You want to go again, or practice standing in the sand?"

"We can do the sand part." Surfing was more fun than she'd ever thought it could be.

As he bent over her to unstrap the leash, she ogled his back muscles.

"Why did you invite me out here?" she asked.

"No clue." A gentleman, Zed carried the board up to the dry white sand. Or was it that he didn't trust her to carry it?

"I was a jerk."

"Yeah, you were."

"So, I don't get it."

"I don't know. You pissed me off when you insulted me like that. I guess I wanted to prove myself to you." He laid down the surfboard.

Eve stared at her toe making a line in the sand. "You don't have to prove anything to me."

"Yeah, once I calmed down, I realized how ridiculous it was."

She glanced up at him. "But you came anyway?"

He smirked. "I didn't think you'd show. Figured I'd just spend the afternoon surfing."

"Oh." Of course, he hadn't expected her to come. And now he'd had to spend his free time babysitting her. "Sorry. I'll go."

"No, don't. I didn't mean it like that." He caught hold of her elbow to keep her from turning away. "I'm getting a kick out of teaching a pretty girl how to surf."

"Right." She gazed at the clouds, wishing she could fly away. He should let her go.

"You don't think you're pretty? Or you don't think I'm enjoying myself?"

Eve shrugged.

He let go of her elbow. "You're nuts on both accounts. You ever look in a mirror?"

She gazed at Zed, trying to determine whether or not he really wanted her there. The thing was, she really wanted her there. For the first time in months, she was somewhere she wanted to be, but not if . . .

"Girls!" He shook his head. "Now, surfing I understand. First thing we've got to do is figure out if you're regular or goofy footed."

"Goofy. Definitely goofy."

He laughed like he thought she was funny. Nobody ever laughed at Eve's jokes. "A goofy surfer puts her right foot forward, and a regular surfer puts her left."

"Oh."

"Close your eyes, and I'm going to push you from behind a little. We'll see which foot you put out to stop your fall."

She raised her eyebrows at him. Did he really think she'd let herself be that vulnerable with a stranger?

In response to her inaction, he crossed his arms and cocked his right eyebrow, silently issuing another triple-dog dare. "Trust me. I'm a cop."

She didn't. She didn't trust anyone, but she closed her eyes; he pushed, and she fell forward.

"How about that—you are goofy."

It took her a second before she remembered he wasn't insulting her. She glanced at her legs. Sure enough, the right one was forward.

Zed said, "Okay, so lay down like before."

"Bet you say that to all the girls." Had she just flirted?

"Only the pretty ones."

And he'd responded in kind? Boop would be so proud. Should she try Boop's staring thing? What if he was being sarcastic? He didn't sound sarcastic.

"Turn your left foot so your inside ankle is touching the deck."

"Deck?"

"Surfboard."

She turned her foot.

He kneeled beside her. "Exactly. Now lift your head and chest again." When he laid his hand on the small of her back, heat seared through the rash guard.

"Slide your right foot forward."

She wasn't sure it was possible to move with him touching her, but she did. His hand fell away and her back grew cold. She shivered.

"Let go and stand up. Bend your knees. Put a little more weight on your front leg." He patted her thigh.

Her breath caught.

"Look straight ahead, not at the board." His hand cupped her chin.

Her body quivered. "That's it?" she whispered, staring at him the way Boop had taught her.

"Yep. Let's go catch a wave," he said, unfazed by Eve's moves.

Guys never noticed Eve like that, she'd been silly to think Zed might be any different. "Right."

He held the board steady while she lay down and scooted awkwardly around trying to get her hands and feet in the right spot. As the perfect wave approached, he said, "Now!"

After paddling for a minute, she felt the wave swell under her, she scooted her leg forward and pushed, but she couldn't seem to budge her body up. The wave passed her by.

"What happened?" he asked.

"I couldn't get up," she answered.

"Try again?"

"I guess."

They tried again, but her sapling arms and core weren't strong enough. No wonder surfers were so ripped. She'd always thought they got ripped for the sake of their vanity since they hung out in tight wetsuits so much, but apparently, it was the other way around.

On her fourth attempt, she finally pushed herself to standing. She was up only long enough to think, "Holy crap, what do I do now?" Then she found herself barreling into the water in a twisty side flop. Water rushed up her nose. By the time she came sputtering to the surface, Zed's face was pinched with worry.

"You okay?"

She nodded.

"What happened?"

"I don't know. Freaked out, I guess." She wiped under her nose, to ensure snot wasn't hanging around.

"I forgot to teach you something."

"What's that?"

"How to wipe out."

"Seems I didn't need a lesson for that." She didn't like surfing. She didn't like making an ass of herself. Coming had been another mistake to add to the list.

"Yeah, but there are safer ways to do it. You could've hit your head."

"Oh."

"Next time, fall backward and protect your head with your arms." He demonstrated.

"Next time? There's not gonna be a next time. I've had enough."

"No."

"What do you mean no? You don't get to say no." She wanted nothing more than to crawl back onto the safe, warm couch.

"Don't be a wimp, Eve. You're this close."

"I don't like it."

"You might if you do it right."

"I can't, okay?" Why did he keep pushing? What difference did it make to him?

"No, it's not okay."

"Whatever." She waved him off and turned toward the shore.

"Give it one more shot. What've you got to lose?"

"My dignity."

"C'mon, Eve. Live a little."

Carpe diem, oh Captain, my Captain. "Fine."

This time, she pulled herself up on the second try and stood for what felt like forever, but it was probably less than a minute. She flew across the surface with every sense in her body alive. Her mind was so overwhelmed by the sensations that she couldn't think, couldn't feel. Never before had she felt so in touch with herself, at one with the earth. As the shore approached, she covered her head, held her breath, and fell backward.

Zed was by her side when she surfaced. "How was it?"

"Totally tubular!" she shouted with only the smallest trace of sarcasm. No wonder people got addicted to surfing. She couldn't think of anything that could top that rush, that was until Zed wrapped his arms around her and squeezed.

"I'm so proud of you," he whispered in her ear.

Was he going to kiss her? Did she want him too?

Uh, yes. She was pretty sure she couldn't handle Zed, but she still wanted him to kiss her.

The leash tugging at her ankles stole her attention. She chickened out, twitched away, and croaked, "The board."

"Right." He cleared his throat and then grabbed the board. "Why don't you take off the leash? I've got to get ready for work."

"Oh." He was sick of her already. Was it because she hadn't kissed him, or because he didn't want to kiss her but knew she wanted him to?

"How long you in town?" He set the board in the sand.

"I don't know. Living on the edge. No plans." In case her boobs had fallen out of her bathing suit, she turned her back on him to take off the shirt.

"It's sweet that you're on a road trip with your grandma."

"Yeah." She handed him the rash guard. "Thanks for the lesson."

"You want me to walk you back to your cottage?" He picked up the surfboard.

"That's okay. You don't have to." They climbed the boardwalk steps.

"I want to."

"Oh." He wanted to? What did that mean? "Okay."

They walked in silence up East Main, the easiness between them disappearing with each step. Eve kept racking her brain for something to say, but all she could come up with was, *Do you have a girlfriend?* Asking that was basically confessing, *I want to jump your bones.*

"Could I call you sometime?" Zed asked.

"I guess," she said before the implications of his question sunk in. Then she wanted to kick herself for her lack of enthusiasm. "I mean, that'd be cool."

"You sure?"

"Positive."

"Good."

They resumed their silent walk. She couldn't think of anything to say because her brain was stuck on, *He wants to call me, he wants to call me.* Eventually though, her mind wandered to the logistics of said call. "Don't you need my number?"

"Nah. I got it last night."

"Oh." She stopped in the driveway of their cottage. "This is it."

"Oh." He repeated, gazing down at her.

Her lips parted. This was it—the big kiss.

"Eve!" her mom's voice shouted from the rooftop crow's nest.

Zed drew back. "Who's that?"

"My mom." Eve should've known she'd show up.

Her expression must've been something else, because Zed's head tilted to the side. "You okay?"

"No."

"Want me to stay?"

She took a deep breath. "No, go to work."

"You sure?"

"Yeah."

"Okay." He bent over and kissed her cheek.

She raised her hand to touch the now tingling spot.

"Eve!"

"Bye," she whispered.

He winked and left.

She gazed after him, taking deep breaths in preparation for dealing with her mom.

CHAPTER 16

What was her mom doing here? Eve's legs were slow and heavy as if they were trudging through quicksand as she climbed the wooden stairs of the beach cottage. She didn't want to face her mom—didn't want to answer her questions, didn't want to listen to her advice, and most of all didn't want to see her disappointment. She'd disappointed her mom in a million and one ways, in ways her mom didn't even know about. She deserved a better daughter.

Justine, foot tapping and arms crossed, was on the porch, waiting.

Eve braced for the tongue-lashing.

"Who was that?"

"A friend." She was starting with Zed? Her mom had a weird sense of what needed to be addressed. The likelihood of a long-distance relationship developing between Eve and someone like Zed was nada. She doubted he'd even call. He'd only suggested it to be polite.

"How old is he?"

Eve shrugged. The less she said the sooner this conversation would be over.

"Too old for you, don't you think?"

Be a good little lap dog, roll over, and play dead. Good dog.

Her mom continued, "I thought we'd agreed you'd wait until after college to date?"

Had they? Her mom had certainly advised that over and over

again, but Eve didn't recall ever agreeing. Of course, Eve's acquies-
cence was a moot point. Such dictates weren't about Eve anyway,
they were all about her mom accidentally getting knocked up and
the consequences ruining her life. Eve said, "So I don't spend my life
chasing after some guy and finally getting knocked up by him and
then abandoned?"

"Exactly."

Eve had been a mistake. "I'm sorry I ruined your life, Mom." Let
that be enough to end the conversation. She nibbled the nail on her
thumb.

"Ruined my life?" her mom asked, as she made herself comfortable on a rocking chair.

Eve wanted to run screaming inside. She'd been foolish to think
she'd get off easy. Her mom hadn't come all this way to make things
easy.

Her mom continued, "You didn't ruin my life. Don't be ridiculous. And stop chewing your fingernails!"

Eve wasn't being ridiculous. Her mom made it very clear that
her life sucked because of Eve. She'd lost Karl, who'd run from the
responsibility, screaming all the way to his trailer park—trapping her
mom in a dull life of suburban mediocrity. Whatever. If Eve wanted
to end the discussion, then she should nod and agree.

Screw ridiculous. "If it hadn't been for me, you and Karl would
still be together; you'd be free to leave your life-sucking job, you
could've traveled and . . ." So much for nod and agree. Sometimes Eve
was such an idiot.

But Justine didn't respond; instead, she studied the hands
clenched together on her lap.

Eve asked, "Can I go inside now?" She put her hand on the sliding glass door, about to make a run for it.

"This isn't about me. It isn't my life I'm worried about. It's yours.
Boop tells me you've been feeling sorry for yourself lately."

Eve flinched. It was true. Only, put like that, it made Eve feel shallow and small, which was also true, but she'd thought Boop had understood. "Is that what she said?"

Her mom waved away her question. "It's time for you to grow up. You want something, you go for it. Life isn't easy. Perhaps I've made it too easy for you."

Did she really think that?

"I'm going to tell you what Trevor always says at meetings, 'Change what you can, as for the rest—suck it up and get over it.'"

"If it were that easy—"

"It is." Justine stood.

"You don't get it. You don't get me."

"I'm your mother. Of course, I get you."

"No, you don't." Eve closed her tear-filled eyes and leaned against the door. "I'm done."

"What? Done with what?" Her mom walked over and brushed her damp cheeks.

"I tried so hard," Eve whimpered. Her breath ragged now.

"Tried what?"

"I tried to be the daughter you wanted." She forced the words out between gasps.

"The daughter I wanted?" Justine lifted Eve's chin, holding her gaze. "You are exactly the daughter I want."

Eve wouldn't be taken in by her lies. She wrenched away. "No, you want me to be a better you."

"I do not!" Her mom sounded mad and defensive now.

But Eve was beyond caring, beyond measuring her words. "You don't even know who I am."

"Then why don't you tell me?" Justine's hands went to her hips and her foot started its staccato tapping.

Who was she? She was . . . she was . . . "That's the thing. I don't know who I am either."

Justine heaved a great sigh. "This is a ridiculous conversation."

There was that word again. Eve wanted to stomp on her mom's fucking tapping toes and smash them into silence. "No, it's not!"

"Quiet. We don't need the neighbors in our business."

"I don't give a rat's ass if the neighbors hear our business." She lowered her voice anyway. "I've been so busy trying to be who you want me to be that I don't know who I am."

"So, it's all my fault?"

"No," said Boop from the top of the porch stairs, having appeared from nowhere. "It's mine."

"What the hell happened to you?" Justine asked her, taking in the bruises and bandages.

"Long story, sugar. We need to talk."

"I don't know where to start," Boop began, or rather, didn't begin at all.

"How about your black eye?" Justine stood and lifted her hand as if to stay Boop's response. "But wait until we're inside to tell me about it."

Eve slid open the door, and Justine and Boop followed her inside where they could trust the walls to safeguard their secrets. An election was under way after all, and it wouldn't do to air the family secrets to the public.

"I took a little spill is all. It's neither here nor there."

"If you say so," answered Justine, but her raised eyebrows indicated that she wasn't about to put a lid on that line of questioning. "What do we need to talk about then?"

Boop's knees were knocking together so hard, she wasn't sure she had the wherewithal to stay upright. She felt too jittery to sit, though, so she clung to the back of a kitchen chair as if to the reins on a runaway horse. She'd spent the car ride back from the library debating with herself about whether to tell Justine about Davey, how to go about it if she did, and what to do about Ally. She hadn't come to terms with any of it yet, hadn't worked out a strategy. Her head was spinning. But here Justine was, and here Boop was, and the secret that lay between them was there too, crowing like a rooster at daybreak. "I guess I'll spit it out." Could she do this?

Boop went to the sink for a glass of water. She chugged it, wishing it were fire whiskey or something equally courage-inducing.

"I'm waiting."

Boop stared Justine dead in the eyes, so she could read her true reaction, rather than the one she would choose to share once she caught hold of herself. "Justine, you have . . . had . . . a twin brother."

"What?"

All Boop saw on her face was confusion. "His name was Davey."

"Is this a joke?" The corners of Justine's mouth were turned down. Her bewilderment was giving way to anger.

Boop plowed ahead. "I had a difficult pregnancy, and Davey was born with some . . . issues."

"Mama, this isn't funny." Justine's body had turned rigid, and Boop had turned into Mama. Not good.

"I don't think she's kidding," Eve said, her face still ashen from her tussle with Justine. She moved closer to her mama now, though. Mother and daughter stood near one another, framed by a soft glow that shimmered through the sheer draperies.

Boop continued, "No. When Davey was born, they—we—sent him to an institution."

"Issues? What kind of issues did he have? What does that mean?" Justine asked.

Boop set her pocketbook on the kitchen table and pulled his photograph from the side pocket. The picture would explain it better than any words Boop might wrangle together. "I have a picture." She offered it to Justine.

Justine examined the photograph. "You never told me."

"No."

"How could you never tell me?"

Eve took her mama's hand.

"Things were different then. I don't know how to explain." Boop paced the tile floor. She'd need every piston firing to survive this conversation.

"Figure it out."

Boop flinched and ducked her chin. "Davey had to be a secret, see?" She pleaded with her to understand, even though Boop was certain she wouldn't. Their relationship had always felt one gust of wind away from fizzling out. This was a veritable tornado.

"No, I don't see," said Justine, her voice shriller than a teapot's whistle.

Boop was flubbing up the whole thing up. She gazed pleadingly for Eve to rescue her, but Eve herself appeared on the verge of upchucking. Eve ought to lie down. Boop wanted to send her off to her room, to protect them both from Justine's inevitable contempt. The likely conclusion of this exposé was that Boop's daughter and granddaughter would hate her. And why shouldn't they? "If people had known, they'd have thought something was wrong with you—with me—with our family. We'd have lost our place in society." A sob caught in her throat and her shoulders shook. Please let her get through this without breaking down.

"That's crap."

And it was. Boop knew that now, but she hadn't known it then. She'd been raised to believe one's reputation was everything. Davey had taught her different, but too late to do him any good. "I always meant to tell you when you were old enough. Then he died and there didn't seem no point in upsetting you."

"Oh, my God." Justine was crying now. Her tears did Boop in. The dam burst, and all three of them stood there drowning.

Watching Eve and Justine hugging each other, Boop had never felt so alone. Not that it was anything less than she deserved. "Vicky and me visited him every Sunday. We told him all about you."

"Sundays?" Justine wobbled like a newborn colt as if her legs were threatening to give out. She nodded and Boop could see her fitting the puzzle pieces together. "You told him about me?" She collapsed in a chair at the table.

"Yeah. He loved to hear stories about you."

Justine closed her eyes and put her head down in her arms.

Boop counted Justine's slow deep breaths—fifteen. Her heart clutched when Justine finally looked up. She'd aged a decade in the course of their conversation. And it was Boop's fault.

"What was he like . . . Davey?" she whispered.

Eve stood next to Justine's chair and rubbed her back. They were blessed to have each other. Whatever else Boop might say about their relationship, it was filled with love. In times like this, that was about the only hope left.

Boop gazed down at Davey's face and remembered him. "He was kind and playful. Stubborn too—like his sister. He had lighter coloring than we do—more like your Daddy's side of the family."

Justine slammed her hand on the table. "How could you? How could you steal my brother from me? You had no right."

"I tried to protect you." Boop's heart ached something awful because even though it was true, it wasn't right.

"You were trying to protect yourself," Justine yelled, yanking a plastic apple from the table centerpiece and chucking it across the room. And then came the banana, pear, orange, each quicker and harder than the one before.

Eve's mouth fell open as she watched Justine lose it.

Once Justine had emptied the bowl, she picked it up and lifted it above her head.

"Mom!" Eve shouted.

Justine smashed the bowl to the floor.

All three of them stood staring at the shards until Eve squatted to gather them.

"Leave it!" Justine grabbed Eve's shoulders to hold her back.

Uncertainly, Eve stood and nibbled at her fingernails.

"I've paid for my mistake." Boop had spent almost two decades punishing herself, but she knew it wasn't enough, that it would never be enough.

Justine made a scoffing sound, but merely asked, "This place got any tissues?" She sat back down.

"Nah, I got a handkerchief in my pocketbook." Boop scrounged inside for it.

"One handkerchief isn't going to cut it for the three of us."

"You and Eve can have it," Boop offered.

"Keep it." Justine sighed.

Boop knew her offer was pathetic, but she'd hoped Justine would take her up on it. Let her have a moment of sacrifice. She should've known better.

"I'll get some toilet paper." Eve left for the bathroom.

"My whole life, something was missing inside me. I thought that's why you and Daddy didn't love me," her voice wobbled. Her tears came so fast Boop couldn't tell one from the next.

"Didn't love you? We loved you." Boop moved closer to Justine, unable to give her the space her body language declared she wanted. She managed to resist the urge to touch. That was something anyway.

"I thought if only you'd loved me enough, then you wouldn't be sad . . . and all this time. . ."

Boop's lips trembled. She'd done this to Justine. "I'm so sorry."

An obscenely loud honk from Eve blowing her nose muted Boop's apology.

"I was even jealous of Eve."

"What?" Eve asked from the bathroom door.

Justine refused to look at either of them. "Because you love Eve more than me. You love her enough to be there for her."

"I don't love Eve more than you!" Boop's eyes darted like squirrels between the two of them.

"No?'

"I love her different. I love her easier."

"What did I ever do to you?"

Boop put her hands on Justine's shoulders and was relieved when Justine didn't shake them off. "Sugar, you ain't never done nothing to me. You ain't never been nothing but my angel. Only, a day don't go by that I don't look at you and feel guilty. . . ."

"You should." Justine pushed away Boop's hands.

"I'm so sorry."

"That's not good enough."

In an act of well-intended futility, Eve handed Justine a wad of toilet paper to clean herself up with.

Boop watched as Justine gingerly dabbed her cheeks and eyes, unable to bear her daughter's pain any longer, Boop closed her eyes. "I know."

"I can't take this." Justine dropped the mascara and tear-soaked wad to the floor, screeched her chair back, and left.

Her car came to life under the house. Then she sped away. By the time Boop stopped staring after it, Eve had shut herself in her bedroom. Boop swept away the mess and followed suit.

CHAPTER 17

Eve hid in her room for hours. Her head buzzing and whirling. When she couldn't stand the bombardment any longer, she chugged some of the Benadryl she'd pilfered from Aunt Victoria. A thief and a druggie—awesome!

But she could only sleep so long, even drugged, and so it was still dark when she woke up way too early the next morning. The beach-cottage walls echoed with anger and fear and grief. She couldn't breathe.

Boop was still asleep. With still no clue what to say to Boop, Eve didn't want to face her yet.

So she decided to take a walk. While she scrounged through Boop's purse for a pen and paper to write a note, her fingers closed in on the picture of Davey, her uncle, her mom's twin brother—so weird. He didn't resemble Mom at all, but he had a nice smile. She couldn't quite wrap her head around the fact that this boy was her uncle. She felt no sense of kinship with the stranger in the photograph. The whole mess was surreal.

For her mom though: Eve couldn't imagine gaining a brother and losing him in one breath. Eve should be with her, wherever she was, but—

ON A WALK, she scribbled on the back of a receipt and then left for the beach. Out of habit, she headed west toward Bird Island and the

Kindred Spirit mailbox she and Ally had taken an annual pilgrimage to.

Eve froze. The email. Ally'd signed it YOUR KINDRED SPIRIT. How could Eve have been so dense? Ally had left her a note in the mailbox. Eve was certain of it. She strode off, anxious to read Ally's letter.

Eve found it easier to think while walking in the moonlight. There was much to think about, and so Eve was grateful in some ways that it was a decent hike to the mailbox. Her mind went to Zed first. He was the easiest to think about. She chuckled, who would've thought that her life could get so complicated that wondering whether or not a guy would call would be her easiest predicament? For all the crazy raining down on her, she might as well be a reality show star. Zed was easy because Eve knew he wouldn't call her. Guys like Zed didn't call girls like Eve. She should prepare herself now, so she wouldn't be disappointed when he didn't call. Because he wouldn't. Crap, she'd forgotten her phone was broken. Since she wouldn't be needing the money she'd saved for her trip to LA, she could use it to buy a new phone—tomorrow—before her mom found out. Then Zed could call. Except he wouldn't.

But what if he did? What would they talk about? Surfing . . .

They had nothing in common. Maybe it would be better if he didn't call. Plus, her mom would not be pleased.

The dry sand spraying in the wake of her flip-flops annoyed her, so she stashed them next to the Second Street beach access post. Then she kept walking, relishing the soft grit of the sand on her bare soles.

She couldn't upset her mom. Not now, not with everything Boop had told them yesterday.

Boop's bombshell changed everything for Eve. Just as Eve had finally found the courage to stand up for herself, she'd have to give up her independence to be Mommy's good little girl again. She'd have to return to school; pull her shit together.

How exactly was she going to do that? If it was as easy as snapping out of it, she'd have surely done it by now.

The sky grew lighter, prompting Eve to peek over her shoulder in the hopes of catching the sunrise. She paused to watch pink and orange and purple splash across the eastern horizon. When was the last time she'd witnessed the daybreak?

Too bad she hadn't brought her sketchbook because the colors were spectacular. If only she could bottle their complexity and then drape them on a piece of fabric where they'd burst like this sunrise. Eve imagined a scarf that could capture the brilliance of this summer dawn year-round. To make her vision a reality, she'd probably have to learn to dye her own fabric, because she'd never seen anything close to this sky and its effect on the ocean below. In fact, the violet hue of the ocean waves would look amazing on Ally.

Ally was going to have a baby. Eve supposed the dad was Ally's agent. Where was he? What was Ally going to do now? Where the hell was she hiding out? Maybe she'd set up a tent by the mailbox. Eve snickered at the image of her high maintenance BFF living on the land. Seriously, where was she? And why was she hiding? Eve suspected Aunt Victoria knew more than she was letting on.

Anxious for answers, Eve resumed her walk away from the sunrise. She'd never pull off the colors for the sunrise scarf anyway. Fashion design was a pointless hobby. She needed to focus on other things now; more practical things, like Mom wanted. Eve was all Justine had. Her mom needed her not be a fuck-up.

Like Karl. Eve didn't want to be like Karl.

The sinking of her feet in the soft sand strained her legs, so she veered to the water where the partly dried sand was hard. If only it were that easy in real life to find firmer footing.

Mom needed her. She deserved a better daughter, Eve wished she could be one. Unfortunately, her mom was stuck with a loser for a daughter.

Out of respect, Eve stepped around the remains of a sandcastle, though it was hardly worth the effort to avoid it. The fact that it was still recognizable after high tide was a testament to its former glory.

Her mom was tough. She'd pull through this.

Would Boop? The Boop of yesterday wasn't recognizable to Eve. Until it came crashing down yesterday, Eve hadn't realized she'd put Boop on a pedestal. Even though Boop's confession had little to do with Eve, Eve felt betrayed all the same.

Could her mom forgive Boop? Could Eve? What kind of person did something like that? Not the Boop Eve knew—her rock, her warm hug. Eve couldn't reconcile the grandma she knew with the story she'd been told yesterday.

The air was still, and muggy, but not hot—not yet. Eve dreaded when the heat would return full force. Not that she enjoyed the muggy—Eve cut herself off mid-complaint. Why was she so negative? What was wrong with her? Nothing excited her. Nothing was fun. Eve hated everything.

Only—that wasn't true. Not since this trip began. She'd had some fun—the fountain, the flirting lessons, surfing. Hell, she'd felt excited twice in the last two days—surfing with Zed, and then a few minutes ago with her sunrise design idea. Was she getting better?

She caught sight of the flagpole that marked the site of the mailbox and jogged toward it, finding it gratifying to rush toward a goal that was actually within her reach.

The mailbox was a normal black mailbox on a wooden post with Kindred Spirit stickered on the side. Eve's hand shook as she reached to open it. The moment of truth.

Inside were three journals, pens, and pencils. She took all the journals and sat down on the wooden bench next to the mailbox. Before opening any, though, she gazed past the deserted beach toward the ocean. The surf had picked up, and along with it the wind. She tucked several ponytail escapees behind her ear. The sun was

brightening, and Eve squinted—kicking herself for carelessly forgetting her sunglasses.

She sighed and opened the journal to the inscription on the front
cover. She knew from past experience it would be on all the journals,
and even though she'd read it a dozen times in a dozen different journals, she read it again:

Thirty-seven years ago, I walked the tide line of Bird Island.
In the distance—right on the low tide line—I saw the silhou-
ette of a rural mailbox. However, either I could never reach
it—or it was a mirage. The very next weekend, I "planted"
the original Kindred Spirit mailbox.

From mirage to reality. This quaint, bizarre little mailbox
brimmed with stories, all heartbreaking and heartwarming in their
own ways. It was like reading other people's diaries. Eve always felt
a little naughty, but it was nice too, sharing in a way that was both
public and private.

At the age of ten, Eve and Ally had walked to the mailbox and had
composed a note together. That journal was long gone, whisked away
by the kindred spirit, but Eve still remembered what they'd written:

Dear Kindred Spirit,
We walked all the way here by ourselves. Today, we promise
to the Kindred Spirit to always stay true to each other. Girl
Power!

Best Friends Forever,
Eve and Ally

And yet they hadn't. Even if there turned out to be a letter in
one of the journals from Ally explaining everything, the reality was
that when the chips were down, instead of finding strength together,

they'd pulled away and fallen apart—alone. Eve wanted to mend their friendship, but it was impossible without Ally, and, so far, Ally seemed to have lost interest in Eve. Eve struggled to push away her feelings of anger and hurt at Ally's rejection, knowing that Ally needed her empathy and forgiveness, not more baggage. Eve hoped that if the opportunity came, she could come through for Ally, but she worried that she'd screw things up between them even more.

Eve turned to the last page of the blue journal and worked her way backward, looking for a note from Ally. Since there was a good chance Ally hadn't signed her entry, Eve read the entries that were unsigned, signed A., or signed with a potential pseudonym. One letter, not from Ally but signed with an A., got to her:

Dear Kindred Spirit,

I am a forty-two-year-old wife, mother, sister, and daughter. Last week, my doctor diagnosed me with breast cancer. Next week, I begin the fight for my life. This week, though, I fight for my soul.

My first inclination is to look back and kick myself for missed opportunities, misguided actions, mistakes. It's tempting to view my life as a series of misses, of which there are many. Only self-flagellation seems oddly indulgent.

My second inclination is to turn to the future and plan how I will live my life henceforth. Perhaps though, I will not have enough time or energy to right all the wrongs and emerge from the cocoon a butterfly.

And so it is that I find myself here at this moment. This precious moment, sitting on this beach, at this mailbox, with the sun warming my back, and a pencil gripped in my fingers. On this fine afternoon, I reach out to all of you, my kindred spirits, you have shared your love, pain, and joy in these pages. Your stories sustain me, refresh me, and remind me I am not alone. We are all part of something greater than ourselves. I will treasure you in my heart for this moment. This moment that is all mine, all ours. This now.

In the coming months, I vow not to wallow in the past. Nor will I escape to the future. Instead, I will treasure the Now. This moment,

... and this one,

... and this one,

... this moment that God has gifted me. And I will make it count.

Yours in the moment,

A.

Eve swallowed the lump in her throat and listened to the seagulls squawking while they dove in and out of the ocean, hunting their breakfasts. She rubbed the worn grains on the seat of the bench. How many people had sat there before her? Where were they now? Where was Ally? Would Eve find her in the pages of one of these journals? How was Ally? Had A. survived?

Would Eve?

Eve finished checking that journal and picked up another journal, this one with taupe and ivory stripes, again she flipped to the end. She let out a hoot of victory when the handwriting on the last entry was Ally's.

Dear Kindred Spirit,

Thank God you made it! I've been at the beach house for almost two weeks. I keep expecting you to show up, but you don't. I'm not sure whether my hint was too obtuse, you are too messed up, or you're done with me. If you're here now though, I guess that's a good sign. Thank you for coming.

By the time you read this, I'll be gone. Grandmother is hot on my heels, and I need to sneak off before she catches up with me. Here are the pertinent details:

I'm pregnant and the doctor says the baby has a birth defect.

I don't know what to do, but my options decrease with each passing day.

I don't want my decision to become about campaign strategy.

I'm going to hide out in K's guest cottage.

Help!

I'm sorry I've been so distant. At first, I didn't want to tell you. I didn't want to disappoint you. I know it's silly, but I've always felt like you needed me to shine, and I didn't want to let you down. By the time I was ready to come clean, I'd grown worried about what my situation would do to the campaign and what the campaign might do to my situation. I knew I could trust you, but I couldn't trust the rest of our family. Then things went from bad to worse and running away seemed like my only chance, but I never intended to run away from you.

I love you! Need you! Come quickly!

Always Yours!

It was unsigned, but Eve knew it was Ally. Ally hadn't dropped her after all. She still loved her and needed her. But Eve didn't know how she could possibly help Ally.

The baby has a birth defect like Boop's baby. Aunt Victoria must've asked Boop to come clean for Ally's sake. Eve didn't know whether to be pissed at more evidence of Boop's secret-keeping, or glad that Boop was protecting Ally.

So, Ally was at Kristin's. Kristin was Ally's aunt on the other side of her family. Eve knew her pretty well, because she and Ally had spent several school breaks at the inn she ran. A year ago, though, Kristin had closed the inn, saying she was sick of having a house full of people. Then she'd gone and bought an RV and had roamed the US ever since then.

Ally. Crap. Eve had no idea what to advise Ally. This dilemma was way out of Eve's league.

The sun was hot on Eve's neck and her lips were dry, reminding her of how unprepared she was for this jaunt. She should go back before her skin caught fire. She stood and opened the mailbox with the intention of returning the journals, but instead, she grabbed a pen and returned to the bench. She opened the journal to Ally's entry and began her own.

Dear Kindred Spirit,
I am lost.

The world around me is crumbling, and I don't have the strength to stop it. My best friend is in trouble—life-altering trouble. She wants advice and support, but I can barely get out of bed most mornings, and I make poor decision after poor decision. She would probably be better off without me.

And my mom got some brutal news yesterday. News that might destroy her and my grandma's relationship, which was already complicated. Me, I'm stuck in the middle, and I don't know what to do.

My mom needs me right now, but she needs me to be someone I'm not—to live a life I don't want. How can I give her what she needs and have anything left for myself? How can I not? I'm afraid if I keep living this alternate reality, I'll disappear.

As for my grandma, she is the poster child for #1

Grandma, but she was a crappy mother. It's like they're two different people who share the same body. She hurt my mom badly. How can I keep my relationship with my grandma after finding out what she did? I can't betray my mom, but I love my grandma too, and I can't abandon her either. Do I even have a right to abandon her for poor choices she made before I was born?

I'm a mess. I don't know what to do about my friend, my grandma, my mom, or even myself. How can I help them when I'm such a loser?

The white glare off the paper stung Eve's eyes, so she squeezed them shut until the sensation of dancing dark blobs passed. She burrowed her feet in the sand and then slowly eased them out so that her feet would leave behind two little caves (or turtle houses, as Boop called them). However, the sand was too dry this far inland, so the sand merely collapsed. She couldn't even make a turtle house.

She stared toward the ocean and frowned at how unfair she was being to herself. No one could build a turtle house with the wrong sand.

She scooped up a handful and watched it seep through her fingers. "Like sands through the hourglass, so are the days of our lives."

Her heart quickened. She turned back to the notebook to capture her dawning realization.

I have to straighten out myself first.
A, in another Kindred Spirit letter, wrote about Now. Maybe I should start there. What do I have right now?

Ally's location.

This beach.

My hands.

My feet.

My head.

A mother who loves me.

A grandmother who loves me.

A father who . . . I don't know . . . a father.

A dream.

The Kindred Spirit.

Feeling Fuller.

Dawn.

CHAPTER 18

From the spot at the kitchen table where Boop had spent an hour staring at the sliding glass door waiting for Eve's return, she came up with eighty-one disasters that might have befallen Eve on her walk. Disaster number six: she'd drowned. Disaster number forty-seven: she'd been captured by ghost pirates. Disaster number eighty-one: she'd eloped with Popeye. Her theories were nothing if not creative.

When Eve returned, at last, Boop greeted her, "You're back."

"Hey."

Before Eve turned her back to close the door, Boop caught a glimpse of her flushed face. She didn't catch enough of her expression to guess at her mood, but it was good to see her with some color. "You okay?"

"Yeah." She stared at Boop square in the eyes like she meant it, but she didn't smile. "You?"

Seemed like a simple enough question. *No, my daughter hates me. My granddaughter might.* Guilt, worry, and grief threatened to reel Boop back into that dark place she'd clawed her way out of so long ago. But . . . she also felt free—freer than she'd felt in decades. That made her feel guilty too, as though she'd unburdened herself at the expense of others.

She shrugged and snapped her eyes from Eve's to stare instead at the groceries she'd picked up from the Island Market that morning. "I bought some breakfast."

Eve arched her eyebrows as she took in the smorgasbord. "You invite company?"

Bread, salt, pepper, bananas, grits, bacon, coffee, chocolate mini-doughnuts, eggs, Yoo-hoos . . . maybe Boop had gone a hair overboard. "Didn't know what you'd be in the mood for, so. . . ."

"I'm not." Eve crossed her arms over her chest. Her stomach grumbled and the left corner of her lips twitched. "Actually, some bacon and eggs sound good."

"Coming right up." Boop pushed back her chair, glad to be busy doing something. Idle hands were the devil's helpers.

"Can I help?"

"Nah, I got it." Boop fetched the carton of eggs and the bacon. When she chanced a glance at Eve, who was nibbling away on her fingernails, she reconsidered. She wasn't the only one in need of occupation. "Sugar, could you clear off this here table and make some coffee? That is . . . you do want coffee?"

"Yeah, I want coffee." Eve fixated on Boop as if she wanted to say something else, something of import. In fact, she even opened her mouth, but then shook herself. All she said was, "I'm on it."

Boop fumbled around the kitchen for two frying pans, which she finally found in the cabinets over the refrigerator. However, even on a chair, she wasn't tall enough to get them out. Whoever last cleaned this kitchen didn't have the sense God gave a goose. "Can you grab them pans for me?"

"Sure." Even Eve had to climb on the chair.

Silently staring at Eve's backside, Boop felt right twitchy. To fill the space, she said, "How was your stroll?"

"Fine." Eve handed her the pans. "No, it was . . . good . . . great, in fact."

"Ain't that something!" After locating the scissors (under the sink), Boop cut open the bacon and set to frying it. "How are you feeling about . . . things?"

"You mean Davey?" Eve asked over the roar of the faucet filling the coffee pot.

"Mostly." Davey . . . and Boop's lies, and Justine and . . . Boop wished Eve would turn around, so she could read her face. Then again, maybe it was easier this way.

Eve poured the water into the rear of the coffee pot. Her finger-nails were a sight. She said, "I don't know. I'm sad for you. I can't even imagine . . ." Boop waited for her to continue while Eve poured grounds into the filter. "I'm sad for Mom. And I'm mad at you, for her sake."

"What about for your sake?" As she cracked an egg into a bowl, Boop's hand shook.

Eve shrugged.

Boop picked out a sliver of shell. "I'm sorry."

"I know."

What else could Boop say? She was sorry, but words were never enough. She threw the eggshells in the trash and stopped to watch Eve as she unpacked groceries into the cupboard. Boop couldn't lose her. "We gonna be okay?"

Eve turned to face Boop with a loaf of bread cradled in her arms. "Yeah."

Boop closed her eyes and exhaled. "You gonna be okay?" She loaded "okay" down with enough weight to ensure Eve knew Boop meant more than "okay." Boop meant everything.

However, Eve's silent frown reminded Boop that Eve wasn't okay and that she hadn't been for a while and that, far from helping matters, Boop's revelation had added yet another wrinkle for Eve to wrestle with.

"I don't have anything to complain about," said Eve.

"Don't you?"

"Nothing important."

Boop flinched at the vehemence of her response.

"But can I ask you a question?" Eve said.

No question Boop had ever wanted to answer had been preceded by that request. Nevertheless, she gave her assent.

"How did you get better?"

Girl didn't know how to ask an easy question. "I spent the ten years after Davey's birth hopped up on tranquilizers. That didn't do much good. It was no more than I deserved."

"What do you mean 'deserved'?"

Boop beat the egg, watching the yolk break and scramble, feeling broken herself as she finally gave voice to her deepest failure. "I hid my child away. I left Davey in that place to be raised by nurses. I should've fought harder for him. I always thought maybe later when he was older, when I'd found my footing again, I thought maybe then I'd bring him home. Only I never did find my footing. Then he died, and my hope of one day being a real mom to him, a real family, died with him. I fell to pieces and did two stints in a loony bin. They helped a smidge, but the results didn't hold up in the real world. On my second visit, the doctors recommended a lobotomy—"

"What?" Eve handed her a cup o' joe—hot and black.

Boop took a sip, hoping it would fortify her. She was willing to strip herself bare for Eve, but it wasn't easy. "At that point, I checked myself out and determined to stay far away from head shrinks. As time passed, Justine grew up, and I grew functional. When Justine got knocked up, I was afraid for her, for you, and was convinced that 'functional' wouldn't be good enough. I needed to be physically and emotionally available for Justine, and I craved a real relationship with you. I grew more desperate than a Yankee at a debutante ball. And so, I found myself once again behind locked doors in rooms with barred windows and zombies wandering around in their pajamas."

"You must've been so scared." Eve topped off her own coffee with an exorbitant amount of milk and enough sugar to fill a Pixy stick. A reminder to Boop of how very young Eve still was.

"Scared I wouldn't get better." A drop of grease popped and burnt her hand, causing Boop to wince. Bacon was like most everything in life—there was a price to pay for its pleasure. "On the second day, I came closer than a shadow to running away again. Instead, I found myself agreeing to electroshock therapy."

Eve's eyes widened bigger than doughnuts.

"I still remember the mortification I felt as I walked along the corridor toward the treatment room in my white flannel pajamas, past well-heeled visitors in their street clothes. A nurse had to lead me by the elbow 'cause they'd dosed me with some drug cocktail that left me floaty."

Boop poured the egg in the frying pan, avoiding Eve's eyes. She dreaded seeing Eve's admiration replaced by sympathy, or even worse, contempt. "When the nurse strapped me to the bed, I had second thoughts."

Eve grunted. "Only second? I think I'd be on my tenth. What about normal therapy, like talking and stuff?"

"Therapy was real helpful in dealing with my divorce, but I'd gotten as far as I could with it, seeing as how I refused to talk about Davey. I'm a fan of therapy—still go off and on, but at that point the doctors thought I needed something more drastic."

When Boop hazarded a glance at Eve, she found Eve shaking her head back and forth. Boop was struck by how much she depended on Eve's love and admiration. Eve was the one person who had never seen her failures, who knew only the best Boop. Their relationship would never be the same after this conversation, and Boop felt that loss deep in her gut. "I remember the nurse patting my shoulder when I shuddered at the big ol' needle full of muscle relaxant. We had quite a crew in there for the spectacle, maybe five people."

"Electrocution by committee," Eve said.

Boop caught a hint of anger in Eve's voice and wondered where it was directed. At Boop? The doctors?

"Weren't you worried they'd fry your brain?"

"Doctor said not, worse-case scenario I'd have some temporary memory loss. Frankly, I had more than enough memories I would have been happy to see the tail end of. I was far more worried that it wouldn't work, and I'd spend the rest of my life in no-man's-land."

"I don't think I could survive misery as long as you did."

"You'd be surprised what you can survive." Boop sprinkled salt and pepper onto the eggs, wishing she'd thought to buy some Tabasco. "The nurse stuffed a bit in my mouth, and I gagged at the bitter leather flavor."

"Were they trying to muffle your screams? This is barbaric!"

"Nah, trying to keep me from biting my tongue."

"Or call a stop to the whole treatment." The plates clattered on the countertop when Eve set them down. Her hands shook.

"Between the muscle relaxant and the anesthesia, it didn't hurt none—just a zap."

"And that's how you got better?"

"It took eight treatments over the following couple of weeks." Boop scooped the bacon between the tongs of her fork and piled it on the paper-towel covered plate.

"You did that eight times?"

"Yeah. I never told a soul before now that I was shocked out of my depression. In fact, I pretend I weren't ever suffering. This world we live in ain't real sympathetic 'bout mental illnesses. Pretty ironic since everybody I know's brandishing around some form of crazy.

Seems to me we'd all be a little less nuts if we spent our energy dealing with our crazy instead of hiding it."

"That was it then?"

"Nah, that was the jumpstart."

"And then?" Eve leaned forward.

"Therapy, newfangled drugs, prayer . . ."

"When you were like that . . . "

"Depressed?"

"Yeah." Eve stared into her coffee as if she were trying to read tea leaves. Too bad she had the wrong drink.

Was she ashamed? Boop knew that feeling well.

"What were you like? I mean, inside."

"Mostly it felt like nothing; like I was zombified. But there were other times I'd catch a crying jag, and sometimes every little thing made me madder than a mosquito in a mannequin factory."

Both corners of Eve's lips lifted at that. Now they were getting somewhere.

"Sugar, there ain't no magic formula for that hurt you got." Boop scraped the eggs onto a platter.

"I'm fine. I'm not like you. I haven't suffered like you. I'm an over-dramatic spoiled baby. Don't worry about me."

"I'll thank you not to insult my granddaughter. Of course, I worry about you." Boop piled eggs and bacon onto both plates then handed one of them to Eve and followed her to the table. "Maybe you should find someone to talk to?"

"You think I'm crazy." Eve hung her head like a kicked puppy.

"I didn't say that. 'Course you can talk to me any time. But there's something 'bout talking to a professional, someone without a vested interest in you, without their own baggage. 'Cause, you know, I carry around a trunk full of the stuff."

Eve shot her a vague smile. "I don't even know what I'd talk about. My life is fine."

"Is it?"

"I'm healthy, and I have a family and food and clothes and college and . . ." Eve picked the extra crispy bits off her slice of bacon. "What do I have to complain about?"

"Being miserable." Boop shoveled in a forkful of egg.

"After all these years, why did you tell us about Davey now?"

"It's complicated, but I'll try to explain." Boop nibbled on her bacon. "Growing up, Justine thought Tommy and me didn't love her. We did, very, very much, only we were too banged up to show her." Boop wiped the bacon grease from her mouth with a paper towel. "Seems to me that maybe if Justine could understand that we were rotten parents for reasons that had nothing to do with her, then maybe she could start to heal from our neglect. And if she healed, then maybe she'd give you a little space to find your feet."

"That's a lot of maybes." Eve pushed the eggs around on her plate. "So it had nothing to do with Ally's baby?"

Boop gasped. "You know?"

"Yeah."

"You know where she's holed up too?"

"I do now."

"We going?"

Eve leaned forward. "You gonna talk to her? That's what Aunt Victoria wanted isn't it?"

"I haven't the foggiest notion of what to say to Ally, but I sure couldn't say much of anything without telling you and Justine first."

"No, I guess not." Eve set down her fork with a finality that declared she was done eating, even though she hadn't eaten nearly enough. "You should tell Ally what you wish someone had said to you."

Eve made it sound so simple.

"I'll think on it." Boop took her plate over to the sink.

Together they tidied the mess Boop had made in the kitchen. Boop sent a quick prayer of thanks to the Big Guy for gracing her with Eve. Boop had tagged along on the trip for Eve's sake. As things turned out, Boop had needed it, and Eve, just as much.

Danielle scooped up a handful of sand, marveling at the variety of colors within such a small sampling. So many different types of rocks crushed by ocean waves over centuries, now shadows of their former selves.

She'd expected to feel elated when she discovered Ally's whereabouts. Listening in on Boop and Eve in the beach house, though, had tested Danielle's allegiances and left her reluctant to report back to Mrs. Liddel. Always the voice of reason, Wyatt had reminded her of her professional obligation.

True to form, when Danielle had called to inform Mrs. Liddel, Mrs. Liddel had failed to express any gratitude. Instead, she'd insisted that it was now Danielle's responsibility to delay Boop and Eve from getting to Ally "by any means necessary."

"What do you mean by that exactly?"

"Do I have to tell you how to do every aspect of your job? For heaven's sake—I don't know—put sand in the gas tank."

"That would ruin the engine."

"You'd be doing Boop a favor. That car's a heap of scrap metal."

"I couldn't. That's illegal."

"Then figure something else out. I don't care, but if they make it to Ally before I do, I'm holding you responsible."

Danielle hung up, unsure of her next move. Mrs. Liddel was wrong—this wasn't part of her job. No way would Wyatt support this move, but she worried about the consequences of not following Mrs. Liddel's orders. Of Mrs. Liddel refusing to pay. Of the travel expenses she'd already incurred doing Mrs. Liddel's bidding. Of Wyatt's medical bills.

A few grains of sand slipped between her fingers and dusted the ground. Danielle squeezed her fingers tighter. She stared down at the sand, noting how the midday sun glinted off a few of the grains. Midday was not the ideal time to commit a crime, but at least it was off-season. She needed to hurry. Boop and Eve could leave at any moment.

Only weeks ago, she'd been patting herself on the back for her ability to manipulate people. That was before she'd met Mrs. Liddel, a true master. She unscrewed the gas cap.

If they caught her, she could lose her license. Hell, she could go to jail.

If she was any sort of decent person, she'd be doing everything she could to hurry Boop and Eve along. She'd always thought of herself as a decent sort of person. Had Wyatt's injury changed her? Did it give her a free pass in morality?

This was wrong on so many levels.

She threw the sand on the ground. She wasn't this desperate. Over her shoulder, she heard a sliding glass door opening. She stuck the gas cap back in, pushed the cubby closed, and hurried off.

It hadn't taken any time to finish packing, since neither Boop nor Eve had gotten around to unpacking. Eve kept listening for a knock at the door, foolishly hoping that Zed would stop by before they left. She kicked herself for not remembering to tell him her phone was broken. She should have gotten his number. Who was she kidding? She'd never have the guts to initiate contact.

Thirty minutes and no knock later, they were on the road and Eve had taken her rightful place behind the wheel, when it occurred to her that in the wake of all of the revelations, she'd forgotten to tell

Boop about her surfing lesson. "By the way, I learned how to surf yesterday." Eve turned on Route 17.

"You went?" Boop seemed so shocked that Eve worried she might have a heart attack.

"Yeah." Eve couldn't help smiling.

"And you are only now mentioning it?"

"I forgot that you didn't know."

"How was it?" Boop looked excited enough to pee in her pants.

Eve's smile widened. "Fun. Real fun."

"Bet he's a dreamboat in a bathing suit."

"Yeah." Eve couldn't seem to wipe away the cheesy grin smeared across her face.

"And surfing was . . . ?"

"Pretty awesome."

"I'm real proud of you."

"Me too. Listen, change of subject."

"Okay." Boop sounded nervous.

"I don't want to hurt your feelings, but the way you told my mom about Davey kind of sucked. Maybe we should practice what you'll say to Ally."

Boop was silent while she absorbed Eve's critique, and then she said, "That's a right good idea."

During their practice session, Eve came to a better understanding of Boop's situation. Any lingering anger she'd felt over Boop's lies disappeared. Her grandmother was more a victim than a villain. She couldn't help thinking that her mom would benefit from hearing all of this too, but when Eve mentioned that to Boop, she fell quiet.

The white lines on the road were lulling Eve to sleep. She didn't want to interrupt Boop's thoughts by asking for entertainment, so she turned on the radio instead. It took a few minutes to find a station. Delilah wouldn't have been Eve's first choice, but, figuring it was music they could both stomach, she left it there. They drove for over an hour without speaking. The silence between them was remarkably comfortable.

But when another love song began crooning about forgiveness, Boop clicked off the music. "I hope you can forgive me for lying to you all these years."

"I might've done the same in your shoes." Traffic on 95 was slow but steady. Eve was grateful it wasn't a parking lot. "I haven't exactly been honest with you either."

"What do you mean?"

"College isn't working out." Eve eased into the left lane, so she could pass the slow Cadillac in front of her. "I'm flunking."

"Oh."

Eve kept her eyes on the road, glad for an excuse not to see the disappointment on Boop's face. "And I don't belong to any study groups or go out or . . ." Eve whispered, "You're my only friend there."

"Oh, sugar, no wonder you're miserable."

"I should've tried harder to fit in." Eve blinked away tears.

"Seems to me, you got uprooted from your home and plopped down in a place where you couldn't find your feet. That'd make anyone blue."

"I guess."

"No guessing about it."

This time the quiet between them was unsettling, but Eve was glad for an opportunity to pull herself together, especially so that Boop wouldn't insist on taking over the driving.

Finally, Boop said, "What are you gonna do about it?"

"I want to drop out, but Mom . . . you know how she is."

"I do." Boop fiddled through her purse until eventually, she found a box of Tic Tacs. "You want one?"

"Sure." Eve popped a few in her mouth.

"You told your mom all this?"

"No. I don't want her to know that I'm even more of a loser than she already thinks I am."

"You ain't a loser. You just been lost. Those are two different things." Boop zipped her purse and settled it back by her feet. "Your mama loves you something awful, and she'd never want you miserable. But she's got her hang-ups and ain't exactly approachable—"

"You can say that again."

"She ain't exactly approachable." They both chuckled. Boop continued, "You want some advice?"

"Sure." Why not? Eve wasn't having much luck on her own.

"You need a plan. Don't tell her what you ain't gonna do. Tell her what you are gonna do and make it good."

"That's a tall order for someone you called 'lost' a few minutes ago."

"Somehow I don't think you'll have to dig too deep for a starting place. There's a footlocker in my trunk chock full of dreams."

Boop was a fountain of wisdom. Guess she'd earned it the hard way.

They got off the interstate and were zooming down some country highway when Eve noticed the yellow light on the dashboard. "What's it mean when your check engine light is on?"

"We should get the engine checked?"

Eve rolled her eyes. "Thanks. Seriously though, car's driving fine. Think we should cross our fingers and keep going?"

"Maybe." Boop's wisdom didn't stretch to auto mechanics.

"Or should we stop and get it checked out? What if it's serious?"

"We can't be too far from Morton's."

"That a friend of yours?"

"Once upon a time." Boop sounded a little too vague.

"Aren't we still pretty far from Leeside? How come you've got friends out this way?"

"The place Davey stayed ain't too far from here. Joe Morton had a daughter there too. Turn here. We got about eight miles to go."

Eve held her breath, hoping the Gray Ghost would make the last eight miles without breaking down.

CHAPTER 19

Morton's Automotive Repair Shop was a two-car garage on the edge of a one-street town. At one time Boop had counted Joe Morton a friend, so she knew they wouldn't get hornswoggled by him like they might at some fancy shop. She held her breath while Eve maneuvered around the higgledy-piggledy parked cars. Somehow, by the grace of God, she managed to find a parking spot with nary a scratch.

The garage door was open, so they moseyed right on in. "Yoo-hoo," Boop hollered.

A gangly boy rolled out from under a pickup truck. "Afternoon, ladies. How can I help y'all?"

"Joe around?"

The boy sat up. "Granddaddy done retired about five years back. My daddy runs the place nowadays."

"Is that right? You Joe's grandboy then?"

"Yes, ma'am. Charlie Morton." He wiped his hands with a rag, but it didn't make a dent in removing the grease from them.

Boop didn't have the heart to tell him he had a streak across his cheek and a dab on his nose too. "Name's Boop. I reckon I knew your daddy when he was knee-high to a grasshopper. Don't that make me older than dirt?"

"Aw shucks, you can't be a day over twenty-nine."

Boop twittered; at her age, she appreciated a bit of sweet talking. "Where's your daddy at then?"

"Gone fishing."

"This time a'day?"

"Don't reckon the fish are the point."

Amen.

Charlie raised his eyebrows at Eve as if inquiring as to her identity.

Boop opened her mouth to make the introductions, but Eve beat her to it, "I'm Boop's granddaughter, Eve."

Boop noted with surprise that she sounded downright friendly.

"It's right nice to meet you," said Charlie.

"Same."

Shoot, was that Eve smiling at a boy? What in tarnation was going on here? Boop gave Charlie another look-see. Tall, thin, brown hair, brown eyes . . . he seemed like a nice enough boy.

"Now Charlie, we done brought our car by 'cause the check engine light's on."

"Is it driving funny?'

"No," Eve said at the exact same time as Boop said, "Maybe."

Charlie grinned. "Now which is it?"

Eve and Boop reversed their answers.

Charlie laughed. "Got it. Don't suppose you got any notion how long the light's been on."

"Fifteen minutes," they answered together and then punctuated with a high five.

"Glad we got that straight."

"At least, that's when I noticed it," Eve added. "Could've been on longer. My mind's kind of distracted."

Charlie handed Boop a form. "Why don't y'all leave me the keys, and I'll have my daddy take a gander in the morning?"

Boop gave him her keys. "We don't live in these parts no more so we're hoping we might could get back on the road tonight."

"No can do. Sorry. I'm only learning. Even if Daddy was here, we couldn't swing it. We close shop in two hours, so doubt he'd have time to fix you up by then anyhow."

Boop frowned. There were many reasons she didn't care for this response. The most pressing of which was Ally. Didn't sound like they had much choice though.

"You ladies got somewhere to stay?"

Kristin's place was still forty-five minutes away. Since there was no cell service in that neck of the woods, and Kristin had cut off the inn phone when she'd left for her trip, there was no way to call for a lift. "You got any recommendations?"

"There's only one motel in town. Might be booked though. Even out this way we sometimes get Garlic Festival overflow."

Mention of the Garlic Festival brought back of a slew of memories.

"Weren't you a Garlic Festival Princess?" Eve asked.

Boop nodded.

Charlie pointed across the garage. "Phone's on the desk in the corner. The number for the motel's on the cheat sheet next to it. Help yourself."

The only room left was a smoking room, but Boop reckoned they could make do. When Boop hung up, she returned to find Eve and Charlie discussing some YouTuber. Boop wouldn't go so far as to say that Eve was flirting, but darned if she wasn't being sociable. Boop couldn't account for it, but at least someone appeared on the mend.

Charlie gave them a ride to the tiny motel a quarter of a mile from Morton's and carried in their suitcases and Eve's trunk. Eve thought it was sweet of him.

While Boop was showering, Eve used Boop's phone to call her mom's cell but didn't get an answer. Then she tried to call her at work, but the receptionist said she wasn't there. This worried Eve. If her mom wasn't at work, something was wrong. Her mom never skipped out early, even on Fridays. She never called in sick, but then she never got sick. Even though Eve was trying to please her mom by calling rather than texting, she decided a text asking her mom to call her wouldn't be misplaced. Only her mom didn't respond, so she tried the house, but got voicemail again.

"Mom, where are you? I'm worried. I haven't talked to you since you stormed out of the cottage. For all I know, you got in a wreck on your way home. Please call me. We left the cottage. We're on our way to Ally, because Boop needs to talk to her. I'll explain when we get home. Oh yeah, about that—the check engine light is on in the Gray Ghost, so we dropped it off at a car shop. They're going to take a look at it tomorrow. Crossing our fingers, they can fix it tomorrow too, but . . . I guess that's it. Call me. Love you. Bye."

Nothing to do but wait for her to call back, which Eve dreaded. Eve searched for a distraction from stressing about her mom going ballistic and the reek of stale cigarette smoke in the room. After opening the window, she turned to her footlocker, figuring it was her best shot at distraction.

She hadn't heard the siren's song from her trunk in ages. Since she had a few minutes of privacy, it wouldn't hurt to check out a couple of the outfits and remind herself of what was in there. Probably a bunch of wanna-bes.

After Boop's thievery, Eve had taken to wearing the key on a chair around her neck. She removed the key and tried to stick it in the lock, but her hands were shaking so much that she missed. Tightening her fingers into fists, she took a deep breath and . . . voila!

The completed pieces were on the top. She laid them out on one of the double beds. Seven pieces were all she had to show for the whole school year. And her sketchbook was buried in a trash dump somewhere. Some fashion designer she was!

Eve heard Boop turn off the shower. She grabbed the dress closest to her, intending to fold it and return it to the trunk before Boop came out and saw it. Only, her eyes caught in the mirror, and she couldn't help holding the dress against her body to get a better look at it. The view only served to tease her more.

She glanced at the bathroom door, wondering how long before Boop appeared.

Eve turned back to the mirror. What the hell.

She scrambled out of her tank top and jeans and into the dress. It fit, which surprised her since she'd made it for Ally's model-thin frame.

Not anymore. Eve could barely wrap her head around the fact that Ally was pregnant.

Eve spun, admiring the flare of the skirt. She hadn't realized how much weight she'd lost.

The dress was a soft pink—a color she hadn't worn since she'd stopped wearing pigtails. Along with the sun from the beach, though, it made her skin glow.

Still in the bathroom, Boop's brush clattered against the sink, causing Eve to skip a little in surprise. Her heart raced. Of their own volition, her hands worked her ponytail free.

The bathroom door opened. "You can have the—" Boop gasped. "Well, spank me cross-eyed!"

In response to another of Boop's crazy expressions, Eve burst into laughter. "Do you like it? It's a little young, I guess, and it would look better if—"

"Hush yourself!" Boop came closer. "Now I don't wanna hear none of that lowdown talk. Let me take a gander." She twirled her finger, and Eve spun again even more awkwardly this time.

Boop whistled.

Eve blushed.

"Honey, you're prettier than a red wagon full of speckled pups."

The warmth of her tone suggested this was a compliment, so Eve took it that way.

"And that dress. Why, I never . . ." Then Boop moved toward the garments on the bed as if she too heard the call of the sirens.

Eve knew that Boop wouldn't criticize her, even if she hated the designs. Still, Eve worried that she'd hear disappointment behind a few fake compliments. Eve's breath stilled.

One by one, Boop picked up the pieces. When she finished, she turned back to Eve, her face wet with tears. "I'm so proud of you, honey. These clothes are the cat's pajamas, and you," her hand fluttered toward Eve, "couldn't be lovelier." She sniffled. "I'm sorry." The back of her hands wiped at her cheeks. "It's only that—this old lady feels as though you handed her the gift of a lifetime. I know what these mean to you, and I want you to know how much you sharing them means to me."

By the time she'd finished speaking, Eve was crying too. And then they were hugging.

They capped the evening off with Eve modeling each piece to the accompaniment of oohs and ahhs from Boop. Eve had never felt so special.

Justine: Good morning.

Eve: Are you okay? It's so early

Justine: Did I wake you? It's 8!

Eve: On vacation. You okay?

Justine: Fine. Sorry, I worried you. What's going on with Ally?

Eve: She is pregnant

Justine: Oh no! Poor girl. She must be a mess and her parents and the campaign. Who's the dad?

Eve: IDK

Justine: What a nightmare. To be so young. Why does Boop need to talk to her?

Eve: You should talk to Boop she's right here she can call you

Justine: No. There's nothing to say.

Eve: There is tons to say. I've been talking to her I get it better now. Listen to her.

Justine: You have no idea how it was back then. This is between Boop and me. You and I need to figure out how to swing your classes and the internship. I put in a call.

Eve: NO! No community college no internship no going back to school in the fall!

Justine: Not funny.

Eve: I'm not laughing I haven't been laughing for months I hate that place. Do you know what I do there?

Justine: What?

Eve: I sleep and I cry and I don't go to class and I don't study and I don't have any friends and I fantasize about dying. And I can't snap out of it. Not there. So don't even say it.

Justine: Why didn't you tell me?

Eve: I'm telling you now

Justine: I'm listening.

Eve: That's pretty much it

Justine: So what's your plan?

Eve: I'm working on that

Justine: I see.

Eve: Can you give me a little time?

Justine: I guess it will hold until you get home.

Eve: Will you listen to Boop then too?

Justine: Fine.

Eve: Thanks mom

Justine: xx

Eve: Love you too

CHAPTER 20

Their motel room smelled like a bouquet of stale cigarettes, must, and bleach. So when Johnny Morton told them the verdict was still out on the Gray Ghost, Boop wasn't real happy about sitting around in that stink hole.

Since there wasn't nothing to do in that there outpost, a stinky dull day lay before them until the desk clerk offered to give them a lift over to the Garlic Festival. The list of reasons Boop didn't want to go was longer than the line for toilet paper in Soviet Russia. But when Eve reminded her that they needed to go to town to get her a new phone, all of Boop's reasons faded into the woodwork.

As Boop set her mind to overcoming her reservations, she was struck dumb by a wonderful idea. "I can't be seen in Leeside in such a state. Not when I haven't seen some of my old friends in years. Getting wrinkly's bad enough, but this—" Boop waved her injured arm across her banged-up face and pointed at her bandaged arm. She was getting right good at this manipulation thing.

Eve frowned. "Can't you wear your big sunglasses and floppy hat?"

"Sugar, you ain't exactly a stranger in those parts neither. You and Ally been visiting Kristin for years."

"No worries. Nobody notices me when I'm with Ally. Speaking of Ally, why don't we Uber to Kristin's?"

Boop wrinkled her nose. "If you think I'm hitchhiking with some serial killer, you've got another thing coming."

Eve opened her mouth as if she was about to start arguing, but then closed it and shook her head as if she thought better of it. "So we're stuck here all day." She wrinkled her nose.

Indeed, the stench was giving Boop a headache. "I'll make you a deal."

Eve seemed wary—as she should be.

"There's a beauty parlor across the street. How about we get them to touch up my hair and face, then we'll get you a phone, and with whatever time we have left, roam around the festival."

Eve's shoulders dropped as the tension ran off, foolish girl.

"And . . ." Boop continued.

Eve crossed her arms.

"You let them take a turn on you too. My treat." Boop attempted to project an innocent smile but suspected that she had failed.

"No way!"

In a mirror image of Eve's stubborn stance, Boop crossed her own arms. "Those are my stipulations."

"This is blackmail."

"Call it what you like." Boop batted her eyelashes. "Oh, and one more condition—you've got to wear that pink number of yours."

Eve's eyes went glassy. "Why can't I just dress like me?"

"That," Boop pointed to Eve's reflection in the mirror, "is not who you are. That is who you hide behind."

"Bullshit!" She said it with vehemence, but her eyes, evaluating her reflection, told a different story.

Boop waited.

Eve chewed on her thumbnail.

And waited.

At last, Eve spat her fingernail onto the floor, wiped her hand on her jeans, and said, "Fine."

Boop needed to do so something about that nail-chewing habit of Eve's. Turpentine?

Lord have mercy! When had Boop turned into Vicky? She felt guilty for jerking Eve's chain. "Never mind. You don't have to do nothing you don't want to do. I shouldn't pressure you like that."

Eve stared at her hands. "I . . . kind of . . . want to." Several minutes passed before she lifted her eyes to meet Boop's. When she did, they were filled with hope.

Now wasn't that something?

Eve's new phone, which Boop had insisted on paying for, held a slew of old messages from her mom, but nothing else. No Ally. No Zed.

Disappointed, they headed over to the Garlic Festival. Boop, Kristin, Aunt Victoria, and even Ally took this Garlic Festival nonsense pretty seriously, but it had always been an inside joke between Justine and Eve. Pageants and garlic are both ridiculous in their own right, but together?

Eve had to admit that the event was fun in an old-school kind of way, though. Who doesn't love funnel cake and Ferris wheels?

Boop and Eve weren't the only ones who'd spent the morning in the salon. For the country-club set of Leeside, this was the place to see and be seen. And boy, were they seen! Someone must've stopped to chat it up with Boop every ten minutes. At some point, they'd inevitably request an introduction to Eve, even though Eve had met most of them several times. Boop insisted that they didn't recognize Eve because of the makeover, but Eve held the opinion that no one had ever noticed her before.

Except, they sure noticed her this morning. At first, it was embarrassing, and then it was flattering, and then it got old. By lunchtime it was hot, and Eve was tired, but they still had an hour before the desk clerk had agreed to pick them up.

At least the messy bun the hairdresser had concocted kept her neck cool, and the pink sundress couldn't have been more perfect for the 90-degree, 100 percent humidity day.

Eve's flip-flops, however, were a fashion disaster, so she kept her eyes out for stalls selling shoes. Only shoes weren't exactly common festival wares. While Eve did eventually find some hemp sandals in the tie-dye booth and some knockoff Teva's in another booth, neither offered much of an improvement.

The clothing options were unfortunate. Granted the Garlic Festival wasn't a market for high fashion, but who in their right mind would wear a T-shirt that said, GOT GARLIC?

They stopped at a silver jewelry booth that was a welcome oasis in the mass of cheap and generic crap. Eve treated herself to a necklace that went perfectly with her pink dress.

After another row of junk, she gave up on finding shoes. She joined Boop, who was chatting with some "cousin" about the time they'd sneaked into their grandmother's pantry to steal some pickled watermelon rind for a tea party with their dolls. Apparently, they'd gotten the "switching of their lives" when they were caught.

They continued to trade similar stories. After a while, the characters blended together, the heat seeped under Eve's skin, and her eyes glazed over. She searched the shops surrounding the town square for some polite reason to wander off, and then she saw it.

"That dress!" In a breach of good manners, she ran over to the store to get a better look at the mannequin in the window, leaving behind a bewildered Boop, and her cousin, to follow if they so chose.

The sign said: Nicholas Russell Studio. Even though she'd been to this downtown square a zillion times, she'd never seen it before. She went inside to get a better look at the dress—to confirm what didn't need confirming. It was the same dress she'd seen in Savannah; the one that had screamed out her inadequacies.

Boop followed her inside. "What have you got there?"

"Do you remember it? It was in Papayas."

Boop considered and then shook her head. "But it's a knockout for sure."

"It's a work of art."

For $299!

"Let me buy it for you."

Knowing that there was no way that Boop had snagged a peek at the price tag, Eve declined her kind offer. "I wouldn't have anywhere to wear it." Nevertheless, she couldn't drag her eyes from it. How had the designer combined these non-compatible elements in such a stunning way?

"C'mon . . ."

"It's not my style—"

"Really?" A male voice cut in.

Eve spun toward the source and discovered a well-dressed guy around her mom's age.

He continued, "'Cause the dress you're wearing is incredible. Who did it?"

Eve blushed.

"My granddaughter designed it herself." Boop pointed at Eve.

"No kidding."

Eve's eyes darted from one dress to the other. "Not in the same ball game as this one though." The dress on the mannequin was perfection.

"Glad you like it," he said.

Eve swung her eyes back to the man. "Are you?" she checked the dress tag, "Nicholas Russell?"

He bowed.

"Oh my gosh! You designed all this stuff?" Eve waved her arm around the small store. She might be obsessed with the dress, but the rest was incredible too.

"Yep."

"You're amazing!" Eve blushed again. She sounded like a little girl with a crush. Heck, maybe she did have a crush . . . on his clothes anyway.

Nicholas lounged on a stool. "Are you going to let your grandmother buy it?"

"Oh no. I couldn't."

"Why don't you try it on at least?" He pointed over to a dressing room.

"That's okay." Eve caressed the lace bodice.

Boop undressed the mannequin and shoved it back into Eve's hands. "Oh, for crying out loud." She herded Eve into the dressing room.

The studio was air-conditioned, but they hadn't been inside long enough for it to work its magic. Eve's pink dress was damp with perspiration, and the new one kept sticking while she shimmied into it. She prayed her sweat wouldn't ruin it.

Boop's voice came from the other side. "And by the way, I'm well aware of the cost, so don't let that worry you none."

Eve stepped out.

Boop whistled. "'Cause it's worth every penny." She turned to Nicholas, who was smiling appreciatively at Eve . . . or at the dress at least. "We'll take it."

"But—" Eve protested. Only she couldn't hold back smiling at her reflection in the full-length mirror. She felt like Cinderella. If only she could trade in her flip-flops for glass slippers.

"No buts! Now you slide back into your other pretty frock, and I'll make arrangements with this gentleman."

As Eve took off the dress, she marveled again at Nicholas Russell's workmanship and wondered if she could ever be that good.

"You married?" Boop's question drifted into her musing.

Not again!

"You seem like a good catch, and I got a daughter round about your age. She's a looker."

Eve snorted. At least it wasn't her this time.

"Thanks, but I'm not in the market for a relationship right now."

My God, couldn't Boop just stop? Why did she constantly have to play matchmaker? Given how her own match had turned out, you'd think that was the last thing she'd be interested in. Eve froze. Was that it? Some kind of compensation? Was Boop lonely? As far as Eve knew, she had never even gone on a date since Grandpa had left her.

Eve focused back on the dress. She'd never wear it. She didn't hang out any place where people dressed like that. Even if she had somewhere to wear it, she wouldn't be able to do it justice. Someone like Ally should wear it. Maybe she'd give it to Ally. Except Ally was pregnant. Plus, Eve wanted to keep the dress. It was perfect. With Nicholas Russell's dress draped over her arm, she stepped out from behind the curtain.

Boop was still chatting up the poor guy. "What the dickens you doing here in Leeside?"

Eve handed him the dress to put in a bag.

"I retired from the rat race in New York. Tired of working for The Man. Thought I'd start my own label. I can design anywhere, and then I make a few trips a year to the city to sell my work. Sell some online. I'm thinking about buying a truck. Like a food truck, but for clothing."

"Juggling designing, and running a business, and marketing sounds exhausting. I hope you got some good help."

Eve's face grew hotter. It was happening again. Boop was going to try foisting her on Nicholas.

He frowned. "I wish. Just me. Leeside isn't exactly teeming with fashion industry experience."

Eve's heart beat faster. Her palms started to sweat. Not another panic attack. She couldn't have a repeat of Papayas. Breathe in. Breathe out.

"By golly, ain't that the truth," said Boop.

The man handed Boop the bag.

Eve inched away, chewing on her fingernails.

"It was nice doing business with you. Take care, you hear?" Boop said.

Nicholas waved and returned his attention to the sketchpad in his lap.

What Eve wouldn't do to see those sketches. Her fingers dropped from her lips, and she craned her neck in a worthless attempt to get a glimpse.

Boop turned away from Nicholas Russell.

Eve waited for Boop to say something else, like how talented Eve was. Only she didn't.

Eve closed her eyes and tension eased from her body. Boop wasn't going to do it.

But . . .

Eve's eyes popped open.

"Would you . . .?" Her knees shook. What was she doing? She should give this more thought.

He lifted his eyes to Eve's.

Don't think about it. Just say it. Eve cleared her throat. "Would you consider hiring me as an intern?" The words spilled so fast she wondered if they were too garbled to even understand. Maybe that would be a good thing. She contemplated the swirl in the marble by her foot.

"You?"

"You said you liked my dress." Eve mumbled. What had she been thinking? Of course, this man wouldn't want her hanging around. "I could help with the sewing and stuff."

"I don't—"

"Never mind." Tears pricked the corner of her eyes. She was determined not to let them fall, not to let him know how much his rejection hurt. She shrugged and forced a smile. "Just an idea. Crazy."

Boop took her hand and gave it a little squeeze. Her sympathy was too much. Eve's breath caught in her throat, and she spun to hightail it out of there before she made more of a fool of herself.

"Wait!" Nicholas Russell said.

Eve stopped but couldn't turn to face him, not when she was so close to losing her shit.

"Do you have a portfolio?" he asked.

Eve was about to shake her head no, when Boop said, "'Course she does. Only we're passing through town on our way to Richmond, so she don't have it handy."

Eve peeked a glance at him over her shoulder.

His eyes were narrowed, and his lips pursed.

Did he know Boop was lying?

"Tell you what. I've got a booth at Arts in the Park in Richmond next month. Why don't you stop by with your portfolio, and I'll take a look?"

An insane laugh-cry escaped Eve. Somehow, she mustered a thank you.

"Now, I'm not promising anything. Just that I'll take a look."

"Okay." At least she had a shot. "See you in June!" Eve dragged Boop out the door before she fell apart from excitement and Nicholas Russell took it all back because he thought she was insane.

Once they were out of sight and Eve thought she could talk without laughing or crying, or both, she told Boop, "I don't have a portfolio. I don't even know what goes into a portfolio."

Boop shrugged. "We'll figure it out."

"Do you think I've got a chance?"

"You bet your sweet bippy I do."

Perhaps Garlic Festivals and princesses weren't such an oxymoron—because Eve was beginning to feel as though she'd stepped into a fairy tale.

Unknown: It's Zed I'm getting off work in an hour want to catch a wave?

Eve: Can't not at beach

Zed: What?

Eve: We left—have to see a friend in trouble

Zed: Everything okay?

Eve: IDK

Zed: Where are you?

Eve: Leeside

Zed: In VA?

Eve: Yep

Zed: When will you be back here?

Eve: ?

Zed: How long will you be in Leeside?

Eve: ?

Zed: Tomorrow?

Eve: Probably

Zed: Can we meet up there?

Eve: No waves here

Zed: I get the message. Never mind

Eve: Wait! JK would you really come here?

Zed: Always up for an adventure

Eve: I guess okay

Zed: Do you want to go on a date or not? Don't do me any favors

Eve: I want to

Zed: Good I will text you tomorrow

Eve: Okay

CHAPTER 21

Mid-afternoon, the desk clerk dropped them off at Morton's. Trailing behind Boop, Eve heard her gasp.

"Now ain't you a sight for sore eyes?" Boop threw her arms around some old guy who was leaning against the counter, grinning from ear to ear.

"You didn't think I'd let y'all run off without a by-your-leave, did you?" the man—who Eve assumed was Joe Morton—asked, as he put his hands on her shoulders and pushed her back a bit. He took in an eyeful. "How you been, Boop?"

"Hanging in there. How 'bout you?"

"Getting old." The man's hands dropped to his side.

"Ain't we all? I was sorry to hear of Joyce's passing in the *Gazette* a few years back. She was a lovely lady. You must miss her something awful." Boop laid her hand on Joe Morton's arm.

Though such a move might be natural given their conversation, Boop wasn't a toucher. A hug and a touch within the space of minutes were noteworthy. It spoke of a bond that shocked Eve. Not shocked like appalled, but shocked like how could Boop be that close to someone who Eve had never even heard of?

That was the whole issue, though, wasn't it? Mr. Morton was part of Boop's secret life. Boop with her double identity.

In an effort to clear away that line of thinking, Eve shook her head.

Mr. Morton said, "Not a day goes by that something don't make me think 'bout her. At least nowadays those thoughts bring a smile. Thank you kindly for the card you sent back then. It helped get me through some dark days." He turned to inspect Eve. "Now who've we got here? This can't be Justine's little girl, can it?"

"On the nose."

"I declare! You remind me of those pictures of your mama that Boop used to flaunt."

"I never flaunted nothing."

"Shucks, I'm only kidding." His warm laugh put everyone at ease.

"You always were a teaser," Boop said.

"I got your car checked out." Mr. Morton pointed toward the Gray Ghost. "Weren't nothing wrong with it 'cept gas cap weren't screwed on—darnedest thing."

"Now that's a relief. What do we owe you?" Boop opened her purse.

"Not a lick. Old friends gotta look out for each other. It's so good to see you." His eyes softened. "After Davey died, we didn't see you no more. We understood, 'course we did, but we missed you all the same."

"I'm sorry, Joe. I went to a bad place after he passed."

"Don't I know it? My Margie died five years later. No one should have to lose a child."

They stood there staring at each other in the awkward silence that falls after all the important stuff's been said and regular conversation feels inappropriate.

"I suppose we best be on our way then," Boop said.

"Don't be no stranger."

"You got it." But Boop's smile was a sad one, more of a goodbye smile than a see-you-later one.

Maybe Mr. Morton thought so too, and maybe that didn't sit right with him because he followed them out to the car. Before they could get in, he asked, "You been out to the Colony lately?"

Boop did a double take. "Not since the funeral." She shuffled her feet. "You must think I'm awful for not visiting Davey's grave."

"You know me, I ain't one to judge. We always tidied his up a bit when we went to visit Margie."

Boop nodded her gratitude.

"Reason I ask is they're tearing it down next month, and I been wanting to go roam around one last time. Say goodbye. Only I can't seem to find the wherewithal to go by myself. Y'all want to join me?"

"I don't know about that." Boop's entire body was trembling. "See we're on our way . . ."

Believing that Boop needed to do this, Eve's gut twisted. Ally had waited this long. What was another hour or two? Boop might regret not going for the rest of her life, and if she went, she might be able to put some of her ghosts to bed.

"I'm real sorry Joe, but—" Boop's voice cracked.

"Mr. Morton, we'll join you," Eve interrupted.

Boop turned terrified eyes to Eve. "Eve—"

In an attempt to seem commanding, Eve narrowed her eyes and threw back her shoulders. "Boop, sometimes all you've got to do is show up. This is one of those times." Not bad!

"But—"

Eve held up her hand. "Get in the car, Boop. I want to go meet my uncle."

Tears rolled down Boop's cheeks, but she got in the car. They put a suitcase in the garage to make room for Mr. Morton in the back seat.

Before they took off, Eve stole a moment to pray for guidance. Because if she was wrong, then this could be bad; very bad.

A Long Time Ago

One Sunday afternoon, Davey sat on the floor of the common room playing with a wooden train. He loved that little blue engine even though he'd never even seen a real train, and likely never would. Davey's world was real small, which was a blessing of sorts. He never knew he'd gotten a raw deal. But Boop knew. And it weighed on her like a rucksack full of sins.

Even though he was four, he still lived in the baby dorm. It always took a few minutes for Vicky and Boop to accustom themselves to the smell. Loads of wee ones meant loads of whoopsies. As hard as the nurses tried to keep up, the place had a distinctive smell.

It took another few minutes to get used to the hubbub. Babies crying and not quite enough arms to soothe them, toddlers tantruming, and children playing. Their noises bounced off the cinderblock walls and tile floors. Eventually, they all got used to both the stench and the commotion because that's what people do. They adapt.

Boop's heart burned when Davey first caught sight of them. His face lit up and he toddled over to throw his arms around her as if holding on for dear life. Or maybe that was Boop. Her poor boy only got love once a week. No matter how kind and hardworking the nurses were, they didn't love Davey. Not like Boop did. Her love was Davey's Sunday treat, but it should've been a staple.

Vicky, Davey, and Boop wandered over to the Gilette Garden for a picnic. Davey was getting right good at walking. The doctors had warned that he might never do so, but six months before, he'd surprised them all by taking his first steps.

Boop had missed them.

She passed Davey a plate of fried chicken and biscuits, which he inhaled. The boy was a good eater.

"Your sister Justine's sick with a cold."

"Something's going around, that's for sure," Vicky said.

Davey didn't say nothing while they rambled on like they usually did. He didn't know but five words: choo-choo, more, no, bye-bye, and duck. Boop wasn't sure what he understood from their conversation, or if he even listened. Still she thought the chatter was good for him to hear.

Once Davey cleaned his plate, he handed it back to Boop. "More, Mama."

Boop about fell to pieces. Mama. In a stunned silence, she sat there shaking while Vicky filled up his plate. Mama. The power of the word crashed over her like an avalanche. Sure, there was the joy and pride any mama would feel in such a moment, but what buried Boop was the guilt. She hadn't earned that title. She had never once tucked him in, never kissed him good night, and never soothed away a nightmare. Showing up on Sundays was insufficient, at best.

Davey dug around in the dirt in search of roly-polies. They'd denied his very existence, as if they could erase him and their sins by locking him away. How ironic, since locking him away had been their real sin. Boop thanked the heavens he never understood that he'd been set aside.

Davey held out his hand so Vicky and Boop could get a better view of the roly-poly he'd found. Boop was intent on watching him. His face, alight with curiosity, reminded her of Tommy. How tragic that Tommy would never know this boy—his boy. The roly-poly curled up in Davey's palm in an act of self-preservation, but it needn't have feared Davey.

Shortly thereafter, Joe and Joyce Morton stopped by with their daughter Margie. Boop got Davey to show off his new word, and the Mortons oohed and ahhed in a way that only other parents in the trenches could manage. Boop was struck by how normal the moment felt. Almost as though they were a real family.

Time travel had always seemed to Boop a fool's ambition, since you can't change what has been, and knowing what will be is a nightmare of a different color.

Yet, she couldn't help feeling their visit to the Colony was a rupture in time. The Colony was like it was, but like it wasn't at the same time. The same old buildings dotted the grounds. They hadn't been shiny new pennies upon her last visit, but now . . . They hadn't been condemned for nothing. She'd expected the dingy, chipped white paint, but the crumbling brick and topsy-turvy porches made her question their very foundation.

"You want me to park?" Eve asked.

"Nah. Them buildings are locked up tight," Joe said from the back seat, his head sticking up between Eve and Boop.

"I'm surprised no one's broken windows and set up camp." Eve slowed to a walking pace.

Vicky used to drive these streets like a turtle, always afraid someone would spring out from nowhere. Now the streets and sidewalks were hauntingly empty.

"Cops drive through here couple times a day," Joe said. "Occasionally catch some kids partying or petting or what not."

Eve laughed.

Perhaps it was another trick of time, but Eve's laugh reminded Boop of Davey's right then. A wave of warmth brought her attention to how cold the dang AC had gotten. She shut it off and rolled down her window.

"Look, Boop, that's where you and me first met." Joe pointed to the dogwood tree where they'd crossed paths, pushing their babies 'round in prams.

His gravelly voice washed over her. The tree in front of her had a cloud of white blossoms that rained petals when the wind blew. In her mind's eye, though, she pictured the tree as it had been on that fall day of which Joe spoke, smaller and covered in red and orange leaves.

"There's the baby dorm," he said pointing toward McAuliffe Hall. Must've done so for Eve's sake, since Boop could've drawn a map of the place in her sleep.

"And over there's where they used to set up the annual carnival. Remember that, Boop?"

"Nah. Those were on Saturdays," Boop said. She'd missed most of Davey's too short life. Davey might've got the best of her, but Justine got the most. There hadn't been nothing left over for Boop and Tommy.

"Joyce and me always admired your grandma's gumption," Joe said to Eve. "Speaking of gumption, how's Victoria?"

"That cat always lands on her feet."

"Suppose so." Joe laughed and then said to Eve again, "You'd have liked Davey. Everybody did. He was real gentle. Remember how he used to rescue critters?"

It came rushing back like those trains Davey used to love. How he'd find bugs inside, put them in his pocket, and free them outdoors whenever he got the chance. She hadn't cared much for that hobby, but it did speak to his kindness.

"Remember how Margie used to pick all them weeds? She'd hand us buckets of them. Davey used to press them in the Bible at his bedside," Boop said. "Must've found a hundred of them when I went to clear out his belongings.

"Now Boop, 'round about these parts we call them wildflowers."

"Aw shoot, what's in a name?"

"Near about everything."

How right he was.

"There's the dining hall," Joe said.

"Joe, you ever feel bad about sending Margie here?" Boop asked suddenly.

"Sure. But I'd have probably felt bad about not sending Margie here too."

"What do you mean?" Eve asked.

"Margie and Davey were different. Folks didn't understand and that scared them. Made them scared of the kids. Fear makes people mean. At the Colony our chillins were safe from that. They had happy lives here."

"That's more that I can say about my life on the outside." For crying out loud, why had she said that?

Joe put his hand on Boop's shoulder. "And what did Joyce and I know about caring for Margie? Not nearly what her nurses knew."

"Things are different now."

"It's hard to believe that nowadays kids like Margie and Davey go to school and read and play sports. I reckon it's a downright miracle."

They were quiet for a bit, each lost in their own thoughts.

Then Joe said, "Take a right. Around the bend's the old cemetery. Why don't you park there, and we can drop in on Davey?"

"And Margie," Boop reminded him.

"Nah. I had her moved next to Joyce. This land's in flux, and Margie'll rest easier with her mama."

Boop's family had a private cemetery at the big house in Leeside. They'd sold the house but kept the family graveyard. Boop had a plot there waiting for her. If she had Davey moved there, they could spend eternity together.

Boop squeezed her eyes shut and bore down on her lips. Her body shook with the effort not to break down.

The car stopped. Eve and Joe got out, but Boop stayed inside pulling herself together.

Joe and Eve chatted on the bumper while they waited for her. Her window was still down, so she could hear the murmur of their voices, but the wind blew their words away.

Once Boop had found her legs, the trio wound around the graveyard, Joe leading the way. Boop couldn't even remember where Davey was buried. She'd only been to the gravesite the one time, and that day had been a blur.

The cemetery had an air of neglect. Here and there, they'd pass a plot that had been carefully groomed. But mostly weeds—wildflowers—ran rampant. The cemetery must've had about three hundred-or-so plots. The markers were simple affairs—no crazy mausoleums or statues. No one spoke during the five-minute walk to Davey's gravesite.

Boop was a little out of breath when they got there. Not because the walk was physically strenuous, but it was emotionally draining.

Davey's plot was so overgrown it was impossible to read the inscription on his commemorative plaque. Boop got to her knees and tugged at the wildflowers with the strength of much younger fingers. As she yanked away the clumps of tangled grass, she was reminded of Davey's favorite books; she could practically feel her grinchy heart growing three sizes.

At last, she cleared his name. With her arthritic index finger, now smudged with grass stains and dirt, she traced the name: Davey Swanson.

Here lay her only son.

From behind, she heard Eve whisper, "Hi, Davey. It's nice to finally meet you."

Tears slid down Boop's cheeks, watering the ground that blanketed Davey. She watched a yellow butterfly flit amongst the buttercups and dandelions. The breeze caressed her like a kiss. Its scent of freshly turned earth and grass spoke of spring and new beginnings.

CHAPTER 22

On the drive to Ally's house, it occurred to Eve that things were about to get real. She longed to crawl back to that spot on the couch with Kafka the cockroach, where she could hide from life instead of living it. Look where living it had gotten Ally. But Eve couldn't abandon Ally, and if Boop had the courage to face her demons, then the least Eve could do was stand beside her. All of which was well and good, but it didn't negate the fact that Eve was on the verge of barfing her anxiety all over Boop's car.

One glance at Boop told her there would be no help from that corner. She looked like a corpse with her signature ruby red lipstick and sickly pale skin. Her mouth was drawn down at the corners, and her eyes were pink. The two of them were quite a pair.

The Mercedes parked in the drive puzzled Eve—a bit highbrow for Ally's usual style, but perhaps it was the influence of LA and all.

Boop climbed out of the car, but her legs didn't seem to be working right. "You coming?"

"I'm scared."

"I know, sugar, but Ally needs you."

"What if I say the wrong thing? What if I fall apart again? What if she's mad at me for taking so long to find her? What if—?"

Boop held up her hand. "It ain't healthy to live a life of 'what ifs.' You gotta deal in the 'what ises.' The fact is that your best friend is in a heap of trouble, and she needs you. You're stronger than you think. You'll get through this."

"Promise?"

"Pinky-swear."

Eve climbed out of the car, and together they trudged up the front walk past the clover patch where Ally and she had killed hours hunting for luck. Ally claimed she'd found a four-leaf clover once, but Eve accused her of tearing one of the three leaves to make it look like four. Ally denied it, said Eve was jealous. Eve suspected they were both right.

"Hold on a sec," Eve said, as she stooped to pluck a clover. Three leaves, as always. Maybe Ally had the right idea. Time to make her own luck. She tore one of the leaves and stuck it behind her ear.

"Should we go to the big house or straight back to Ally's guest cottage?"

"Seems in poor form not to try the front door first, but that peach in the drive is giving me the jitters," Boop said.

Eve raised her eyebrows.

"It don't strike me as Ally's taste or budget—though I suppose she's got her trust fund. . . ."

"I was thinking the same."

"I don't know how she'd a managed it, but I'm thinking the car's—"

Her prediction was cut short by the front door opening. "It'd have been thoughtful if you could have given me thirty more minutes," announced Aunt Victoria.

"You? The loose gas cap? You had us followed," Boop sputtered.

A slow, crowing grin spread over Aunt Victoria's face. "Don't be silly."

"You conniving little snit," said Boop. "I can't believe you." Boop marched up the stairs, pushed past her sister and continued ranting inside.

When Aunt Victoria turned to follow her sister, Eve had flashbacks to her invisible days. Only this time she recognized the opportunity that she'd been handed and, instead of following them, she slipped around the big house and headed straight to the guest cottage, where she hoped she'd find Ally.

After sprinting through the herb garden, she knocked on the cottage door. "Ally, it's Eve."

No answer. Eve turned the knob. It was unlocked. "Hello?" she called into the dark foyer.

"Go away!" Ally's voice came from her bedroom.

Having spent many holidays there, Eve knew her way around and headed straight for Ally. Since the door was shut, Eve knocked but got no answer. She eased the door open into another dark room. She could just make out a lump on the bed, which she supposed was Ally.

"Can I turn the light on?" Eve asked.

"Whatever." Ally's voice was muffled by the cream blanket she had over her head.

"I won't if it bothers you."

Ally clawed out from under the blanket. "Do what you want."

Ally clearly didn't want Eve there. And yet she'd left her the note. Only, that had been a while ago. What had changed? Stupid question. "Never mind."

"Just turn on the damn light." Ally sat up.

Eve flipped the switch and stifled a gasp. Ally looked like shit—at least, by Ally's standards. Though Eve supposed, if she were being fair, Ally was still better looking than 80 percent of the population. She had dark circles under her eyes, her tan had a yellowish hue, and her hair was sticking up all crazytown, probably static from the blanket.

"I'm hideous." Ally said it like she was daring Eve to . . . Eve wasn't sure . . . was she supposed to agree, or disagree?

"No. Not at all. . . ." Eve wasn't equipped for this. She had no clue how to deal with this Ally. Too bad she and Boop hadn't role-played this conversation too. It had never been hard to talk to Ally before.

Eve wandered over to the dresser and picked up a picture of the two of them at Ally's prom last year. Ally had gotten one of her guy friends to ask Eve so they could double. Eve hadn't gone to prom at her own school, but it was all good.

Ally said, "Morning sickness is one big fat lie. All day sickness is more like it, and I'm past the first trimester too. I don't know how much longer I can take this." She rolled out of bed and put her hands on her hips. "You sure took your sweet time."

Eve couldn't help staring at Ally's baby bump. Ally was preggo—so weird. Her body at least wore pregnancy well. All the weight was in her belly. It was cute. "It took me a while to figure it out."

"And you didn't want to have to deal with my mess." Ally walked over next to Eve. Her eyes shot daggers at their reflection in the mirror.

"What? How can you think that?"

Ally's face fell and the anger seemed to zap right out of her. "I don't think that."

"What's going on with us? Why all the cloak and dagger business?"

"My grandmother, my parents, your mom. You're my weak spot. They all know that. I needed to deal with this without you, because once you found me, they would too." She pointed in the direction of the big house.

"We didn't know she—"

"I know. That woman." Ally shook her head.

Eve wasn't sure what to say, so to stall she picked up the clothes strewn around the room. Ally was usually so meticulous with her clothing. Eve had picked up five things when it hit her that not one of them was her design.

Seemed Ally was too good to wear her stuff now.

"Awful aren't they?" Ally nodded to the clothes in Eve's hands. "None of my regular clothes fit, so I'm stuck wearing crap maternity wear. You want to get rich? Design something decent for pregnant women."

Eve gazed at the clothes in her hands. She'd never thought of that. She wondered . . .

Ally plopped on the edge of her bed and picked up her hairbrush from the nightstand. "I missed you."

"Then I don't get it. I set up the secret account. You could've made this a lot easier. I called you. I emailed. I wrote you. And nothing. I got nothing!" Eve hurled the clothes into the hamper and continued to glower at it long after she was through. She was too proud to let Ally see the hurt in her expression.

"I couldn't do it," Ally said.

Eve spun around, her eyes flashing. "Couldn't do what? I needed you too, and you disappeared."

Ally's eyes welled with tears. "I suck. I'm sorry."

Her apology didn't make Eve feel any better. "I don't understand. You're pregnant. How could you not tell me? How could you not need to tell me? Something goes wrong in my life and I need you, but you—"

"I know. I'm sorry!" Ally didn't sound sorry. Her hair was back to its usual perfection. She set the brush back on the table with an odd delicacy.

"You keep saying you're sorry, but I need something more. Help me understand."

Ally swatted at the brush and sent it flying across the room. "I need. I need. It's all about what you need! Well, I'm pregnant and my baby isn't right, and I can't exactly deal with what you need. Do you get it now?"

Eve twisted the rod to open the blinds and peered through the slats at the swing set. The metal slide was caked in yellow pollen. It made Eve want to sneeze just to look at it. How depressing that the imaginary circus apparatus of her childhood was merely a potential allergy attack to her now.

Nothing was the same. Not Eve. Not Ally. Not their friendship.

Maybe she was being selfish. Sure, she was depressed; but Ally's situation . . . God, how could Eve even compare?

Did she even have the right to be angry with Ally? Because she was. Ally had shut her out. Instead of reaching out, instead of giving Eve a real chance to help, she sent her on some wild-goose chase. Eve went to Ally for help, and all she got was silence. Why couldn't they have gone through everything together? Like they always had.

"Fine. Tell me what you need. Please. I'd love to know." Eve regretted the words as soon as they garbaged out of her mouth. They'd come out all wrong, but it was too late to take them back.

"I need you to fly away, little girl." Ally went back under the blanket.

Eve flinched. She'd been dismissed. Ally could see the emptiness inside Eve and knew that Eve was too weak, too useless, to support her. So why was Eve still standing? Why was she letting Ally heap this guilt on her? It wasn't Eve's fault Ally was pregnant. It wasn't Eve's fault her baby had a birth defect.

Through Ally's open closet door, Eve could see her designs hanging. As if somehow rubbing the fabric between her fingers would reassure her, Eve walked over to touch her pieces. She touched the shirt Ally had worn on the first day of school their senior year. Eve's designs were featured in Ally's first day of school pics for the entirety of high school. They were a team—Ally and Eve.

What did it matter who was right and who was wrong when everything had ripped apart?

So.

Eve wasn't going to walk out. She wasn't going to leave Ally to figure out this mess on her own. That wasn't what friends did. Even when said friends were acting like total bitches.

Eve marched over to Ally's bed and yanked off her blankets. "No. You're stuck with me."

Ally was lying curled up in the fetal position, her face awash with tears.

Eve's anger cracked.

She slid into bed and wrapped her arms around her best friend. At first, Ally stiffened, but gradually she relaxed and sank into Eve's embrace. They lay there for a while. Ally cried a lot. Eve cried a little. And when they had both run through their tears, Ally sighed and reached for the box of tissues on her nightstand. She handed Eve one and kept one for herself.

Eve blew her nose, sounding like an elephant.

Ally chuckled. "When I found out I was pregnant, I tried to call you. I left a message with Carrie."

"I called you back. I left you a message too. What happened?"

"I couldn't stand the thought of you feeling sorry for me."

That didn't make any sense. Eve shook her head.

Ally continued, "You always, sort of, I don't know, looked up to me." She blushed.

It was true. Ally was the golden child.

"And there I was pregnant and running away. A total fuck-up."

Ally wasn't the first person to find herself in this predicament. She was being too hard on herself. "You aren't a fuck-up."

"Hah! Look at me." She pointed to her reflection.

Sure, she was blotchy and tired and pregnant . . . but she was so much more. "You're more than beautiful. You know that, right? You're kind and smart and fun."

"Try dumb and screwed. I've blown everything. Nice clover, by the way."

Eve fingered the fake four-leaf clover that wasn't bringing her luck after all. She didn't know what to say. This was a total disaster. If Ally had the baby, bye-bye modeling career. If she didn't have the baby, who knew what she'd sacrifice? "You don't know that. Everything's gonna be okay." But would it?

"Easy for you to say." Ally walked across the room to throw away her used tissues, and, Eve suspected, to establish some distance between them.

Why did Ally keep pushing her away? "Easy? Easy? No. I wouldn't say anything's been easy lately. But then, what would you know about that?" Eve couldn't seem to let go of the bitterness. God, she was such a jerk.

Ally said, "I'm sorry I ignored your messages. I told myself you had enough going on, and that I was doing you a favor by saving you from my mistakes."

She had a point. If Eve couldn't even manage to shower, it seemed unlikely that she'd have had anything left to help Ally. Ally's problems could've pushed Eve further over the edge.

Ally continued, "But the truth is . . . it was the other way around. I'm sorry I wasn't stronger. I'm sorry I haven't been a better friend."

Eve heard her own words in Ally's, and Boop's were in there too. Maybe none of them were strong enough on their own. "You aren't alone. I'm here now."

"There's nothing you can do." And now it was Ally staring out the window into the yard. Eve wondered what Ally saw when she looked out there. Their childhood? Her baby playing? Nothing?

There had to be something Eve could do, but she still didn't have a grip on the situation. "Tell me where you are in all of this. What's the deal with the father?"

Ally sat down in the desk chair. "He's an asshole. I'm not telling him about the baby. He wouldn't give a rip." She opened last month's issue of *Vogue* and thumbed through the pages. "And if he did, I wouldn't want him within ten feet of my kid."

"That's pretty harsh. What'd he do?" Eve leaned against the wall so she could watch Ally's face.

"That's a story for another day."

"I see." So they weren't back to normal. Eve wished Ally would put down the damn magazine.

"No, really, I'll tell you about it, but give me some time. Okay?" Ally lifted her gaze to Eve's as if searching for reassurance.

Eve sighed. "Yeah."

Ally turned back to *Vogue*. "So—the baby—you know she has a birth defect?"

Eve nodded, not that Ally noticed. Must be some issue. "But I didn't know it's a girl."

"Yeah."

Ally's refusal to make eye contact was unsettling. Eve asked, "So what are you going to do?"

"I don't know. When I first found out I was pregnant, I decided to keep the baby. But now with this . . . my parents will push for having it, maybe they'd raise it or arrange a hush-hush adoption. It would be hard though to find someone who wants a special-needs baby. And I can't see how they'd have the time for a newborn, let alone one with issues. And Grandmother—I'm supposed to be packing my bag right now for a secret trip to London where doctors will discretely make my problem go away, and Grandmother will reward my good behavior with an audition in the West End."

"What do you want?"

Ally shrugged. "Depends on the day."

"I guess having a baby complicates your modeling and acting dreams."

"That wasn't going so hot anyway. I don't know how much longer I'd have lasted in LA. I was already thinking about going into social-media marketing, maybe." Ally turned another page.

Eve moved so she could stand behind Ally. If Ally was going to rudely read a magazine in the middle of their conversation, Eve might as well look on too, seeing as how she'd missed the last few issues.

Ally was staring at a bathing suit spread.

Upside down.

"After the disaster in LA, I want something stable and real."

"And the baby? Where does she fit in? Or does she?"

Ally closed the magazine she'd been hiding in and shoved it across her desk. "I don't know. Everything would be easier if I let her go, but I don't know if I can. She's my daughter. I already love her. Isn't it my job to protect her? But I don't know the first thing about being a mom and throw in a birth defect . . . I'm terrified."

She spun in her chair to face Eve. "I'd have to do it alone. My parents would help, I'm sure, but with the election—I don't know what sort of time they really have—and their motives are suspect. It's like my head and my heart are at war with each other. What do you think I should do?"

Eve had no business doling out advice. "Talk to Boop."

"Huh?" Ally wrinkled her nose.

"Boop, well . . . I'll let her tell you, assuming Aunt Victoria hasn't taken her out. How about I go get her?"

"Um. All right." Ally walked Eve to the door. "Can you ask her to give me five? I've gotta pee and maybe clean myself up a bit." Ally grabbed Eve's elbow. "We okay?"

Eve smiled over her shoulder. "Always."

Ally returned her smile, and then walked toward the bathroom. When Eve was at the front door, Ally's voice stopped her again. "And you? God, I'm so self-centered. Your messages sounded miserable. You want to talk?"

Eve did, and she would, but for now this was enough. "Later."

"No, really." Ally stepped toward Eve.

Eve held up her hand. "Look, you need to pee, and I'm doing all right. I'll fill you in later."

"Promise?"

"Promise."

Eve found Boop with Aunt Victoria in the sitting room. They fell into an icy silence when she stepped inside.

Eve cleared her throat. "Boop, Ally wants to chat with you, but she needs a few minutes."

Boop leaned forward from the leather armchair. "How'd she seem?"

"Been better." The sitting room was stifling. Sweat beaded on Eve's forehead. The walls closed in.

"And you?" Boop asked

Eve fanned her face. "Went as good as it could have." How they could sit in this room, Eve didn't know—she could barely breathe. She opened a window and drew in a deep breath.

"Then that's something," said Boop.

Aunt Victoria jumped in. "Betty, I don't see any need for you to get involved, after all. I'll go tell her to hurry on with her packing." She stood.

Eve turned from the window and held a shaking hand out. "Stop."

"I beg your pardon?"

Eve took a deep breath and steeled her spine. "You've had your say. Now it's Boop's turn. I won't let you browbeat Ally."

Aunt Victoria swung to Boop. "You going to sit idly by while she back talks me like that?"

"If she wins this round, I might stand up for an ovation, but I reckon that ain't what you had in mind." With a smirk, Boop leaned back.

Eve watched as the two sisters locked eyes and fell into a staring contest that would've impressed any eight-year-old. Clearly, decades of practice had commenced before this moment.

Finally, Vicky winced and blinked. "Darn dry eyes! Eve, you'll do as you're told and so will Ally, or I'll—"

"Aunt Victoria, you should stop there because you won't be able to unsay whatever threat you're about to unleash. I know you love Ally. I love her too, and so does Boop. We all want what's best for her. You don't hold a monopoly on that." Eve had had about all she could take of Aunt Victoria's machinations. It was one thing to spy on them and to mess with Boop's car, but this business with Ally was too much. Fury threatened to consume her. If Aunt Victoria didn't back down, she wasn't sure how much longer she could maintain her self-control.

Aunt Victoria sighed. "Seems like our girl's got a bit of Justine's spark after all."

"Spark?" Boop scoffed. "Her mama's an inferno."

"I'll shoot for a warm campfire then," Eve said.

"That's a step up from the marshmallow I thought you were," Aunt Victoria retorted.

Boop put her hands on the arms of her chair as if preparing to stand. "Now see here!"

Eve put a comforting hand on Boop's shoulder. "It's okay, Boop. Just go to Ally."

Boop stood and left the room, clapping.

Boop hadn't an inkling what to expect when she laid eyes on Ally. Eve's newfound pluck gave her a small cause for optimism though.

Ally was putting on her face when Boop stepped into her bedroom. Mascara's a tricky beast, so Boop waited until Ally was done before greeting her.

Meanwhile, Boop nosed around Ally's room. Boop had never been in the room before, but it was clear that Kristin had made every effort to give Ally a home away from home. The walls were cotton-candy pink and her bedspread was trimmed in lace. A giant dollhouse was displayed in the corner. The effect of a pregnant woman still living in her childish bedroom was jarring. Babies having babies.

"Boop, it's good to see you. You okay?"

"Aw, these old bumps. Never you mind. Give me some sugar, honey child." Boop threw her arms wide and Ally, always a good girl, air kissed her cheek—wouldn't want to smudge her fresh lipstick. "You've gotten yourself into quite a pickle here." Boop patted Ally's belly.

"Yeah, I know." Ally blushed. "Eve said you wanted to talk to me?"

And with that opening, Boop spent the next twenty minutes filling Ally in on Davey. Ally mostly listened, so Boop didn't find it necessary to veer off her practiced script too much, though she couldn't help but splash in a little color here and there for effect.

Only when she'd run through the tragic tale in its entirety did Ally ask, "So I guess all of this is the lead up to your big advice? Let's hear it."

Boop regarded the ceiling, reminding God that this would be a good time for the gift of clarity. Either he didn't hear her, though, or she wasn't listening right because her thoughts were still a muddle. This was the part she'd been dreading. Of course, she'd expected it, and she'd tried to prepare for it, but any advice she might give required a certainty that she didn't feel.

"Way I see it, you done got five choices. One, you birth the baby and raise it; two, you birth the baby and offer it for adoption; three, you birth the baby and house it in an institution; four, you get your parents in on the game; or, five, you don't have the baby."

Ally put her hand on the small of her back and sat herself in her desk chair. There weren't any other chairs in the room, but Boop didn't mind—relishing the opportunity to stretch her legs after driving to and fro all day.

Ally said in a tone laced with bitterness, "Except a baby with a birth defect probably won't get adopted. And my parents didn't even have the time or energy to raise me. Don't forget, they sent me off to boarding school when I was six. Kristin feels more like my parent than they do. Are they really going to agree to raise my child? And an institution? No offense, but nothing about your story encourages that."

Now that hurt. As the truth often did. "I ain't offended." At least Boop shouldn't be. A little pacing was in order. "So, you've narrowed it down to raising her yourself or terminating the pregnancy." As her feet wore down Ally's floorboards, her thoughts paced alongside. "I don't rightly know what would've happened had we chosen to raise Davey in our home. Who knows what those ignorant folks might've done to our family, to Davey. And his health? I didn't have no nursing skills. It might've all come crumbling down. Then again…"

"So, what are you saying?" Ally's voice shook like sea oats on a windy day.

"I don't know. I made the most practical decision and listened to the advice of others. It nearly destroyed me. But had I followed my heart I might've just created a mess of a different sort."

Ally's entire body was shaking now.

Hell's fire, Boop's pessimistic outlook weren't the thing right now.

Ally rubbed her temples. "So basically, you're saying either way I'm screwed."

"I don't know about that. Davey was my sunshine on a rainy day. He was joy and laughter in a ball of a boy. It wasn't Davey who ruined my life. It was living in a world that wouldn't accept him. A world that made me feel shame and pushed me to make choices that felt wrong."

Ally tossed her head back like a spirited mare. "I don't live in that world. It's not like that anymore."

"And ain't that the berries." Change didn't automatically mean progress the way young people reckoned, but in this particular case—they'd practically wrought a miracle.

Ally folded her long willowy fingers across her belly. "I love my little Madeline."

Boop stopped pacing. "That's a right beautiful name."

"But I don't know how I'd even pull it off. I don't have a job or a house, or a clue. . . ."

Boop moved to Ally's side and laid her hand on Ally's shoulder. "Now, I don't want to overstep here, but I'm gonna find myself at loose ends once my shoulder's fixed up. Should be feeling right spritely by the time your little one arrives. I'd be honored to help you care for Madeline while you go about the business of putting on your grown-up shoes."

"Would you move here? Well, not here as in Kristin's, but here in Leeside? I guess I wouldn't have to live here, but it's the closest place to home I've ever known. And right now, that feels awfully comforting."

"Why not?" Boop wandered over to examine Ally's bulletin board plastered with programs from school plays and fashion shows. As long as Boop could remember, Ally'd dreamed of life in Hollywood. And here she was. Here Boop was.

"You hate this place." Ally reminded Boop as if she'd gone senile.

Home. "No, I hated who I was here," echoes of Eve's words, "but I ain't that person no more. Might be time to put some ghosts to rest."

"Seriously?"

This idea was as much a surprise to Boop as it was to Ally. Boop hadn't thought it out, couldn't say where it hailed from. Maybe God had decided to get in on the action after all. But whatever the case, it felt right, it surely did. "I could rent a little house. Y'all could move in. I could be your nanny."

"You would do that?"

"In a heartbeat." Wasn't everybody who got a second chance. "But Ally, if you do decide to terminate the pregnancy, if that is the right choice for you, I'll support that too. You could go to London with your grandma. Or do it here even. I'd hold your hand. Heck, I'd even drive you there."

"Might be better if I did the driving."

"That's enough of your cheek, Little Lady." Boop wagged her finger. "Point is, don't you let nobody tell you what to do. This is your baby, your life, your decision. And whatever decision you make, I'll do everything in my power to make it easier for you."

"Thank you." Ally stood and threw her arms around Boop, almost bowling her over.

Boop sniffed and wiped her sleeve across her cheeks. "Now, your grandma's gonna come barreling in here any minute. I'll go hold her off. You take your time and come down when you're ready."

By the time Boop stepped out of the guest cottage, Vicky was already halfway across the garden.

"How'd it go? She all right? What'd you say?"

"Went fine. She's coming 'round."

"Thank heaven. Now that Ally knows what she's up against, I pray she won't let it ruin her life. She wouldn't listen to me. Stubborn girl."

"Well, hello there, Pot."

Vicky humpfed her umbrage, but it was just for show. Even Vicky had to admit she was more stubborn than a fact.

Overcome by a sudden exhaustion, Boop searched the garden for a place to sit for a spell. Since bird droppings splattered the picnic table, she decided to wander over to the old swing set. On arrival though, she discovered the rusty swing was coated in pollen. Without other options, she sat on it anyway. "I think you should know I didn't offer her no advice."

"What do you mean?"

"I told her about Davey. And then I told her that no matter what she chose I'd support her."

"What?" Vicky flinched as if she'd been slapped.

"Turn your hearing aid up." Boop toyed with the bandage on her arm trying to let in some air.

"I don't wear a hearing aid."

"Maybe you should." The rusty chains holding the swing squeaked a bit, but they seemed sturdy enough. Boop didn't plan to test them by actually swinging anyway. With her luck, she'd break her neck.

"Nothing wrong with my hearing. I can't believe you dropped the ball. Telling her to make her own choice. Like she needs that kind of pressure."

"All these years, ain't you learned nothing?"

"Like not to trust you to get this right?"

Boop straightened her spine. "Like to quit bossing folks around."

"Betty, did you do this to spite me?"

That woman! "I did this in spite of you. We ain't got no right to tell Ally what to do. This is her life, her problem, her decision. We need to stand behind whatever she decides with whatever force we got left."

"Well, I never!"

"No, you never did understand that."

"What a simplistic bunch of hooey. Life is more complicated than that. It doesn't matter how much I love Ally, if she keeps that baby her life is ruined. If anyone finds out she's with child, my son's race for the governorship is over. She needs to have a very secret, very quiet termination, and I can help with that." Vicky crossed her arms over her chest and bit down on her lips.

"I might've been a little slow to catch on, but we are kin and you aren't the only one who can dig in her heels. Your plan is dependent on her pregnancy staying a secret, but secrets have a way of getting out."

Vicky's eyes narrowed. "You'd do that to your nephew? Ruin his dreams?"

"I value that little girl more than his political career."

"Don't you see, this is best for both?

"What I see is a woman who is far too certain that what's best for everyone is coincidentally the most convenient for her as well. That's how it was with me back then and that's how it seems now." Even though Boop's heart hammered in her chest and her pulse raced, she tried to keep her tone even. Wouldn't serve to let Vicky know she'd gotten Boop's goat. "Having Davey didn't ruin my life. Keeping him a secret did. Being too weak to stand up to you and Tommy did."

Vicky's sharp intake of breath alerted Boop to the upcoming show. "I knew it! You've always sold short all I did for y'all. I was there for you when no one else was. But did you ever, even once, thank me?"

"Thank you? Thank you? For locking away my child?" Boop stood.

Vicky's face was redder than a tomato in August. "For protecting him."

"Protecting yourself."

"I won't argue that keeping Davey a secret was in my best interest, but it was in everybody's, even Davey's."

Clearly, Vicky's cheese had slid off her cracker. "You still think that? After everything that's happened? You still don't see what that secret did?"

"How convenient of you to judge history in hindsight."

"How convenient of you to refuse to admit fault."

Vicky said, "Enough. I've held my peace too long."

Boop found that difficult to believe.

Vicky slapped her hand against the old slide. "I didn't make Davey different. I didn't make society a bunch of bigoted fools. All I did was try to protect you and drive you to visit him every Sunday for a decade. But I'm the villain? That's fair, Betty. Really fair."

"But . . ." Forgetting about the bird poop, Boop plopped down at the picnic table. "You . . ." My God. "I don't . . ." Vicky'd always driven her bonkers. Blaming Vicky had felt so natural, so right. "I never . . ." Every Sunday. Not to mention all those times Vicky had covered for her, dragged her out of bed, chased down Justine. "Ah, hell . . ." Vicky'd come through for her. And she'd . . . "I'm sorry." The words stuck in her craw.

"What did you say?"

"You heard me." Vicky'd never let her live this down. Boop needed more time to wrap her head around this because there wasn't any way that Vicky got a free pass. Still . . . "I might owe you an apology."

"You might?"

"I might."

Just like Vicky not to accept her apology with grace. Bet she'd keep harping on it too. Even now she was probably plotting how she could rub Boop's nose in it.

But Vicky said, "What's done is done. Getting back to Ally, that girl's got a bright future. Having a baby, any baby, but especially one with issues, will ruin it. You're the one person in the world she might listen to. That's your obligation."

"No. You're wrong. I can't go back and fix what we did, but I can do for her what no one did for me. Not even you." There. Take that!

"What did I not do for you?"

"Trust me." The sun had set, leaving behind a lingering twilight. It was Boop's favorite time of day. "Believe in me."

"Hogwash."

Boop sighed; as usual, conversations with Vicky went in circles. "We appear to be at an impasse."

"That we do." Vicky's rounded shoulders spoke to a resignation that surprised Boop.

Seemed about time to wrap up the conversation, but Boop

couldn't think of a way to ease into farewells, and she didn't want it to appear she was rushing off with her tail between her legs.

Vicky said, "I suppose I should tell you that Justine called me this morning."

"Did she now?" That did not bode well.

"Not to bore you with the details, but she asked plenty of questions about Davey. You must've bungled the telling something awful."

"I . . . I did." Boop kicked at the worn-out mulch.

"Then I straightened up your mess, as usual."

Had she? Or had she sold Boop down river? Nah, Boop reckoned any story that made Boop look bad, made Vicky look worse. "Then I thank you." Vicky had come through for her again.

"You're welcome."

Boop was overdue for some heavy thinking around her sister. "Victoria?" There now, the show of courtesy hadn't been as painful as she'd always imagined.

"Yes?"

It was time for Boop to put on her big girl pants. "I hated what we did to Davey. I hated myself, and I heaped all my leftover hate on you. That wasn't fair. I'm sorry." Boop braced herself for Vicky's predictable barbed response.

"Me too."

Hell's bells and buckets of blood! Perhaps it was a shot in the dark, but her soft response gave Boop the courage to try one last time. "But Ally . . . she needs you. Only not the way you think. She doesn't need our outdated advice. She doesn't need to carry out our judgment. Ally needs to own this. She needs you like she's never needed you—behind her. No matter what."

"She's got that."

Whatever else might be true about Vicky, she was faithful. All those years and she'd never given up on Boop. "Then instead of telling Ally what to do, tell her that."

"She knows."

"Nope." Sometimes Boop wondered if Vicky knew how intimidating she was.

"She—"

"She don't." Other times Boop was certain she did.

Boop waited. And this time she refrained from mind-reading.

"Just that?" Vicky asked. "I'm tempted to call your bluff. I don't think you'd really go public with her pregnancy."

"Seems like a big risk. Anyhow, Ally might decide to take you up on your offer, but it needs to be her unpressured choice."

"Bite my tongue?"

"'Til it bleeds."

Vicky chuckled. "I'll think on it."

"That's a start."

So, it appeared you could teach old dogs new tricks. Seemed they both had thinking to do. Boop started toward the house to meet up with Eve and figure out the next step of their journey. She'd made it to the door when she heard: "I love you, Boop."

Boop's eyes stung. "I . . ." her breath caught, "love you too."

CHAPTER 23

The fried chicken in the backseat of Zed's pickup truck smelled like greasy heaven. When Eve asked what other goodies were stashed back there, he said she'd have to wait and see. Then he turned off-road, picked up speed, and Eve was too busy hanging on for dear life to ask any more questions about their mysterious date.

"Can you slow down?" Eve yelled.

In response, Zed pushed the gas down harder.

Wondering what sort of insanity she'd been struck by when she agreed to go out with this guy, Eve closed her eyes and prayed that she'd survive the ride and the date. If this was his idea of foreplay . . . Unfortunately, her stomach was rebelling at the closed eyes, and so she was forced to watch the woods flash by, to see the car wobble to the right.

Then Zed took a sharp turn and headed straight toward a stream.

"Stop! There's no bridge."

"Don't need one." Zed grinned like a maniac. Eve wondered for a minute if he was one. Then they were in the stream, water splashing all over the car as if hit by a wave. Once they were through the stream, Eve understood the practicality behind the size of the truck's giant tires.

Several hair-raising minutes passed before they reached a clearing of grass surrounded by black-eyed Susans, where Zed brought the truck to an abrupt halt.

"How was that?"

"Are you insane? Who drives like that? That was the most dangerous, frightening experience I've ever had. You could've warned me. You could have asked if I wanted to risk my life tonight."

"So, you liked it?"

"Hell yeah, it was awesome!" Eve looked through the splattered window at the stunning meadow before them. "Where are we?"

"A friend of a friend owns this land—said we could come run around out here."

"Cool."

"Hungry?"

"Starved."

Zed laid out a cotton blanket that Eve had the sneaking suspicion had come off his bed, as it didn't have a picnic blanket look to it and it had a faint odor of man rather than laundry detergent. They sat down, and Zed unpacked the cooler and grocery bag. In addition to the fried chicken, there was also potato salad, cheese straws, watermelon, deviled eggs, and pecan sandies.

"You make all this?"

"Nah, I ordered it from some gas station outside of town that caters."

"A catering gas station?"

"Why not?'

"Why not indeed."

Zed and Eve got down to the business of eating and talking and laughing. By the time the meal was finished, they were full and happy. After they cleaned up their mess, Zed pulled a gun out of the glove compartment.

Eve's heart picked up the pace. What did she really know about this guy? She reminded herself that Zed was a cop. He was allowed to have a gun. He had a good reason to have a gun. But why did he have it out when it was just the two of them in the middle of nowhere?

Determined not to panic, Eve threw her shoulders back and steadied her voice, "Why do I feel like Gretel all of a sudden?"

"Got a ways to go before you're fat enough to eat." Zed's smile struck Eve as more predatory than it had before.

"Seriously though, what's going on?"

Zed lifted a box of empty cans from the floor behind the driver's seat. "You ever shot a gun?"

Eve sighed in relief. "Uh, no."

Zed set the cans up on a rock across the clearing.

"Here let me show you." He slid on a pair of safety goggles and some headphone-looking things, loaded, aimed, and shot. One of the cans fell to the ground.

Eve clapped.

"Your turn." He strode over to her.

"You're not going to even ask if I want to shoot a gun?"

"Nah. I decided to skip the part where you say 'no' and then I have to talk you into it."

"Hey." But Eve was laughing because he had a point.

"Safety first." Zed tossed Eve some goggles and headphones of her own. "Okay, so before I hand you the gun, a few things—always point it downrange, do not ever point it at a person, even as a joke."

"You're cute when you're serious."

"I am serious. I've seen some dumb-ass accidents with guns. Also, first thing check that it isn't loaded. Like this." Zed removed the magazine and pulled the slide back. "See there's nothing in the chamber, so we're good."

He handed her the gun, placing it in her right hand, then moved behind her, so he could better guide her body into the proper position. "Now put your left hand under the gun to help support the weight."

Eve's heart picked up the pace again, but whether it was the thrill of Zed's body pressed against her or of the gun in her hands, she wasn't sure. Either way, his presence was making it difficult to concentrate on his words.

"All right, feet hip-width apart."

Eve slid her legs apart, feeling a tingle of excitement as her butt brushed against him.

"Move your left foot up a step. Lean forward." He pressed gently on her shoulder. "Not that much. Don't lock your knees."

Sounded like a good idea, except her legs were trembling, and locking them was the only way to get them to stop.

"To load the gun, you'll want to pull back the slide and release." He put his hand on top of hers and guided her fingers. "Level the gun—the sights should line up. When you're ready, fire."

Eve's entire body was tingling now. With slightly trembling hands, her shot went wild, landing somewhere amongst the black-eyed Susans.

Zed backed away giving her more personal space. "Next time, try closing your left eye."

Eve missed his warmth, but her hand was steadier this time. Her shot hit the rock.

"Closer. Let's work on your follow-through. After you pull the trigger, hold your position and hold the trigger in for a few more seconds."

She followed his advice. "I hit it!" Eve hopped up and down.

"Fantastic!" He glanced up at the sky, which was a deep purple. "The sun's going down. We better wrap this up." He reached out for the gun, unloaded it, and put it back in the car.

They locked gazes and Zed approached her. Eve's smile slipped away. Her lips parted. Zed leaned in and their lips touched softly at first and then harder. They fell to their knees. Zed's hands threaded through her hair. Eve let out a soft moan. Zed leaned against her until she was lying on the picnic blanket, and he was on top of her. She wriggled to get more comfortable, and he groaned and rolled off of her so they were lying side by side on the blanket.

"How's your friend?" His voice came out all breathy, but Eve appreciated his effort to sound casual.

She attempted to match his tone. "Verdict's still out."

He rolled onto his side and propped his head on his hand so he could look down at her. "What's going on? Can I help?"

"Nah, but thanks. It's probably best if I keep her situation to myself for now. Until she figures it out."

"Sure." Zed looked away, but not before Eve thought she caught glimpse of hurt.

"It's not that I don't trust you." She tentatively touched his arm.

Zed forced a smile as if he knew he was being overly sensitive. "No. I get it. What's next on your grand adventure with Boop?"

"We're headed home tomorrow."

"You don't sound happy about that." Zed's free hand came to rest on her stomach.

Eve shivered. "My mom's a nightmare. We're fighting."

"About?" His hand lazily drew circles on her stomach.

Seeing this as an opportunity to show Zed that she did trust him, she unloaded her life story. By the time she finished, he'd laid down and was staring into the sky. She was suddenly aware of how much she'd monopolized the conversation, how much she'd shared, how young and dysfunctional she sounded, how much this guy was probably completely turned off by her, and she wanted to crawl under the picnic blanket.

"Look, there's Venus." He pointed to what looked like a super-bright star.

"Cool." Eve measured her words, wishing she could take back everything she'd shared, wishing she could run back to the safety of Ally and Boop, and wishing she knew how to talk to Zed. If only a shooting star would flash across the sky. Although a meteor shower might be required to fix all of her problems. She wondered how long before Zed suggested they pack up and head back so he could escape her.

"My mom left when I was little. My dad raised me. He was pretty much a piece of crap. Stories about that another time." He waved his hand in the air as if brushing aside those details. His reference to "another time" didn't escape Eve's notice. He continued, "The point is that he died a few years ago. The crazy thing is that I miss him. Not him, I guess, but I miss the hope that one day we might make things right between us. I get that your mom is overbearing, but I'd give anything to have someone love me that completely."

Eve bit back the inclination to volunteer. Instead, she said, "She doesn't even know me. How can you say she loves me? She loves her idea of me."

"What if she loved you no matter what? Then it wouldn't matter if she knew you."

"Maybe."

He twirled a strand of her hair around his finger. "You're beautiful you know."

Eve couldn't believe that she was lying on a picnic blanket under the stars with this man, who as far as she could tell, was everything. She rolled over, reached up, and pulled his head down to hers. They kissed open mouthed this time. Zed darted his tongue into her mouth. His hands reached under her sundress, pushing it up, so they could get to her breasts. He reached under her to unhook her bra, and Eve couldn't help noticing how adept he was at the maneuver. And then her breasts were free and his lips were on them and she stopped noticing or thinking about much else, except the taste of him and the feel of him and how much she wanted him inside her. Her legs straddled his waist. Fully clothed he pushed against her, and she could feel his hardness. Her underwear grew damp with desire.

Zed stripped off his T-shirt. His lean muscles, coated in a sheen of sweat, glinted in the moonlight. Eve's hands stroked his back.

He touched the waistband of his shorts. They made eye contact. "You sure?" he asked.

Sure? Sure she wanted him? Yes. Sure this was a good idea? That would be no.

Eve shook her head, sat up, and cleared her throat. "I want to do this. I really like you. But . . . I think it might all be too much too fast for me."

Zed nodded as if he had half way expected that response. "Then we have something to look forward to."

"You're not mad?"

"Mad? No. Disappointed, hell yeah. But when we do have sex, I don't want you to have any regrets." Zed leaned over and kissed her on the forehead. With their arms wrapped around each other, they sat staring at the night sky for a long time.

"Have you thought on what you're gonna tell your mama?" Boop asked Eve on the drive back to Richmond the next morning.

Eve snorted. "Yeah. Butt out and back off."

Boop whistled. "Seriously?"

"No, but I'm not going back to Florida, and I'm not going to medical school." And her mom couldn't make her. It didn't escape Eve that she sounded like a two-year-old.

"Okay. What about fashion? And Zed? And college?"

"I guess I've got to tell Mom about fashion designing."

"You nervous?"

"You mean since Mom's going to crap all over my dream?"

"She might not."

"Maybe not." But they both knew she would. "I have to get that internship. If I don't. . . ."

"You'll figure something out. And Zed? How was your date?"

"Awesome. Zed is perfect."

"I hear a 'but.'"

"It's hopeless."

"Why?"

Was it that hard to figure out? Did Boop want to hear Eve admit it? "He lives hours away. He's a grown-up. We don't have anything in common." Eve tapped her steering wheel to punctuate her points. "Not to mention he's way out of my league."

"I beg to differ."

"You're my grandma. Hardly an objective bystander."

"Sugar, you ain't exactly an objective bystander either. Let's not quibble over this. The point is you don't reckon it'll work out."

"Right. I mean why go through all that. . . .?"

"Through all what?"

Boop couldn't be this dense. Had she forgotten the trauma of the dating scene? "Embarrassment, awkwardness, and heartbreak."

"Risk?"

"Yeah." There she said it. "What do you think I should do?"

Boop pulled a compact out of her purse and observed her reflection in its little mirror. Eve wondered what she saw. Did she begrudge every nook and cranny, or did she see a different version of herself—a secret version, a younger version? Boop asked, "Why don't you tell me all about this dreamboat of yours?"

"First off he isn't mine, but you're so right about the dreamboat part. He's fun and a great listener. He was patient while he taught me to surf and shoot a gun."

"Shoot a gun?"

Eve chuckled. "Yeah, we did some target practice last night. He's forgiven me for acting like a big B when we met. And when I was upset at seeing Mom, he offered to come face her with me, even though he was on his way to work."

"So, a good catch?"

"If I were fishing."

"Are you?"

With every fiber of her being, Eve wanted to fall in love, but she was terrified of the mess. "Maybe."

Boop reapplied her lipstick. "You'll never get anywhere without risk. Mind you, that ain't a free pass for stupidity."

"I'm scared to get my hopes up." Needing a break from the arctic wind, Eve flicked the A/C off.

"But that's the fun part."

"Until it doesn't work out."

"That'll hurt something awful whether your hopes are up or not. Might as well enjoy the daydream. Might be all you ever get."

"Always a fountain of optimism."

"Seriously, life's full of rotten eggs. Hope's what keeps the chickens laying. You lose that and—"

"You end of on the couch befriending Kafka."

"The author?"

The cockroach. "Never mind." This train wreck of a trip had gotten her off the couch. Who knew a road trip would be what the doctor ordered? Boop had. "How much of this trip has been about Ally, and Davey, and Vicky, and how much was about me?"

"Hmm. Fifty-fifty."

Seemed Eve had underestimated Boop. Again. Eve felt like the victim of a WWE SmackDown, but at least her bruises were invisible. Boop's bruises were yellowing. This trip had literally beaten Boop inside and out. She'd taken one for the team. For Eve.

"You think I'm better?"

"Do you?"

Goldenrod was in full bloom in the median. What a surprise after miles of monotonous interstate driving. "Yeah, but I feel fragile."

"You are."

"Say Zed breaks my heart, and Nicholas Russel rejects my portfolio; how do I keep going?"

Boop clasped her hands together and brought them to her lips. "I can guarantee that if you don't give it a whirl with Zed, it won't work out. And if you don't put together a portfolio, you won't get an internship."

"Yeah, but I won't get rejected either." Failure might squash her like a June bug. Eve inwardly chuckled at the turn of phrase—Boop was rubbing off on her.

"True, but you'll be exactly where you started because you never left. Stalling isn't victory. But if you go for it, you got a shot at living your daydream. If you don't succeed, bet you can find some side streets that'll make the journey worth it."

"Making lemonade isn't my strong suit." That kind of mind game was beyond Eve. Some things sucked. Period.

"Then you ask for help from me, from your mama, from Ally, from a therapist. And you keep asking until you get it."

But that required Eve admitting to the world that she couldn't hack it, that she was weak. Like Boop.

Only Boop wasn't weak. Not anymore. A string of steel ran through her that Eve had never appreciated before, or even noticed. But on this trip, Boop had carried Eve. And Ally, and Mom, and Aunt Victoria. Yet, all the while, her own shit had been hitting the fan. Eve didn't know how she did it, and it wasn't over yet. "How do you think Mom's going to react?"

Boop turned the air conditioner back on. "Don't know, but she spoke to Vicky yesterday, and Vicky says she explained about Davey better than I did—straightened it all out."

"That's promising."

"Yeah, except Vicky and me don't have the same interpretation of events, so I'm worried she filled Justine's head with tall tales that I'll never unravel. And even if Justine understands why I did what I did—she doesn't have to forgive me."

"She loves you. She'll come around."

"I ain't certain of that. I lied through her entire life so far, and I bungled my mothering gig big time."

"You loved her. That should be enough."

"It ain't." Boop tossed out such a soul-wrenching sigh that Eve was tempted to pull over on the shoulder to give her a hug, but she didn't.

Boop said, "Not if Justine didn't know I loved her. Not if she didn't feel it."

"I'm not sure that's totally true." Eve's whole life, Boop had been there for her mom. Maybe part two didn't negate part one's neglect, but her mom couldn't have missed how hard Boop had worked to make it right. "Either way, she knows now."

"We'll see." Boop watched the road ahead.

"If she won't see reason, I know exactly what we'll do."

Boop turned to Eve. "What's that?"

"Drag her on a road trip."

CHAPTER 24

The woman who greeted them at the door wasn't Justine. She had her face, her clothes, but the rest of her was all wrong. Her hair was in a ponytail, which according to her was "only appropriate for planned sweating." She'd forgotten to put makeup on one of her eyes. Heck, she hadn't even put on shoes.

"Mom, are you okay?" Eve reached out to give her a hug, but her mom backed away like a skittish kitten. Was this about Boop and Davey? If that was the case, why would she be acting weird with Eve? She'd had plenty of time to armor up since they'd last seen her, but she struck Eve as broken, and her mom didn't break easily, or ever, as far as Eve knew. Eve was at a loss.

Her mom still hadn't said anything, when Boop asked, "What's the matter?"

Instead of answering, her mom glared and then gestured for them to follow her upstairs. Halfway up, Eve's stomach sank when it dawned on her where they were headed and what it might mean.

When her mom flung open the door to Eve's bedroom, the room spoke for itself. Eve's old sketchbooks carpeted the floor and at least thirty of her designs were draped across every piece of furniture in the room.

Boop gasped.

Eve felt naked and proud, and terrifyingly nervous.

Her mom glowered into the room like she was staring down the enemy.

"Um . . ." What did her mom want her to say? She wasn't sorry. Did her mom want an explanation? Didn't the sketchbook and clothes tell their story? "I was gonna tell you."

"When?" She still hadn't looked at Eve.

"Today." Her mom was acting like Eve had done something wrong, like Justine had found a stash of drugs in her closet. When in fact, she was the one who'd invaded Eve's privacy. "I told you not to go in my closet."

"I didn't want to wait around for you to unpack it." At last, she turned to Eve. "I didn't mean to snoop."

Eve pointed toward the footlocker she'd left behind when she'd gone to college. Its lock had been pried open.

"That was later. After I'd already found . . ." She kicked an empty cardboard box by the door.

Eve had forgotten about that box. How careless. "You had no right."

"Don't turn this around and make it about me." Her mom's voice shook. "You've been doing . . . this for years, and you never told me. I don't get it. Why did you hide it?"

"I didn't think you'd understand."

"Understand what? What does this mean?"

No time like the present to get your dreams squashed Eve always said. She took a deep breath. "I want to be a fashion designer. Not a doctor."

Her mom pulled back as if Eve had smacked her. "Why didn't you tell me?"

Eve hugged her midriff. "I wanted you to love me."

"And you thought I wouldn't if . . . if . . .?" Her mom sank to the floor, covered her face with her hands, and sobbed.

Deep, wrenching sobs that plucked at Eve's own gut. But to Eve's surprise, she didn't take up her mom's cries. Eve felt many things, but none of them were sadness. If anything, she felt vindicated, like somehow her perfect mom's breakdown made her own okay and somehow it also reassured her that her mom did, in fact, love her and that maybe there weren't as many strings attached to that love as she'd thought.

With great awkwardness, Eve patted the top of her mom's head. However, her taps went unacknowledged by her mom who continued to weep. Thus far, Boop had remained silent. Eve shot her a silent plea for help with calming down her mom.

Boop, though, wore this crazy, wide-eyed expression like she was as lost as Eve, but she finally managed to say, "She really was gonna tell you today. We talked about it on the way here."

"You knew?" Justine glared at Boop. "How could you keep this from me?"

Boop flinched. "I've only known for a few days. I found out through a bit of accidental snooping of my own."

"You should've told me."

Eve hadn't meant for Boop's save to mean taking her mom's heat.

"It wasn't my secret to tell."

"Dammit. Forgive me if I don't trust anything you say. You hid Eve's depression from me. You hid my brother from me. And now this? Is everything that spills from your lips a lie?"

Boop squeezed her eyes shut.

"Mom, back off," Eve protested lamely, afraid drawing her mom's attention might incite her mom to return to berating Eve, but still wanting her mom to leave Boop alone.

"Why doesn't anyone trust me?" her mom asked.

Trust her? Was it a matter of trust? Eve supposed so. She hadn't trusted her mom with her dream, because Eve didn't think her mom would respect it. How could she say that though?

As she scanned the room, Eve tried to see the situation from her mom's eyes. The clothes had been carefully laid out. She pictured her mom smoothing down the wrinkles. She'd even put together outfits from separates. It was the sketchbooks, though, that made Eve gasp. Each was opened to a page that reflected the piece next to it. How long had her mom spent among Eve's designs? What had she thought of them?

"I can't look at this room any longer," her mom said.

The disgust in her tone said it all—she hated them. Eve had been right not to trust her.

"C'mon, let's go downstairs where we can sit on the furniture at least," she continued.

Once they made it downstairs, Eve flopped facedown on the couch. Boop sat in the rocking chair, but her mom paced the room instead of sitting. Her mom asked Boop, "What made you finally decide to tell me about Davey?"

"I couldn't tell Ally and not tell you," Boop said.

Her mom's eyebrows knit together. "Tell Ally? Why would you tell her?"

Eve sat up and winced, she probably should have already explained this to her mom. She cleared her throat. "I might not have told you everything." Her fingers flew to her mouth, groping for the comfort that chewing on them somehow gave.

"What a surprise." Her mom tapped her foot.

Eve hadn't thought real people actually tapped their foot when they were mad, but there it was.

"I'm waiting," her mom said.

"Ally's baby has a birth defect."

"Oh, God, no." Her mom stopped pacing and froze as if she couldn't process and walk at the same time. "What's she going to do?"

"I don't know." Eve flicked away her pinky-nail sliver. It landed on the blue couch.

Her mom scrunched her nose at it.

"Guess you'd tell her to get an abortion," Eve said. "No sense having Ally's life ruined like I ruined yours, right? Best to clean up your mistakes while you still can?"

Her mom's eyes bugged out and a strangled sound exploded from her lips. With the back of her hand, she wiped sweat from her forehead. Then her hand fluttered around until it knocked into a pot of geraniums on the window, which then crashed to the floor.

Eve's questions hung like toxic radiation.

Boop left and returned moments later with a dustpan, small broom, and the kitchen trashcan. She tossed the clump of traumatized flowers into the trash. Justine stared at Boop as if she'd never seen anyone clean before and didn't quite know what to make of it. One by one, Boop threw away the broken pieces of pottery. Then she swept up the rest of the mess. It was on the second swipe of the dirt that it occurred to Eve that she could help—should help. But she didn't. She watched Boop and so did her mom, as if the words had frozen them. It took Boop four rounds of sweeping and dumping before she finished.

"You weren't a mistake," her mom said.

Eve arched her eyebrows.

"I mean. . . ." Her mom stared at her with wide eyes. "I got pregnant on purpose."

"You what?" What sort of recrafting of history was her mom up to?

"Please, don't tell Karl any of this," her mom said.

"Why'd you do a stupid thing like that?" Eve asked.

Her mom blushed.

Eve couldn't remember ever having seen her mother blush before. She said, "I didn't want to be alone anymore, and I thought if I got pregnant Karl would finally grow up and marry me."

"Seriously? That was—"

"Pathetic, huh?" Her mom tugged on her ponytail. "I was getting older and I felt stuck, like I couldn't move on to the next phase of my life, like I couldn't grow up."

"Appears we all got our share of secrets," Boop said.

Her mom rubbed her neck and gazed out the window. A cardinal flew by, but she didn't even blink. Eve doubted the bird's visit even registered. Then her mom shook her head as if coming to her senses and mowed Boop down with an intense glare. "If it weren't for Ally, you'd still have your little secret."

"That's not the only reason." Boop's manic rocking back and forth made Eve worry about the direction the conversation was moving.

"Do go on," her mom said.

"You reckoned I didn't love you. You blamed yourself for my failure. Those perceptions have misguided you."

Her mom crossed her arms. "And you thought that telling me you'd lied to me my whole life would lead me to believe that you loved me?"

"More like, if you understood why I fell apart, you'd know it had nothing to do with my love for you. And if you could accept that I love you and have always loved you—" Boop's glance cut to Eve, "then maybe you wouldn't be so dependent on Eve."

"Dependent on Eve? What are you talking about?"

What was Boop talking about? Wasn't it the other way around? Surely, Eve was the one who couldn't hack the real world and was running home to her mommy.

Boop said, "Just maybe, you're so focused on loving and contr—raising her, you haven't given her the space she needs to grow up."

"Space? She just spent a year hundreds of miles away and look at where that space got her!" Her mom pushed against the window frame as if they were prison bars.

Eve knew that feeling. She was dying to jump out of the window and . . . go surfing or something.

"At a school you chose. Taking classes you picked," Boop said.

"It's my money." Her mom yanked dead leaves off the surviving geraniums on the windowsill.

Boop winced. Eve wasn't sure if she was reacting to her mom's words or the fate of the dearly departed flowers. "It's her life."

Her mom opened her fist and stared down at the dead flowers she'd collected. "I only want what's best for her."

"How can you know what's best for her?"

"Because I love her." Her mom's eyes wore a softness Eve couldn't recall ever noticing before. Eve's stomach clenched.

Unswayed, Boop kept going. "Like you loved Karl? Like you knew what was best for him when you decided to trap him by getting pregnant?"

Her mom pressed her lips together so hard they whitened. "Having Eve didn't fix anything with Karl. We were doomed from the start."

Eve wondered if this desperate woman was really her mom.

Justine continued, "It did fix something inside me though."

Nothing she said made any sense to Eve. "What?"

"I finally had a daughter who I could love with my whole heart and who would love me back."

"Oh." Love? Is that what her mom called it? Try suffocation.

"Eve, you haven't ruined my life. You saved it. You are my life."

That, right there, was the problem. "Arghh!" Eve yelled. "I am not your do-over."

Her mom leaned against the wall and closed her eyes. She looked beaten. "I never meant to make you feel that way. You're the best thing that ever happened to me."

What else was there to say? Eve couldn't keep kicking at her, but she wasn't ready to stand down either. When watching her became too painful, Eve glared at the floor wishing she was elsewhere, which she supposed was a step up from nowhere.

Finally, her mom changed the subject. "By the way, you got some packages—one's from Karl. I'll go get them."

Eve couldn't blame her mom for grasping at any excuse to leave the room and escape the toxic atmosphere.

While her mom was gone, Eve rubbed the goose pimples that dotted her arms. Since when did Karl send her packages? She couldn't recall him ever even sending a card. Birthday presents (when he remembered) were presented in person on his next visit, sometimes months after the fact, but whatever.

Her mom returned with two packages. The smaller was square, about the size of a book. Her mom handed it to her first.

Eve checked the return address. From Carrie. She must've forgotten something. "I'm shocked you haven't already opened it," she said to her mom as she dug her finger in under the crease.

"You don't know how much I wanted to."

"You didn't show such restraint in my room. What made this different?" The tape gave way and Eve slid one of her sketchbooks out of the wrapping.

"I guess I figured it would mean more if you shared whatever it was with me."

There was a Post-it note on top with a message from Carrie: THIS DOESN'T BELONG IN A TRASHCAN. Eve hugged the book to her chest.

"What if I don't?"

Her mom flinched. "I guess that's your right."

Eve set the sketchbook on the coffee table, knowing that at some point she'd cave and show it to her. Wanting to withhold that satisfaction from her a bit longer, she motioned for Justine to pass her the package from Karl. It was flat and light, the size and shape of the window, or she gulped, a painting. Could it be? No, it wouldn't do to get her hopes up.

But Boop's suggestions about allowing herself to enjoy the daydream nagged at Eve. Dare she imagine that Karl had sent her one of his paintings?

No, surely not. Probably some random painting he'd discovered at a flea market and thought she'd want for some obscure reason. Though how Karl thought he could guess at her taste in artwork was beyond her.

But if he had sent her one of his own paintings, that'd be huge. Her hands trembled as she opened the card taped to the outside:

Dear Eve,
What can I say? "I'm sorry" doesn't cut it. You deserve a better father. I hope this package will show you how much I love you even though I fall short.

Love,
Karl

Eve couldn't get past the lump in her throat enough to read it aloud, so she passed the note to Boop, who was closest. While waiting for her to read it, Eve picked at the packing tape. Only, without fingernails, it was a lost cause.

Not even Karl would be so stupid as to write that message and then send her a painting by someone else. Would he? Eve heard Boop's sharp intake of breath and knew she was thinking similar thoughts. Boop passed the note to Justine. Eve abandoned the tape struggle, opting instead to grab inside the coffee-table drawer for the pen she knew was always in there. She stuck the point into the tape along the seam and pulled to slice through it.

By then her mom had read the note too, and she muttered, "This had better be good."

Eve slid the gift from the box and unfolded the brown paper Karl had wrapped around it. Her jaw dropped; he had painted it—no doubt about it. It was of Eve. She was about thirteen, sitting on the bank of a river, fishing. It was stunning. The Eve in the painting was way more beautiful than the Eve in her mirror. She looked beautiful in the way that a loving father might see his daughter. Eve swallowed.

"You're killing me! Let's see it," Boop said.

Eve flipped the canvas around. Her mom gasped and neither spoke for an eternity. Until finally her mom said, "He's gotten better."

"Great day in the morning!" Boop said. She and her mom weren't exactly fans of Karl, so for them to acknowledge this painting, his talent—that meant something.

Eve set the painting against the couch and moved next to her mom, so she could take it in at some distance. She frowned. Poor Karl. To have that kind of talent and that kind of love and to be so afraid to share them with the world was a tragedy.

Then again, he had shared his talent with her, hadn't he? Her dad had mailed her his heart.

Eve's shoulders shook with silent sobs. Her mom put her arms around Eve, and Eve leaned into her. For a few moments, Eve luxuriated in the comfort of her mom's embrace. When, awash in the love of her parents, Eve felt strength welling within, she eased from her mom to stand tall by herself. "If Karl can find courage, so can I."

"What do you mean?" her mom asked.

"I don't want to hide my art. I don't want to be afraid any longer. I want to study fashion design."

"I don't know, Eve."

"I knew you'd say that."

"Say what?"

"That you hate the idea."

Watching her mom wince and then frown and then pull off some weak-ass smile was like watching a silent film.

"I just want to protect you. A career in fashion isn't practical," she said.

"Every person in the world wears clothing. Sounds pretty practical to me."

"You're young. You don't know what you want. Sure, you have these dreams, but you have no concept of reality. The real world is a hard place. It's got a history of smashing dreams."

"The world isn't smashing my dreams—you are." Under the strain of not screaming, her voice cracked.

"I don't want to watch you make a huge mistake."

"Following my dream isn't a mistake. I might fail. I probably will fail, but that doesn't make it a mistake."

"Nonsense." Her mom started pacing again.

"I don't want to be some robot who goes through the motions."

"Like me? Is that what you think? I'm some robot?"

"I didn't say that. This isn't about you."

Her mom rubbed her temples. "What exactly are we talking about here? You want to major in fashion design?"

"Not exactly. Maybe later. I don't know. I do know I can't go back to school in the fall, though. That place was killing me."

"So you're going to drop out?" her mom asked.

Boop smacked her hands together and stood. "That's enough. Sit down, Justine."

For a moment, her mom watched the still-rocking chair that Boop had emptied, and then she did in fact, take a seat in her recliner. Eve couldn't remember another time when her mom had followed Boop's orders so easily. Of course, Boop didn't usually take such a domineering stance. The role reversal was unsettling.

Boop took Justine's hands and squeezed them. "You're a good mom, way better than me, but Eve's an adult now. She needs you to let her grow up. Let her scramble it all up. Let her fall on her behind."

Justine snatched her hands back. "That's reckless."

"Mom, Boop's right. When I went to school, I fell apart." The time had come to admit out loud what she hadn't before. "I wanted to die."

Her mom looked like she might vomit. "You mean—?"

"I wanted to kill myself." Now that her mom and Boop knew how weak and pitiful she was, Eve's face burned in mortification.

"Did you know about this too?" Justine asked Boop.

Boop shook her head.

Eve continued, "I'm only now, since this trip, starting to figure out who I am and what I want. You can either help me follow my dream, or you can get of my way."

"You don't leave me much choice. You're serious about this."

It wasn't a question, but Eve affirmed it anyway. "Yes."

"Do you have a plan?"

Eve told her about showing Nicholas Russell her nonexistent portfolio. To give her credit, her mom listened and even managed to seem somewhat excited by the prospect.

"I can't say I'm comfortable with this, but if this is what you want, then let's give it a shot."

"Thank heavens that's settled!" Boop sat back down on the rocking chair as if a huge load had been lifted off her shoulders.

Quiet settled comfortably around them. Sometimes Eve forgot to think of her mom and Boop as daughter and mother. Maybe it was because Justine called her mom, "Boop," or because her mom always seemed like the one in charge. Maybe it was that they didn't look or act anything alike. But as Eve watched the two of them, both stripped of their secrets and their usual masks, damned if they didn't wear the same expression.

It was her mom who finally broke the silence. "Thanks for bringing my girl home."

"I reckon she's the one who brought us all home." Boop's arthritic hands gripped the arms of the rocker. "I always hoped that if I was a good enough grandma to your baby, somehow it would make up for failing you as a mother."

"I should've let you start over a long time ago," Justine said.

"Now's as good a time as any."

Boop rocked. Justine closed her eyes. Eve watched them from the couch, feeling grateful. The fact that these women had found enough courage to forgive was a miracle of sorts. How many families could come through this intact? They were lucky.

When her mom flicked her eyes open, she asked, "Did you make the outfit you're wearing?"

Now that was an unexpected turn of conversation. Eve glanced down at her shirt and shorts, resisting the urge to tuck her knees into her chest. They weren't her best work, but still. "Why? You hate them?"

Her mom frowned. "No, you look cute. Much better than the usual black crap you wear."

"Hey," Eve protested, but since she couldn't detect any malice behind her mom's words, Eve's response was a mere formality.

"Why Backstitch for the label?"

"It's the final stitch in a seam, keeps the whole piece from unraveling."

"And I took away Heathcliff, the very thing that was holding you together. I'm so sorry. I didn't know."

Eve nodded.

"I feel like I'm losing you both," her mom said.

"Funny. I'd say you're finally finding us," Boop said.

"Do you still love us?" Eve asked, knowing her mom did, but needing to hear her say it anyway.

"Of course." Justine beckoned them to join her in a group hug. "Boop, I've made meatloaf for dinner. Do you mind whipping up some mashed potatoes?"

"Be delighted." Boop squeezed them and beamed.

Justine continued, "And Eve, I'm going to a wedding next weekend. Maybe you could whip up something for me to wear?"

"Be delighted," Eve mimicked Boop, facial expression and squeeze included.

They bathed together in the laughter that followed. Like seams, their family was only as strong as their ability to mend, and mend they would.

EPILOGUE

September

*H*old on to your hats Leeside, because Boop is back, and she's better than ever. According to Ally, that was the word floating around the town grapevine. Boop got a real kick out of the last part.

Ally and Boop received visitors from the swing on the front porch of their new place. They'd had five so far, all new neighbors, and they'd come bearing gifts—beaten biscuits, pickled watermelon rind, brownies, fresh dill bread, and hand-picked apples. This neighborhood was wreaking havoc with Boop's girlish figure.

With the rest of the crew busy with the heavy lifting, Boop felt downright guilty enjoying her visitors. She got to sit out of the moving hoopla on account of her healing shoulder and advanced age. Ally got to sit out on account of her advanced pregnancy. Poor Eve was left to direct the slew of young men who'd volunteered to help the three of them move.

Eve stuck her head out of the front door and yelled down to the U-Haul, "Hey, Zed . . . forty-four hours."

Ally and Boop rolled their eyes, as they'd suffered hourly updates all the day before as well.

But Zed, to his credit, grinned at Eve. "You're gonna rock your internship, Eve." He was good for her, even Justine admitted it. Well, not out loud, but she had stopped referring to him as "that man," which was as good as an admission.

Eve had stationed Justine in the kitchen—unpacking. A strategic move that took full advantage of Justine's nitpicking tendencies but kept her from under Eve's feet.

"Where should I put this box of birdhouses?" Zed asked Boop.

"Why don't you set it right next to me? It's about time I culled this collection." They'd been with her so long, the thought of saying goodbye left a lump in Boop's throat, but the living within the walls of her new home deserved the space, not a bunch of empty birdhouses. Maybe she'd donate them to a senior center.

Boop glanced over at Ally, checking to see that the heat wasn't getting to her too much. There was no need to worry though, she looked fresher than a farmer's market in her new maternity sundress designed by Eve, of course. Boop, though, was feeling quite parched.

As if on cue, Justine came out with a pitcher of lemonade and a stack of paper cups for the troops. Work halted as everyone gathered for a break. Boop counted six young men whose names she hadn't gotten straight. If the besotted glances they kept throwing at Ally were any indication, Boop reckoned she'd get a handle on who was who over the next few months. Tommy sure hadn't looked at Boop like that when she was eight and half months pregnant, but then Boop had never looked like Ally, so there was that.

"How are you doing with the whole empty nest thing?" Ally asked Justine.

"Oh." She blushed. "I signed up for up for two night classes, so I don't guess I'll have a whole lot of time to think about it."

"You what?" Eve asked.

"If you aren't going to college, I figured someone should."

Eve laughed until she cried. Then the child sat there laughing and crying at the same time.

The boys looked on her like she was kind of crazy, and she was . . . the best kind of crazy. Boop reckoned they all were.

Dear Reader,

Thank you for reading *Boop and Eve's Road Trip*!

I value you and your opinions. Please consider helping others discover Boop and Eve by leaving an honest review of the novel with your favorite bookseller or on Goodreads.

Disappointed the story is over? Head over to my webpage https://maryhelensheriff.com/boop-and-eves-road-trip/ for book club questions, cut scenes, and more bonuses. Be sure to sign-up for my author newsletter while you're there for a secret scene.

Finally, if you or someone you care about is in distress, you can call the National Suicide Prevention Lifeline (1-800-273-8255) for free and confidential support. Please know you are important and hope is real.

Peace & joy on the road ahead,

Mary

ACKNOWLEDGMENTS

First and foremost, I'd like to thank my husband Dan for his support of this novel. This book would not exist without your encouragement, critiquing skills, and financial investment. Your belief in me and this book is a testament to the wonderful partner and husband you are. I love you.

I've been overwhelmingly blessed with many supportive family members, friends, other writers, and publishing professionals on this book's long journey to publication.

Thank you to Brooke Warner, Samantha Strom, and supportive sister writers from She Writes Press for guiding this book to publication. Thank you to my editors, Sheena Billett and Megan Hannum, for your keen eyes. Thanks to Rebecca Lown for the terrific cover design.

Thanks to my publicists Crystal Patriarche, Taylor Brightwell, and Paige Herbert for your hard work in spreading the word. Thank you to Mark Raper for sharing your marketing expertise. Thanks to Carol Wampler for your financial support of my marketing endeavors and ready help with the children. Thank you to my Writer Road Trip author friends. It's quite a journey we're on.

Thanks to Michael Neff, Phil Hilliker, Melissa Bybee, Jessica Rowland, Jillian Sullivan, Anne Westrick, Libby McNamee, Meriel Martinez, Ashley Gregoire, Bethany White, Joetta Curie, Malesa

Mayhall, Susan Miller, Jennifer Radgowski, Julie Valerie, and Mona Jain for your insights on early drafts. I hope you are proud of this book we created together.

Several organizations have provided me with key learning opportunities. Thanks especially to Hollins University, James River Writers, Women's Fiction Writers Association, Highlights Foundation, Algonkian Writers Conference, Capital Writing Project, Visual Arts Center, and Author Accelerator. With so many wonderful writing teachers, it is hard to know where to start, but I'll give a shout out to Jim Bulleit, Mazan Saah, Han Nolan, Hillary Homzie, Lisa Rowe Fraustino, Alexandria LaFaye, and Leslie Shiel.

On a personal note, a special thanks goes to my parents, Beth and John, for your life-long support of my writing passion. Whether it was sending me to writing camps or babysitting the kids so I could write, you've always been there for me.

Thanks also to Jake, Zoe, Jim, Deborah, Alan, Kathryn, Lex, and Jackie for your love and encouragement.

ABOUT THE AUTHOR

© Caleb Keiter

Mary Helen Sheriff spent fourteen years in classrooms teaching elementary school, middle school, college, and professionals. During that time, she also had the pleasure of dabbling in writing for children, teenagers, and adults in a variety of forms including fiction, poetry, blogs, and nonfiction. She spent several summers immersed in an MFA program in children's literature at Hollins University. Currently, she lives and writes in Richmond, Virginia, with her two kids, two cats, and husband. Check out her "…the gift of story" blog and newsletter at https://maryhelensheriff.com/blog/.

SELECTED TITLES FROM SHE WRITES PRESS

She Writes Press is an independent publishing company founded to serve women writers everywhere. Visit us at www.shewritespress.com.

The Moon Always Rising by Alice C. Early $16.95, 978-1-63152-683-1
When Eleanor "Els" Gordon's life cracks apart, she exiles herself to a derelict plantation house on the Caribbean island of Nevis—and discovers, with the help of her resident ghost, that only through love and forgiveness can she untangle years-old family secrets and set herself free to love again.

Eden by Jeanne Blasberg $16.95, 978-1-63152-188-1
As her children and grandchildren assemble for Fourth of July weekend at Eden, the Meister family's grand summer cottage on the Rhode Island shore, Becca decides it's time to introduce the daughter she gave up for adoption fifty years ago.

A Drop In The Ocean: A Novel by Jenni Ogden $16.95, 978-1-63152-026-6
When middle-aged Anna Fergusson's research lab is abruptly closed, she flees Boston to an island on Australia's Great Barrier Reef—where, amongst the seabirds, nesting turtles, and eccentric islanders, she finds a family and learns some bittersweet lessons about love.

Arboria Park by Kate Tyler Wall $16.95, 978-1631521676
Stacy Halloran's life has always been centered on her beloved neighborhood, a 1950s-era housing development called Arboria Park—so when a massive highway project threatens the Park in the 2000s, she steps up to the task of trying to save it.

True Stories at the Smoky View by Jill McCroskey Coupe
$16.95, 978-1-63152-051-8
The lives of a librarian and a ten-year-old boy are changed forever when they become stranded by a blizzard in a Tennessee motel and join forces in a very personal search for justice.

Anchor Out by Barbara Sapienza $16.95, 978-1631521652
Quirky Frances Pia was a feminist Catholic nun, artist, and beloved sister and mother until she fell from grace—but now, done nursing her aching mood swings offshore in a thirty-foot sailboat, she is ready to paint her way toward forgiveness.